THE COLLETTA CASSETTES

ALSO BY BRUNO NOBLE

A Thing of the Moment

THE COLLETTA CASSETTES

BRUNO NOBLE

Indie Novella

First published in Great Britain in 2022 by Indie Novella Ltd.

INDIE NOVELLA www.indienovella.co.uk

Commissioning Editor Jodie Evans

A CIP catalogue record for this title is available from the British Library

Paperback ISBN 978 1 739 95994 4

Printed and bound by Clays Ltd in the United Kingdom.

Indie Novella is committed to a sustainable future for our readers and the world in which we live. All paper used are natural, renewable and sustainable products.

For Collettiani, past, present and future

ONE

'And I thought the French were bad!' said Sebastian's father through gritted teeth as he gripped the mahogany steering wheel of his red Alfa Romeo. The late afternoon sun in his rear-view mirror and the bright headlights of the eager cars close behind conspired to blind and bewilder him. His sunglasses were of little use; no sooner did he put them on than he had to whip them off in order to be able to see his way in the Italian coast road's many tunnels. 'In retrospect,' he continued, 'the French habit of driving on your tail at a hundred miles an hour with the overtaking indicator permanently on seems positively courteous. At least you don't feel that the French are actually *trying* to kill you. And where's the respect? Alright, I may have a British number plate but, after all, I am driving an *Italian* make of car.'

'Don't be nasty about the French,' said Dominic coura-geously, his compulsion to stick up for his mother overcoming his reluctance to reprimand his father. 'After all, Mummy is French. And Sebastian and I are half French!' he added, as though this were news, opening his eyes wide at his elder brother on the back seat next to him.

Sebastian exaggerated the effect of a turn and brought his elbow down into Dominic's side.

'Ouch! You're squashing me!' Dominic giggled.

'I thought I'd told you to put your seatbelts on?' said Peter Kentish, glancing in the rear-view mirror at his sons.

'It's not compulsory,' said Sebastian. 'I know my rights,' he added as he sat upright and fumbled for his seatbelt.

'It is compulsory in this car,' shouted Mr Kentish, having to raise his voice above the noise of car engines in a tunnel. It was so hot that they had to drive with the windows down.

Sebastian didn't like to say so for fear of upsetting his mother but he didn't feel French or even half French: he didn't feel French at all. France had lost to Italy and then to Argentina in the group stage of the World Cup and not progressed to the second round and he hadn't felt sorry, not really. Nowhere near as distraught as when England had failed to qualify for the tournament and not even boarded the plane for Argentina. Although both born in England, his paternal grandparents had been Scottish, so Sebastian could at least try to feel Scottish with some legitimacy, but Scotland had lost to Peru and only managed a draw with Iran. If Peru beat Iran that evening, Scotland was unlikely to beat Holland and go through to the second round. He thought then that he wouldn't like football so much, after all.

Jacqueline Kentish raised her sunglasses to the top of her head and waited patiently for the car to leave the tunnel so she could consult the map on her lap. The improvised hairband resembled a visor on a blond helmet. Sebastian marvelled at his mother. While the wind blew his buffeting hair about his eyes and ears, Mrs Kentish had not so much as a hair out of place.

While his father lost himself in childish enthusiasm, his mother never lost her composure. She had what Sebastian thought of, at times, as class and distinction and, at others, as snobbishness and indifference. Sebastian imagined a border that ran down the middle of the car, separating his mother and him on the left from his father and Dominic on the right. Tall and blond versus short and dark. The four didn't resemble a family so much as natives from two different countries.

'Not far to go now,' said Mrs Kentish once she could see again. She kept a finger on their destination as she lowered her sunglasses and looked out of the car window, out over San Bartolomeo Al Mare and the Ligurian Sea. 'Another twenty minutes on the *autostrada* and then another twenty or so to Colletta.'

The coastal road, when not winding its way in and out of tunnels, twisted up and down vertiginously high viaducts, the stilts and buttresses of which plunged hundreds of feet into ravines and dry river mouths. Sebastian watched the needle of the speedometer rise as his father accelerated down a long straight and then fall as he braked, took the turn and dropped a gear to accelerate up a long climb into the clear sky ahead.

'Where are we going on holiday again?' Sebastian had asked when told to pack a suitcase.

Mrs Kentish had shown him on the map. A long day's drive to Lyon for a couple of days' stay with his maternal grandparents – *Le général* and *Mme la générale* – and then another long day's drive to Colletta di Castelbianco.

'But that's in the middle of nowhere!'

'It's in Liguria, in Italy. In the mountains. You'll love it, you'll see. And it has a swimming pool.'

'But why are we going *there*?'

'Daddy has to meet someone for work there and we thought it would be nice to make a family holiday of it.'

'I'm sure it's going to be perfectly boring.'

'No. I'm sure there'll be other children there. It'll be really exciting. It's a very old village, medieval in fact. Apparently, it's been left untouched on the outside while the houses and apartments have been modernised on the inside. No cars. Olive and cherry trees. Wait and see.'

Sebastian had winced when his mother had said *children*. His ten-year old brother had said, 'Oh, goody!' but, at sixteen, Sebastian neither liked the term nor felt he quite had the right to object to it. Actually, he didn't care, so long as there were girls his age. Last summer had been spent on a German exchange misunderstanding the signals of his pen-friend's sister, a girl of fifteen who had spent a week making eyes at him and slept with her bedroom door open only to scream when he had entered her room one night. 'I am sorry, I must have mistaken her bedroom for the bathroom,' had been offered to her pyjamaed parents in his best, sleepiest German. Sebastian hoped that this Italian holiday might be more successful than the German one.

Sebastian looked out of his car window onto the sunlit Ligurian hills and admired the view of villages and houses that dotted the hillsides like raisins on buns. He reflected that Colletta might just be better than the out-of-season ski resorts his family usually holidayed in during the summer, principally because they were cheap but also because they allowed his mother to paint and his father to work. He wasn't actually certain what his father did for a living and had heard him describe himself variously as a journalist, a historian, a researcher, an adviser and a political analyst. As far as he could see, whatever time his father didn't spend traveling, he spent reading and writing.

Mr Kentish pulled off the motorway and up at the tollbooth half a mile down a single lane road. '*Buongiorno!*' he said cheerily to the uniformed woman behind an open window, leaning across his wife and flashing a smile. '*Quanto?*' he asked, reaching for his father's *Teach Yourself Books' Italian Phrase Book (First printed 1954)* should he need it. 'Ah,' he added, 'damn it. The *lire* are in the boot.' Mr Kentish got out of the car and popped the boot open where he located the old leather sponge bag he had promoted to travel bag. In it, he and his wife kept passports, car insurance papers, travellers' cheques and foreign currency safe in one place.

The tollbooth sat in a no-man's land, with low mountains to one side and a plain that led to the sea on the other. The colours were bright, distinct, even the olive green of the trees, the grey of the dusty tarmac and the faded yellow of the booth, so that Sebastian had the impression of looking at a world in a Polaroid picture. He admired the tollkeeper's cap that struggled to contain a mass of brown hair, and her tight, blue regulation shirt that, he noticed, also had the attention of his father.

Mr Kentish slapped the travel bag down on the booth's sill and extricated first the envelope marked, in Mrs Kentish's looping hand, *francs* and then the one marked *lire*.

The tollkeeper looked as though she might have been asleep. She smiled with an open mouth, dreamily, and rubbed her eyes with the knuckles of one hand while she held the other out for the toll and Mr Kentish counted out the requisite number of notes. The only noises were the intermittent whooshes from the distant motorway and the throaty purr of the Alfetta's engine at rest.

'*Grazie!*'

5

'*Prego.*'

Mr Kentish and the tollkeeper looked up at the sound of a car approaching at speed, the squeal of its tires audible above the howl of its engine, that braked late and hard so as to not run into the back of the Kentish's car.

'Steady on!' said Mr Kentish to no-one in particular.

'Hey! *Ragazzi!*' The tollkeeper leant out of the booth and waved at the car's occupants. Her face was inches from his father's.

Mrs Kentish, Sebastian and Dominic looked out of their car's rear window, at two men in a Lancia that was the colour of the dust that covered it. They each had an arm hanging casually out of a window and appeared unperturbed, oblivious to the notion that they might have been driving too fast. The driver extracted a comb from behind the car's sun visor and swept his brilliantined black hair back while looking in the driver's mirror. The passenger waved indifferently at the tollkeeper and resumed his drumming on the car door in time with the beat of a jolly Italian pop song played loudly enough to be heard in the Kentish's car.

Mr Kentish stood a moment, as though overcome by the sudden shift from summer torpor to noise and movement. It seemed to Sebastian, reclining on the warm leather seat of his father's car, looking up at his immobile father and at the attractive, expressive tollkeeper, that time stood still a moment, that they were all participants and spectators both in the soundtrack of a sunny day. The tollkeeper tucked some hair under her cap and fixed her smile more widely and her eyes on the men. Mr Kentish looked admiringly from her to the car and back. The song ended in a gurgling diminuendo, disappearing suddenly like water drained from a sink.

'Hey! *Sbrigati!*' The driver raised his eyebrows and both hands.

'One of them is called Ragazzi and she is called Sbrigati,' noted the observant Dominic, kneeling on the back seat.

'No,' said his mother, '*ragazzi* means *boys* and *sbrigati* means *hurry up* – Peter! They want you to hurry up!'

'*Allora! Sbrigati!*' The driver had his head out of his window.

'Oh!' said Mr Kentish and then, 'Damn it!' as he dropped the Italian phrase book in his hurry. Some of the pages had come loose from the binding and a cajoling wind blew them about the dusty ground and up against his car's back tyres. He scrabbled for them with one hand while holding the other up in apology and then shuffled them together, reinserting them higgledy-piggledy between the book's covers. He ran to the driver's door, slammed it shut behind him, dropped the phrase book in his wife's lap and accelerated hard over the short distance to an intersection.

'Left here,' said Mrs Kentish, 'in the direction of Garessio and away from Albenga. Come on, what are you waiting for?'

Mr Kentish had been looking in his rear-view mirror. 'It's funny, they don't seem in a hurry. Unless it's simply a hurry to chat,' he said and took the turn.

'Drive on the right,' said Mrs Kentish automatically.

They drove north, passing olive groves, industrial estates, fields of rosemary in pots, vineyards and hamlets and then left over a bridge by a deserted petrol station. They entered a wood and then passed a working quarry, an open-pit mine according to Mr Kentish, that lay quiet and still, as it was a Sunday. The quarry formed a deep scar on the landscape, its benches widening as it climbed the mountainside as though spreading an achromatic disease of ash and granite greys, bleeding the light and colour from the surrounding vegetation. At its base, behind rusted iron fencing and padlocked gates, pools of black water had formed and reflected the quarry's dark stepped sides and the concrete shells of some yet to be completed buildings squatting sinisterly beside them. Giant bulldozers stood silently by in enclosures, sleeping animals in a malevolent, mechanical zoo.

And then west into a narrow valley on a winding road that followed the river that had shaped the valley over millennia. Shaded in the valley but driving in the direction of the setting sun now, the back-lit mountainside trees and bushes presented gradations of muted greens and of browns, greys and, furthest away, purples, much as a stage set might. Butterflies and other flying insects above the meandering road caught what little sun broke through the trees. The Kentishes stayed speechless as though in unspoken agreement not to break the spell of what felt, to Sebastian, after the heat and noise of the motorway and the gloom of the quarry, to be an enchanted, mystical place. But then he forgot himself and exclaimed, 'Look!' sitting up and pointing straight ahead in the distance. 'Interlocking spurs! I've just studied them in geography,' he explained to Dominic, settling back in his seat.

They drove uphill on a gentle incline, up and out into the open, leaving the river at some distance below them.

'Are we nearly there yet?' asked Dominic as a joke, knowing full well that *Are we there yet?* and *Are we nearly there?* were allowed and tolerated by his father but that the tautology wasn't.

'Yes. Not long to go now,' said Mrs Kentish. 'In fact, not long at all if your father continues driving at this speed.' She looked from the speedometer to Mr Kentish. 'Peter, what's got into you?'

Mr Kentish nodded in the direction of his rear-view mirror. 'It's those chaps who were behind us at the toll. They've been following us. And now they want to overtake us.' Mr Kentish changed down a gear before he took a corner and accelerated out of it. The Alfa Romeo's engine noise reverberated off the rock wall bordering the road.

'Peter! Slow down!' Mrs Kentish gripped the door handle.

Sebastian swung into Dominic again.

Mr Kentish changed up for a straight and put his foot down. 'I can't believe it! He's making a move!' The road narrowed. 'Ha! That'll teach him!'

'Peter!'

Mr Kentish, in a right-hand drive car, couldn't always see what was coming before his wife could. She emitted a cry. The four breathed in deeply. The van's long hooting faded into the distance behind them.

They came out of the turn into a short straight and then a left turn. They passed a couple of cottages in the blink of an eye.

'I can't believe it!' exclaimed Mr Kentish. 'Now he's flashing me!'

'Peter! Think of the children!' Mrs Kentish gripped the dashboard with both hands.

Sebastian didn't know whether to be afraid or elated and decided he was both. Dominic felt for his brother's hand and held it tightly.

They came out of another turn into another straight.

Mr Kentish double de-clutched and accelerated. Sebastian was pressed into the back of his seat. The sound of an Alfa Romeo in full voice was the most glorious sound in the world, he decided.

'Damn!' Mr Kentish's knuckles were white on the steering wheel. 'He's stuck fast behind me!'

The road widened ahead. The Lancia pulled to the left and drew parallel with the Alfa, its driver laughing, his black hair beating about his clean-shaven face in the wind. The passenger was so close that Sebastian fancied he could reach out and touch him and as the Lancia pressed ahead the passenger, now just inches from Sebastian's mother, turned sideways in his seat and stared at her. Sebastian could see his beard's stubble, flecks of grey in his sideburns, the oil in his hair, a scar on his chin, the gold of one molar in a row of stained, yellow teeth and the thick links of the gold chain around his neck. The whine of the Lancia's labouring motor, only just heard above the Alfa's bellowing exhaust and, above them both, what sounded like the same tinny pop song they had heard at the tollbooth, receded as the Lancia pulled ahead.

Mrs Kentish rested her hand on her husband's arm. 'Let them,' she said. 'Let them, just let them go. Don't do anything stupid.'

Resignedly, Mr Kentish decelerated. 'Well, we *are* fully laden,' he muttered. 'Still, to be overtaken by that rust-bucket...'

The Alfa slowed. To Sebastian's surprise, so did the Lancia. Having sped ahead of the Alfa by a good distance, its brake lights flashed red and then stayed red. It skidded and stopped in the middle of the road, its brake lights illuminating the cloud of dust behind it like the red eyes of a mythical monster in a fog. Mr Kentish had no alternative but to brake too and the Alfa came to a stop only a car's length from the Lancia.

The sun lit the mountains' peaks and forested sides, but the valley and they were in shadow. Above and ahead of them, the series of interlocking spurs that diminished in the distance seemed to suggest that this was a replay of an event that the valley had witnessed many times before.

Mrs Kentish tightened her grip on her husband's arm. 'Wind the windows up. Lock the doors,' she commanded her family calmly, but the driver had already left his car and was striding towards them, a silhouette of a person now, dark against a pinking sky. The passenger had got out too but stayed by the open car door, leaning nonchalantly against it, one arm along its top and the other along the car roof, his legs crossed at the ankles.

The driver drew close and Sebastian saw that he was still laughing. And then there he was, right by the passenger door of the Alfa, leaning down and looking in and holding up the Kentish's leather travel bag.

'Hey! Mister!' He inclined his head briefly at Mr and Mrs Kentish and acknowledged Sebastian and Dominic with a narrowing of his eyes. 'You left this at the – *come si dice, casello?* You left this,' he finished by saying, holding, in a hand extended through their car's open window, the bag that contained their passports, their money – their life in mainland Europe.

Sheepishly, Mrs Kentish took receipt of it. 'Thank you. *Grazie,*' she said weakly.

Mr Kentish looked from the driver to the travel bag and back again and opened and closed his mouth.

The driver leant forward a little and said, across Mrs Kentish to her husband, 'That was fun! Yes? Great, much funs! Where are you going? We raise you there!'

'No. No thank you,' said Mrs Kentish. 'We don't race anymore.'

The driver looked from Mr Kentish to his wife and back. '*Bene!*' He nodded. 'We don't raise any more.' It was implicitly understood that, were it not for his wife, Mr Kentish would have relished a race. The driver stood straight and drummed his fingers on the roof of the Alfetta, directly above Sebastian. '*Bella macchina! Arriverderci. Buonasera!*' His back to the Kentishes, he waved goodbye as he returned to his companion and his car. They drove off.

Sebastian noticed the butterflies again and a large number of dragonflies that, strangely, were somehow more visible in the absolute silence. At some point, Mr Kentish had pulled the car to one side of the road and cut the motor. Mrs Kentish rifled through the travel bag and the envelopes it contained. 'It's all there,' she said.

'Well, of course it would be,' said Mr Kentish.

An insect entered the car from Sebastian's open window and made a lazy escape out of Dominic's. The boys watched it come and go.

'I must admit,' said Mrs Kentish, 'to feeling a little ashamed.'

'So do I,' said Mr Kentish, looking straight ahead.

'Come on,' said Mrs Kentish, 'let's get to Colletta before the sun sets.'

TWO

Mrs Kentish looked from the road to her finger on the map and back again. 'Right here, by the *osteria*,' she instructed, and they turned and followed the road around again so that they were now heading east up a steeper, narrower road that clung to the mountainside under an overhang of rocks.

Sebastian reflected on the exhilaration he had experienced as they had driven the winding country roads at speed. Dominic had said that he hadn't been afraid at all and, to his father's only mild irritation, expressed by a dismissive wave of the hand, that it had been a good thing the stranger was a faster driver than Daddy. Now, Dominic repeated his question, 'But why were you distracted, Daddy?'

'Yes,' said his mother, 'I wonder. Why were you distracted?' she asked her husband.

'Fair enough, fair enough,' Mr Kentish repeated, grinning. 'I forgot the bag.'

The Alfetta slalomed up, its engine's reverberations magnified at intervals by the shallow caves the weather had carved out of the rock, and then rounded a stucco-fronted church that was small and so simply perfect that it might have had a child for an architect: wooden double doors with a window and a flower box either side and, above, a niche in which sheltered a plaster Virgin Mary. At the front of its gently pitched tiled roof was a steel crucifix and, to one side, a short bell tower. Just past it, was a sign on which was written *Colletta di Castelbianco* and another with *Parcheggio* and there was the car park with the Lancia and a dozen other cars in it and room for a dozen more.

The Kentishes got out of their car and stretched and walked to the edge of the car park to look down on the village nestled in the last of the day's sun. The valley they had left earlier was now in deep shadow. Rising from it directly in front of them, Colletta sat perched on a rocky outcrop like a stone promontory in a green sea, a jewel in a verdant setting, sparkling and winking where the sun caught its windows. It seemed to have grown organically, upwards and out of the hill in the middle of that wide valley, vertical sheets of bedrock transformed into the massive walls of a citadel. The village appeared, at first inspection, to have evolved higgledy-piggledy and, at second, along lines established by an ancient biological and primary imperative – a succession of piggy-backing, leap-frogging, odd-angled habitations that had formed themselves into a stone community of cobbled paths, stone bridges and arches, coloured shutters and painted doors. It sat in the centre of the valley it commanded, the ground falling away from it on one side to a stream that fed the river in the valley the Kentishes had just driven up. Immediately all around it were terraces given over to wild grasses and a herb garden, to cherry, fig and olive trees. Across the running water, wooded land rose to form peaks that surrounded the village as though there to shelter it from the worst of winter winds and rains.

Opposite the church was a little gravel-covered space with

red carnations in pots and a fir tree and a stone house on either side. A sloping cobbled path led down to the village's principal and only square. The Kentishes, having unloaded four suitcases, Mrs Kentish's easel and Mr Kentish's cassette recorder and satchel, paused with their luggage and looked down on it. It was small, perhaps half the size of a football pitch's penalty box. Terraced stone houses lined the path on its right; to the left, it opened out onto a patch of lawn and a small public terrace from where to admire the magnificent mountain opposite, its sheer, vertical stone face rose-tinted in the setting sun.

A young woman stepped out of a turquoise door marked *Ufficio* and said, '*Benvenuti!*' with a smile just as the plaintive guitar of *Hotel California*, playing on a cassette player behind her, ended. She had chestnut hair that hung straight to the small of her back, to the string bow of a loose-fitting dress of greens and browns with baggy sleeves. She wore gladiator-type leather sandals laced up bare, suntanned legs and bracelets on both arms that glittered in the sun when she raised her arms to push her hair back. She smiled with parted lips and hazel-coloured eyes.

In the seconds in between tracks no-one spoke, and then the breezy twang of *New Kid in Town* started and Mr Kentish put his suitcase down and opened his phrase book. 'Ahem. *Fa degli esercizi al mattino?*' he asked confidently.

The woman gasped and laughed and caught herself, her hands to her mouth.

'Give me that,' said Mrs Kentish, dropping her suitcase and taking the phrase book from her husband. 'The pages are in the completely wrong order,' she said, rolling her eyes at her husband. 'You just asked her,' and she ran her finger down a page, '"Do you do physical jerks in the morning?"'

'As a matter of fact, I do!' laughed the woman again. 'But I think you want to ask me if I have a reservation for you. I assume you are the Kentishes, yes?'

'Oh, you speak English,' said a relieved Mr Kentish.

She introduced herself as Francesca and Sebastian regretted his inability to return her generous smile as nonchalantly as he would have liked. His father was as warm in his greeting of her as his mother was cool. Dominic's mouth hung open and, keeping a grip on his mother's easel with one hand, he extended the other to be shaken in turn.

Francesca flung one arm behind her in a gesture that took in the mountain, the village, the square. 'Welcome to our paradise! Did you have a good journey?'

They did.

'Would you like me to show you to your apartment?'

They would.

Francesca ducked back into her office for some keys.

'Close your mouth,' Mrs Kentish commanded Dominic.

Francesca stood before them with a set of keys. 'Can I help you with your luggage?'

She could help Mrs Kentish. Francesca swung her head and her hair arced over her shoulder, opening and closing like a fan, and she took Mrs Kentish's suitcase from her.

The Kentishes and Francesca descended the long, inclined steps to the square in which a number of people sat on the stone benches that bordered it on two sides. Others stood, looking past an open red door into the village bar that had a television on.

'Of course!' exclaimed Mr Kentish. 'The Scotland Holland game will be on soon.'

Francesca stopped, so the Kentishes stopped.

'Hello!' said some people.

'Welcome!' said others.

'*Buonasera.*' A swarthy, severe-looking Italian stepped

forward and introduced himself as Dario, the barman and restaurateur. He carried a dishcloth over one shoulder and a couple of days' growth on his chin and cheeks, and had black, oily hair, swept straight back up from his forehead and down over his collar. He wore pointed black shoes, tight-fitting black trousers and a striped black and white short-sleeved Breton shirt like a matelot, which he had once been, he said, pointing at the tattoo of an anchor on one bicep. One rolled-up T-shirt sleeve contained a packet of cigarettes, the other, his lighter. Sebastian was rather impressed by this. Dario delivered the illusion of having recounted his life story in the time it took him to shake hands with all four Kentishes and he dropped Dominic's hand to catch a dark-haired woman by the elbow as she passed with an empty tray. 'And this is my sister, Claudia.' The *au* was pronounced *ow* and not *or*. The welcomes and handshakes were repeated. Claudia tucked her long black hair behind both ears and unnecessarily untied and tied her apron string behind her back. 'My older sister but still my beautiful sister,' said Dario addressing Dominic and putting an arm around Claudia who blushed brighter than Dominic.

Claudia took the dishcloth from Dario's shoulder, flapped it at him and continued on her way into the bar.

Sebastian watched Claudia go from the corner of his eyes and then surreptitiously at the people around him. Were all the women here going to be as attractive as Francesca and Claudia? No, there was a grey-haired witch in a leopard print sarong and with a face like a prune sloppily decorated with crimson lipstick and blue eye shadow. She was talking to a long-haired younger man in flared, patched jeans and a tie-dyed shirt with a guitar held over one shoulder, like a gun. And were they all going to be as old? Francesca had to be nearly thirty and Claudia over forty. Sebastian recalled his mother's promise of teenagers with annoyance, when along came a girl of Sebastian's age, cutting the corner of the cobbled square, carrying sheets and towels in a pile in both arms, and Sebastian's vexation vanished.

'Rosetta!' Dario called her over.

She stopped by him and looked at him impassively.

'This is the family Kentish. They are staying in...?' Dario raised his eyebrows at Francesca who spoke the name of the apartment.

'This is Rosetta. You can ask her for anything.'

Rosetta gave Mr and Mrs Kentish a barely perceptible nod and Dominic the briefest of smiles while ignoring Sebastian completely. She said to Dario, '*Hai finito? Posso andare?*' She and Dario exchanged a few more sentences in Italian and several raises of eyebrows and shoulders.

She was as cool as the others were warm, Sebastian thought. Her black hair was long and wild with a fringe of sorts behind which thick eyebrows disappeared as she spoke animatedly to Masssimo. Her arms and legs and face were tanned, with just the faintest hint of freckles, alleviating an aura of severity that would otherwise have made Sebastian feel she was completely unapproachable. He watched her turn on her heels and disappear down a cobbled path to one side of the bar.

Dario advised the Kentishes that dinner would be served at eight in the *piazzetta* but that they should appear for *aperitivi* in the square beforehand.

Francesca said, 'Follow me!' and the Kentishes followed her down some stone steps opposite the bar and turned right onto a stone-flagged path. More steps led to a rough path of hewn rock through a short, arched tunnel; their apartment was then up some steep steps on their right.

'This is all so... so... medieval,' said Sebastian, unable to find a better word.

'Late medieval,' specified Mrs Kentish stopping to admire a fig tree.

'Spooky,' said Dominic.

But the contrast between the village exterior of grey, roughly-hewn stone and the apartment couldn't have been greater. The two-bedroom apartment was all smooth white walls, modern furniture and gleaming kitchen and bathroom appliances. Dominic baggsied the bed by the window and Sebastian pretended not to care.

THREE

Robert Bravo had taken to walking before dinner because the exercise provided him with the excuse for a drink. Or with the justification for one. Or pretext, even. He was unsure of the difference between the three but didn't let that trouble him; he had other things on his mind. Out of breath, he sat down heavily on a garden chair that protested under his weight and he bent to undo the laces of his walking boots. The tinkle of running water in the valley below was drowned out by the whoosh of blood to his head. He sat back up and waited for his head to stop spinning. He scratched the grey stubble on his chin and ran his fingers through his shaggy white hair, staying his hand momentarily, as if to suppress his mind's activity. He had the evening's World Cup soccer game to look forward to, of course, and, particularly, the following day's commencement of a string of interviews with Mr Kentish.

He had done his research on Kentish and on other journalists, using his contacts and resources in the Agency to compile a dossier on them: photos, copies of the articles they'd written, their résumés. He'd gone about it prudently, he thought, discreetly enough so as not to raise any questions about why he, now retired, required the information. He'd dismissed Italian and American journalists and chosen Kentish from a short-list of English journalists. He'd read enough about and by Kentish to decide that Kentish would do, that if he were to – well, he didn't quite know how to put it to himself – *open up*, tell his story, tell *the* story, spill the beans, *'fess up* – it could be to Kentish and not only because Kentish, as a journalist, researcher and writer had some integrity, it would seem, but because he was already on the tail of the story that he, Bravo, wanted to tell. Kentish had written a nuanced article on political ideologies following the hijacking of the Munich Olympics by Black September, the Palestinian terrorist group, which focused on their collaboration with a German neo-Nazi group that had provided them with logistical support. He'd written scathingly of The Widgery Tribunal, that had absolved the British army from blame for the murders of unarmed civilians in the Bogside's Bloody Sunday. In a recent article, he had even managed to make the split of Cornwall's nationalist party sound interesting. He had interviewed people in Munich, London-derry and Cornwall for his articles and here he was – or would be soon – about to interview Bravo in Italy, having read the Pike Committee report. Bravo liked that; he believed that a journalist should be prepared to travel to his sources, should want to glean information first-hand.

The sound of a motor car gunning up a hill and the screams of children playing in a swimming pool brought him out of his reverie. He left his boots by the front door to his stone cottage and stepped into his kitchen, moving empty grappa bottles aside with one socked foot as he did so.

Bravo stood by his kitchen table, an old oak butcher's block, he suspected, with a concave centre, dark stains and one drawer.

He tugged the drawer open. Amongst the string, Scotch tape, scissors and screwdrivers was a FP-45, a pistol called a *Liberator*, still in the clear plastic bag it had come packaged in together with ten rounds of .45 A.C.P. cartridges. It was an ugly steel handgun, manufactured by General Motors Corporation with the explicit intention of being distributed to Europe's clandestine resistance forces during World War Two and designed to be cheap to produce and easy to use. What Bravo liked best about it was the twelve-step diagrammatic instruction pamphlet that contained no words, so that whoever received one would face neither language nor literacy barrier. He, personally, had overseen the distribution of hundreds of these FP-45s to Italians and demonstrated its assembly. He weighed it in one hand and considered its removal from the plastic bag. He could load it and shoot it in just six seconds, he reckoned.

Then he looked at his watch. The soccer would be starting soon and the Kentishes would be arriving in the square for their first dinner in Colletta, he presumed. He returned the gun to the drawer that he pushed shut with his hip while scanning the grappa bottles for one that might not be completely empty. A shot of grappa, a shower and a clean shirt in that order, he thought.

FOUR

Having unpacked and washed, the Kentishes made their short way back to the *piazzetta*. A television set had been placed on a bar stool in a now defunct stone bread oven that was the height of a person and resembled a grotto. A number of holidaymakers and locals had gathered around it as if before a shrine.

'The game's about to start!' said Dominic.

Dario offered people glasses of white wine from a tray poised on four fingertips, while Francesca proffered trays of *antipasti*. On the terrace just above the square, Rosetta was shooing wasps and laying the dining tables.

The Kentishes stood at the edge of the small crowd, glasses and *antipasti* in hand, exchanging polite hellos and good evenings. Mrs Kentish held her glass tightly in both hands and stood close to her husband. Sebastian was surprised that his mother, who was so confident most of the time, had moments of insecurity. He gave her a hug.

A tall man with a copper tan and shoulder length blond hair under an orange cap introduced himself as Kees Langemensen, adding that he was Dutch.

Mr Kentish introduced his wife and his children and checked, 'Case?'

'Yes. Kees. Short for Cornelius. And this is my wife, Anouk.' He pulled her gently to him by the elbow. She too was tanned and blond but with hair shorter than her husband's. 'And over there are my friends.' He waved to a couple who waved back. 'Of course, you'll be supporting Holland this evening,' he said to Sebastian mischievously, nodding in the direction of the television.

'No,' said Sebastian resolutely, 'we'll be supporting Scotland.' He felt he really did want Scotland to win as soon as he said that.

'But Scotland will never win by the three goals they need to go through to the second round!' said Kees. 'And, anyway, England and Scotland are enemies, aren't they?'

'No,' said Dominic, 'they're both British.'

Kees smiled broadly at them all, winked at Mr Kentish and ruffled Dominic's hair. Sebastian knew that Dominic hated it when people did that to him, as he sometimes did. Funnily enough, when someone else did it to Dominic, Sebastian felt protective of him.

Francesca showed the Kentishes to their table. 'Don't worry about the wasps,' she said. 'They'll be going to sleep soon.'

From where they were seated, they could just about see the television screen on which the two captains shook hands. The referee blew his whistle and Scotland kicked off. Everyone shifted on their feet in anticipation. The cave-like oven in which the television squatted magnified the roar of the crowd in Mendoza.

Sebastian had wondered at the Dutch, at the fact that they all seemed to speak English so well. 'It's because,' his French grandfather had explained, 'their foreign language television programmes are never dubbed but subtitled, unlike ours. Which is why France will always be at an international disadvantage.' Sebastian never tired of hearing English and American actors speaking French when watching television in his grandparents' house; he thought it was hilarious. His French was only passable by virtue of his having a French mother and his having to speak French with her parents, especially with his grandfather whom he liked to quiz about his time as a soldier in the Far East. Somehow, overshadowing so much of Sebastian's adolescence had been the Vietnam War, that had only ended three years ago, and, before that, the Indochina War, that had ended before he'd even been born but overshadowed his mother's childhood. *Le Général* had served there as a *Capitaine* initially and had taken his young wife with him, who, Sebastian had come to understand, had been reluctant to go.

'I never understand why he talks to you about it but never to us, to his children,' Jacqueline Kentish had said to Sebastian about her father's time in Vietnam.

'Why didn't *Grand-maman* like it there?'

'It was hot. She got bored. There was nothing for her to do and *Grand-papa* was always away.' Jacqueline Kentish had been born there, in Cochinchina, in Saigon.

Francesca and Rosetta, now wearing waitresses' aprons, brought food and wine to the table.

Sebastian lolled back in his chair in the hope of communicating complete indifference to the fact that the most beautiful girl he had ever seen was serving him. And of hiding his embarrassment at his father's open admiration of Francesca.

'This food looks delicious,' said Mrs Kentish, drawing her husband's attention to the food.

A roar went up in the stadium in Mendoza and a small cheer from the crowd in Colletta's square.

'Ah, *nee!*' said Kees.

'Scotland has scored,' shouted Dominic who had slipped out of his chair to watch the replay.

The crowd in the square took a step closer to the television and then a step back with a gasp. 'It's been disallowed!' reported Dominic.

Kees hugged Anouk.

'Look behind them,' said Sebastian, 'that chap sitting on the bench. He's the passenger from the car, earlier.'

Mr and Mrs Kentish looked and saw indeed that it was – a swarthy, unshaven, middle-aged man sitting impassively on a stone bench by the bar, his eyes on the television. Next to him sat an older man in shorts who appeared more pink than tanned and had voluminous grey hair. He had a bottle of beer in one hand and another at his feet.

'Maybe we should go and thank him,' said Sebastian, moving his legs so that Dominic could resume his seat.

'That won't be necessary,' said Mrs Kentish, shifting in hers and looking at her husband. 'We've thanked his friend once already.' She looked around, pulling her cardigan more tightly over her shoulders. 'I can't see him, though.'

'Who?'

'The driver.'

Sebastian couldn't either but, in looking around, he'd noticed that the older man was now looking intently at his mother and that his father was looking equally intently at him.

'He's American,' said Dominic following his father's look. 'I know. I heard him speak.'

The American, as if suddenly aware that he'd been caught

staring, looked away abruptly, drank deeply from one bottle and then reached for the other.

'Do you think –' started Mrs Kentish.

'Yes,' said Mr Kentish, 'I do.'

'Think what?' asked Dominic.

'Mummy means, do I think that's the man I've come to interview and, as a matter of fact, I think it is.'

'Maybe when you interview him, you could inform him that it's impolite to stare at ladies,' suggested Mrs Kentish.

'I thought he'd been looking at *me*,' said Mr Kentish.

'Penalty!' shouted the crowds in Mendoza and in Colletta.

Dominic slid from his chair and reported from the square, 'Holland have scored!'

Kees hugged Anouk.

Francesca appeared with more wine.

'It's a Vermentino?' asked Mr Kentish, appreciatively.

'The courgette flowers and goats' cheese in olive oil were just delicious,' said Mrs Kentish before Francesca could reply.

'Where's the American gone?' wondered Sebastian after the first-course plates had been removed.

His parents shrugged and turned their attention to bowls of *trofie* pasta and pesto.

'It seems,' observed Mr Kentish, 'from what we can hear, that the crowd in the stadium is behind Scotland.' There had been encouraging cheers with each Scottish attack followed by collective groans as the Scots had fallen to a succession of offside traps.

And then a roar – 'Goal!' cried Dominic, spilling pasta from the bowl he'd been given.

'If you two want to join him, do,' said Mrs Kentish.

'Well, it's half time now,' said Mr Kentish, 'and we can see well enough from here.'

Francesca and Rosetta brought clean plates and a rabbit stew and roast potatoes to the table. Dominic resumed his seat.

A couple approached the Kentishes' table with a bottle of wine and introduced themselves as the Betters, Clifford and Eva, English but just retired and living in Italy. They both had *big hair*, as Sebastian called it, Eva's blond and Clifford's pepper and salt. She carried a cloth handbag on a long strap over her shoulder and he a cream linen jacket over his, a finger through the loop below the jacket's collar.

'We saw you arrive. Have you settled in alright? How are you enjoying the food?' Mr Better pulled up a couple of chairs. Sebastian knew that his mother would be thinking that it was rude of him to do so without even asking but Sebastian liked the familiarity of it all. 'It's a very friendly crowd here. We have English, Germans, Dutch, Norwegians and even some Italians!' Mr Better laughed at his own joke.

'And an American,' said Sebastian.

'Yes, there's him too,' said Mr Better. He ran a hand through his hair and hung his jacket over the back of a chair. 'Well, what do you think? Does Scotland stand a chance?'

Sebastian had noticed that football-related questions were always asked of him or Dominic, as though children were incapable of discussing weightier topics. He had questions of his own – How does an English boy chat up an Italian girl? What did his father do for a living *exactly*? Could his mother *really* be jealous of Francesca? Was this a holiday or a business trip? It was both, he supposed. The family had gone to Colletta for a holiday precisely because his father had business in the village. At least it had got him out of school early. It might have been worse: he remembered the family's Cornish holiday in 1976 – it had rained for two weeks while there had been a heat wave in the rest of the British Isles, but they had holidayed there so his father could research an article on the first-year anniversary of the Cornish Nationalist Party.

Sebastian listened to Dominic explaining why Scotland stood a good chance of beating Holland but a slim chance of progressing to the second round and then asked, 'But why does Argentina still get to host the World Cup? After the coup and all,' he added. He thought this a rather grown-up question.

'A good question, a good question,' said Mr Better sitting up in his chair and topping up the wine glasses.

Sebastian liked him even better immediately.

'Yes, not a contentious choice when chosen as host nation over twenty years ago but now, what with the *National Reorganisation Process*' – Sebastian thought that if Mr Better could have spoken in inverted commas he would have – 'you know, the junta and the Dirty War and all that...' Mr Better's voice tailed off. He loosened what Sebastian guessed to be his old school tie.

'Yes,' said Mr Kentish, 'it's fair to say that the junta's chosen means of combating so-called international terrorism is not without a great deal of controversy.'

'If they hadn't the Americans' support, I dare say they'd have had the privilege of hosting the cup taken from them.'

'Not by FIFA. They're a pretty spineless lot,' opined Mr Kentish.

'Quite right,' said Mr Better in the tone of someone who was too polite to disagree with someone he'd only just met. 'Anyway, Argentina – as a footballing nation – has got a pretty poor reputation from previous World Cups. For being thuggish. They're hoping this one can redeem their nation's image – politically too.'

The Scottish and Dutch teams ran out of the stadium and onto the pitch for the second half and the *Collettiani* re-emerged from the bar. The noise level rose. Dominic ran off and stood by Kees. The Dutch kicked off. Mr Better's chair scraped the floor as he pushed it back and stood. 'Right,' he said.

'Look at that,' said Mrs Kentish and all turned to look at her pointing at the television. 'A beautiful colour picture. The Argentines have had new stadia built and a new T.V. centre from where they're sending their colour pictures all around the world. But – do you know what? – the games are being broadcast to their own people only in black and white. What do you think of that?'

'Well, I think it's pretty awful.' Mrs Better emptied her wine glass and spoke quickly, in the voice of someone who, having overcome her timidity, wasn't going to stop until she'd had her say. 'Argentina has had to spend a fortune building motorways, hotels and stadiums, apparently. The newspapers say that the junta is burning millions despite the country being broke. I read that the one person of any influence who didn't want to spend any money on the World Cup and to comply with all of FIFA's demands was General Actis, the chairman of the organising committee, and that he was murdered on his way to the first press conference.' She smoothed her dress down and placed her hands on her lap as though to signal she'd finished talking.

Mrs Kentish considered Mrs Better approvingly. 'The junta gives the military a bad name everywhere. And as the daughter of – '

'Murdered?' repeated Sebastian. Football risked losing what shine it had. 'Who by? Why?' He didn't want to sit through another recitation of his mother's family's military background.

Mrs Better pushed her hair behind her ears. 'Who knows? Some say by an urban guerrilla group aligned with the Left. Others say by Admiral Massera. At the first meeting of the junta after the coup, apparently, he persuaded General Videla that the World Cup had to go on, that it was of vital interest for Argentina's image. Videla thought it was a waste of money but gave in to Massera's arguments and, as Actis didn't want to spend the money, he was assassinated.' Mrs Better shrugged.

Sebastian turned his attention to the television. He couldn't reconcile murder to *the beautiful game*, he could only vaguely grasp the notion of sport as a political tool, and he wasn't that sure that it interested him. The good thing about being British, he felt, was that that kind of thing – the misallocation of resources, the assassination of political opponents – would never happen in Britain. He decided he really wanted Scotland to win the match and leant forward in his chair.

There were shouts of 'Penalty!' as a Scottish player was fouled and then cries of 'Hooray!' when the penalty was converted.

'We could do this,' Sebastian heard himself saying to no-one in particular.

'We?' said his mother.

'Well, you know, we're British when we're not English,' said Sebastian. 'Where have the American and the passenger gone?'

His mother shrugged. 'What a good idea to put olives in the rabbit stew,' she said to Rosetta who'd come to clear the table.

'Is what we do in this region. In Liguria,' said Rosetta, dinner plates in both hands. Night had fallen and the flickering television light, the weak moon and the candles on the table lent her an elfin quality.

'Is this where you're from then? Here?' asked Mr Kentish.

'No. But now my family lives down the road. Past the career. Martinetto.' She indicated somewhere with her chin.

'The career?'

'*La cava – come si dice?*'

'The quarry,' said Mr Better, helpfully.

'Yes, the quarry,' said Rosetta.

Sebastian struggled to associate Rosetta with the quarry. Her English was better than she'd let on earlier, he thought. 'Are you always working?' he asked.

'Always,' replied Rosetta and walked off the terrace, through the square and towards the bar. There was a kind of music to the way she walked, the way she side-stepped around the children who ran about her feet; to the way in which she swung her hips as she dodged the diners and drinkers who had their eyes on the T.V., all the time holding the plates high and her head higher. It felt to Sebastian, when she disappeared from view into the bar, as if a song had come to an end.

Their dinners finished, more locals appeared in the square and then a Scottish forward got to a loose ball before a Dutch defender and rounded three more and scored with a left foot cross goal shot. The Mendoza crowd went wild and its echo in a little village of holidaymakers in Liguria did the same. Everyone in Colletta's little square stood, aware that they had just seen one of the greatest goals of that World Cup, and Sebastian found that he and his father too, were standing.

'Yes!' Mr Better and Dominic punched the air.

'It's not over yet,' Kees pointed out.

'We need just one more goal!' shouted Dominic.

'I don't think I can eat any more,' said Mrs Kentish as Francesca placed a bowl of yellow cream in front of them.

'Custard?' asked Mr Kentish.

'It's *zabaglione*. It's very light,' said Francesca.

'Lovely!' said Mr Kentish.

'Yes, the *zabaglione*, it is lovely,' said Mrs Kentish.

'And where are you from?' asked Mr Kentish.

'Yes, that's exactly what I was going to ask,' said Mrs Kentish. 'Where is this delicious dessert from?'

Francesca's reply was lost in another cry and a gasp from the crowd as Holland scored.

'That's it. There's no coming back now,' said Sebastian and watched as Francesca deliberated whether or not to repeat her reply. She ran a finger across her fringe and tucked her long hair behind her ear while simultaneously shrugging it off her shoulder. Sebastian wished that his father wouldn't stare. His father was too old, he thought, to find a woman besides his wife attractive and he found it all rather embarrassing. Francesca bunched her hair in one hand and then shook it down her back as she walked smiling through the throng of people in front of the television and into the bar.

The game over, Dominic trudged back to his seat and to his dessert. 'Three two,' he said, 'but just not enough to go through to the second round.' He returned Kees' raised fist with a wave of his dessert spoon.

Dario stood behind Sebastian and Dominic, a hand on the back of each chair and a cigarette wedged in one corner of his mouth. '*Tutto bene?*' he asked, 'You like?'

'It was all quite delicious,' said Mrs Kentish. 'Compliments to the chef.'

'*Il cuoco?*' replied Dario. 'Is my sister. Claudia. I will tell her. She will be very pleased.' He inhaled deeply on his cigarette and looked up. 'A beautiful night. Tomorrow will be a beautiful day.'

Sebastian leaned back and looked up to a cloudless night sky. 'What *are* we doing tomorrow?' he asked. On the periphery of his vision rose mountains and Colletta's tall stone walls. He wondered what secrets these stones held. If they'd been there for 700 years, well, that was over thirty generations of people, wasn't it? He wondered if Rosetta had days off work and when they might be.

'I'm going to do some drawing,' said Mrs Kentish.

'I'm going to go swimming,' said Dominic.

'I'm going to work,' said Mr Kentish, 'you know, interview that American. Assuming it is indeed him and that he reappears.'

FIVE

Bravo reclined on a sun lounger with his back to the swimming pool so he could watch the sun rise above the olive trees and the valley ahead. He wore bathing trunks and an open dressing gown. His hairless legs were extended before him, and his stomach had grown just portly enough for him to be able to rest his saucer on it as he lifted his first coffee of the day to his lips. At such times, he would wonder why his chest had retained its bushy mat of now white hair while his legs had come to resemble denuded tree trunks, and conclude that this had something to do with those years in French Indochina where, a junior officer in U.S. naval intelligence prior to his assignment to the Office of Strategic Services, he had had to wear abrasive woollen socks that ended at the knee and just below his regulation white shorts. He had discovered coffee in Indochina, where the French had quickly learned the climate was conducive to the cultivation of the coffee bean, and he had been delighted to rediscover it in Italy, where, it appeared, no café-owner could fail to make a customer a bitter-sweet espresso or *ristretto* that tasted, to him, of redemption, of a guilt-free future.

He knew that at any moment Godehard would appear with towels that he would distribute across the sun loungers nearest the swimming pool, laying them out neatly and, alongside, placing books, suntan lotion and swimming pool toys for his family, thereby effectively reserving the sun loungers for the day. He would say, *Guten Morgen*, and Bravo would acknowledge him with a wave of the hand without turning around to look at him. Godehard would then head to the bar to buy bread and return home for breakfast, re-appearing with his wife and children for a swim before lunch and again in the late afternoon for an hour or so. In between times the sun loungers would lie unoccupied, the towels on them steaming briefly under a hot sun, and other holidaymakers would have to make do with the sun loungers and deck chairs amidst the olive trees.

He knew, too, that, no sooner had Godehard laid his towels out and left, Kees, Clifford and Renzo, a resident Italian, would arrive at the pool for their early morning swim, during which they would talk incessantly about the German's inconsiderate monopoly of the best-situated sun loungers. Renzo, who was thin and offended some people by wearing the tightest and smallest of swimming trunks, would speak admiringly of the German's chutzpa, a word he had been delighted to learn from Clifford, while Clifford just laughed about it. But Kees would seethe in anger on principle and make a point of removing a towel from a sun lounger, folding it and placing it to one side before straddling the sun lounger, while hoping, or so he claimed, to have to justify his actions to the returning German.

Bravo extended one arm carefully and placed his cup and saucer on a paving stone and closed his eyes. He imagined himself one of the many lizards he'd seen in Indochina, crawling out from beneath a rock to warm itself in the day's first sun. He saw red, a deep, profound, violent and yet beautiful crimson as the sun beat down on his eyelids. Maybe that's what the beginning of the world looked like, he thought. Or what the end of the world would look like. Or maybe it was just a case of his having had too much to drink again.

He'd had a shock when he'd seen the Kentishes arrive. Not Mr Kentish, but Mrs Kentish. So much so that he hadn't stayed in the square long and had then regretted having missed the rest of the soccer game. He had returned home and, having found a bottle of grappa that still had some grappa in it, had drained it and lain on his back on his bed in the dark and stared out of the open bedroom window. The mountains opposite were black against an inky sky. The only sounds were the rustling ones of small animals in the undergrowth and the occasional faint, distant cheers from the crowd in the square. Yes, he'd done his homework on the journalists but had failed to even ask himself if they had families. He hadn't bothered himself with whether Kentish had a wife and, if so, children. It had never occurred to him that a journalist might travel to an assignment with his family in tow. And such had been his urgency to divest himself of the baggage of secrets that he carried with him like a sack of snakes over his shoulder, that he hadn't for a moment stopped to consider the danger his story posed once in the open. For a journalist, well, alright, there was such a thing as professional hazard even though, in this instance, the journalist could have only the vaguest idea about what he would be getting into. But for his family, for his wife and children... Bravo winced at the term, *collateral damage*.

Seeing Mrs Kentish standing there in Colletta's square, tall, slim and blond, with a glass clutched in two hands, had transported Bravo back to 1941, when he'd taken the stairs to the rooftop bar in The Majestic Hotel in Saigon. There, he had seen a young French woman, tall, slim and blond, standing alone, a cocktail glass held in both hands and looking dully out over the darkening Saigon River. She stood outside a group of French officers and their wives, close enough to hear their conversation but not to take part in it. He had walked up to the group, introduced himself and said that he'd been told he could find *Le Capitaine* Panetta amongst them. In reply, he'd been told that the captain was out of town but that *Madame la Capitaine*, indicated with a jerk of the head, was just here and might know something about her husband's return. And so he had approached her, repeated his introduction, and explained that he had been assigned to work with her husband during this difficult period of Japan's occupation of Indochina, to gather intelligence for his country and to provide whatever assistance he could to the French. All the time, even while answering that her husband was 'in the *jongle*' and that he'd be gone for weeks at a time and that she never knew when he'd return, she had never stopped looking out over the river and holding her glass so tightly he'd feared it would shatter. He'd imagined holding her bloody hand as he removed shards of glass from it.

'I'm sure you needn't be worried,' he'd said, and she had rounded on him.

'Worried? Why should I be worried? I am not worried. I am bored. Bored nearly to death by my compatriots, by their Bridge, their cocktail parties, their... their *soirées*. I could have stayed in France if I'd wanted... this.'

She had spoken passionately but not loudly and, anxious that her outburst not be overheard, he had taken a couple of steps away from the group and to the balustrade and looked over it. The river, several stories below, was now an eastern diamondback rattlesnake thanks to the lanterns on the fishing and basket boats, stretching to a horizon that met a starlit heavens. The effect was dizzying. As he had hoped, she had followed him and looked down on the street immediately below them.

'To think, I have been here a year and have not once left Saigon,' she'd said, lifting her head. He could see the lights of the bar behind him reflected in her blue eyes.

'You don't want to know what the enemy does to French officers' wives if they capture them.'

'I know. I mean I know that I don't want to know,' she'd replied.

'If you want, I can show you around,' he'd said to the street below and that had been the start of the affair.

'*Guten Morgen!*' said Godehard.

He waved the back of one hand to the German behind him and stroked the stubble on his chin and cheeks with the other.

The prospect of an encounter with the daughter of a former lover was a sweet one, no matter how improbable. The extent to which the daughter looked like the mother had shaken him: Colletta's square had dissolved from his view and been replaced by the Majestic's rooftop bar as he'd travelled back in time in a vertiginous freefall, landing with a thud at the thought that Mrs Kentish might be his daughter. He'd staggered to his feet and fled the square, as though to leave that idea behind him, and gone to bed hungry.

Bravo swung his legs off the sun lounger and sat up. He watched Godehard's receding back. In the warm light of a new day, he could persuade himself that his was a ridiculous notion. He rubbed the stubble on his cheeks with both hands. Today he would shave. Today he would start talking to Mr Kentish. Today was to be the end of something and the start of something else.

. . .

Mr Kentish, in a white short-sleeved shirt over tan shorts and in long socks and sandals, was standing at the counter of the bar, struggling with the loose leaves of an Italian phrase book when Bravo came in. On the stool next to him were a satchel and a cassette recorder in its carrying case.

'Mr Kentish, I presume? Good morning.'

'Ah!' said Mr Kentish, shuffling pages before reciprocating. 'May I buy you a coffee?'

'You may,' said Bravo.

Claudia appeared behind the bar. '*Ciao*, Bobby,' she said to Bravo.

Mr Kentish held a finger up and then jabbed it quickly into the phrase book to prevent some pages from spilling out. '*Le piacerebbe vedere al rallentatore...*' and his voice tailed off. 'This wretched book,' he said, smiling weakly. 'But it was my father's,' he added proudly.

'May I see?' asked Bravo politely. He completed the sentence. '*Le piacerebbe vedere al rallentatore un bel film sugli animali?*'

Claudia covered her mouth with her hand but her black-mascaraed eyes betrayed her incredulity.

'Mr Kentish, the pages of your phrase book are not in page number order. Ah. Found it. "Would you like to see a good animal film in slow motion?" is the translation given here. Perhaps you wanted to order coffee?'

'Yes,' said Mr Kentish, 'but perhaps she speaks English?' He looked at Claudia who was bent over, searching for something below the counter, it seemed.

'*Due caffè, per favore, Claudia,*' said Bravo and returned the book to Mr Kentish who stuffed it hurriedly into the satchel that he then slung over his shoulder. 'No, Claudia doesn't. But Dario, Francesca and Rosetta do. The locals don't, as a rule, but at this time of year there are as many English-speaking visitors as there are Italians, you'll find. You possess no foreign language?'

'Not even French,' said Mr Kentish, raising his voice above the noise of the coffee machine and adding, by way of explanation, 'My wife is French.'

The American gripped the bar. 'Your wife is French,' he said.

'Yes.'

The American took a moment to steady himself. He decided that the emotion he felt was his habitual irritation at the reluctance the English had to learn a foreign language. His fellow Americans, he'd decided, were poor travellers who, once abroad, made an effort to learn their host's language while the English were formidable travellers who expected everyone to speak English. Well, at least Mr Kentish had a phrase book, even if its pages were in the wrong order. And of course one French woman might resemble another French woman – in fact, it was more *likely* that Mrs Kentish would be French than otherwise, given her resemblance to Bravo's former French lover. Bravo knew, deep down, that his reasoning might be suspect but didn't wish to examine it. 'Come.' He took Kentish by the elbow. 'Let's take our coffees with us.'

The American and the Englishman sat at the far end of the empty terrace. Bravo peeled the cellophane off a cigarette packet slowly, seeking time in which to order a confusion of thoughts. He'd looked forward to this moment with elation and some trepidation, with joy tempered by a small amount of apprehension that brought to his mind the sentiment that had swept Italy at the time of its liberation at the end of the last war.

On this occasion, however, the liberation was to be his. Surrounded on three sides by the stone walls of an ancient citadel and on one by steep woods and rock faces, he felt alone in a vast arena. He thought of the amphitheatre in the shallow valley between the terrace he sat on and the rocky, wooded mountain to his left and imagined a Roman circus into which he'd been thrown to combat the lions of his personal history. He thought to cover his confusion by pointing to the eagles that typically hunted in the morning sun and lifted his arm to point one out to Kentish but, not seeing one, he turned the gesture into an extended, elaborate offer of a cigarette that left him feeling a little foolish.

Kentish declined with a raised palm.

Bravo blushed to find himself asking after Kentish's family, asking whether they'd had a good journey and a good night and how was Mrs Kentish and how were the boys. He adjusted his lighter flame.

Kentish replied easily and expressed the consensus that Colletta was a find, a pearl, a jewel, a charming and exquisitely pretty village by day and an eerie and intriguing one by night.

Bravo, having heard it all before, just nodded. First-time visitors always gushed at the place, and rightly so, he thought. Having lit a cigarette, he exhaled, upwards, as if out of courtesy, but still in the hope of seeing an eagle. From where he was sitting, he'd once seen an eagle plummet into the woods above the church and rise with a snake in its talons and then drop it and catch it repeatedly, as if in a game. He had wished for binoculars. The great bird might have been playing, toying with its food, or a young and inexperienced hunter and the snake an old and wily campaigner whose luck had run out.

Kentish turned to the sound of running footsteps behind him. 'Hello,' he said, and to Bravo, 'This is my son, Dominic.'

'Dad,' said Dominic breathlessly.

'He never walks when he can run,' explained Kentish.

'This place is so exciting! I nearly got lost in a tunnel! And there was this old woman in it and she gave me a fright! Seb and I are going to explore. And then we're going for a swim.' His voice tailed off. Sebastian had followed him to the table and Dominic seemed to have noticed the American staring at his brother.

'And this is my son, Sebastian.'

Bravo couldn't help himself. The elder boy was very unlike his father and, for that matter, his brother. His blond hair and blue eyes were those of his mother but, colouring aside, Bravo thought he might have been looking at himself fifty years ago. He turned from Sebastian to his younger brother and tried to shoehorn Dominic into the sepia photographs he had seen of his father as a boy; Dominic had the colouring of a Sicilian, he fancied. If one of the boys were his grandson, the other one would be too, of course. He wanted to weep with the pleasure that the novel sensation of perhaps being a father and a grandfather brought with it. He had been looking at them, he realised, almost tenderly, too intently and so he coughed and said, 'Enjoy the exploring and have a good swim. And say hello to your mother for me,' which immediately struck him as a very stupid thing to have said and he wondered what Kentish would make of it.

He watched the boys go, Dominic skipping the length of the terrace and onto the square where his brother stopped to exchange words with Kees, who, still wet from the pool and with just a short bathing robe over his trunks, stood to drink his coffee. No doubt he was complaining about the Germans' poolside etiquette and, on this occasion, lamenting Holland's having lost to Scotland.

Bravo said abruptly, 'You didn't tell me you had a family. That you had children.'

Kentish scratched his chin, 'I didn't think it important. Relevant.'

Bravo leant forward and felt the warmth of the table on his bare forearms. He pushed his cup and saucer to one side. 'I wonder, do you know what you're letting yourself in for? Potentially, I mean?'

Kentish said nothing.

'This could be,' said Bravo speaking quietly, 'the greatest coup of your career. And possibly the last.'

Kentish raised his eyebrows.

'It could be the biggest story to break in – a very long time – anywhere. There are a lot of people who will not want the story to be told.'

'The story of Operation Gladio?'

'And everything that goes with it. You realise that you will be putting yourself and, possibly, your family at risk?'

Kentish frowned.

Bravo realised that the hand holding the cigarette was shaking. 'Actually, not necessarily.' He sat back. 'It will depend on what I tell you. You'll be safe with the big picture – you'll get the idea and maybe others will pick up from where you leave off. I'll keep you safe, I'll keep the names out of it. It's the names people object to. Of course, *my* name doesn't get mentioned,' he added.

Kentish nodded. 'As agreed in our correspondence.' He looked around him. 'How shall we do this? Where shall we conduct the interviews? Our rented apartment – well, I fear it lacks the necessary privacy.'

Bravo extinguished his cigarette. 'That won't be a problem. There's an empty office below the car park there,' he said, indicating the car park above the amphitheatre and not wishing to invite Kentish to his own apartment, his cottage. 'And then there's always the restaurant dining room downstairs from the bar. No-one ever eats there in the summer.' He opened and closed his cigarette packet. He only smoked when it was too early to drink. He was perspiring from the temples and wiped his brow with the backs of his hands. 'If you don't mind, though, we'll start tomorrow.' He needed a day in which to savour the indulgent fancy of having discovered a daughter and grandsons and to come to terms with implicating them in his story. 'We'll meet here and fetch the key from Francesca and go to the office below the car park.'

Kentish looked disappointed.

'I think I'll use today to – you know,' Bravo gestured expansively and ran a hand through his hair. 'I need to find the order in what I'm going to tell you.' He pushed his chair back and stood and looked up. Still no eagles. 'My only hope,' he said, 'is that you won't live to regret it. I mean I hope you will. Live, that is. But not regret it.'

SIX

Sebastian sat on his unmade bed in a T-shirt and shorts and gazed out of the open window. The hills appeared as though a giant hand had ripped the baize off a giant billiard table, scrunched it up and discarded it.

He turned his eyes from the brightness, back to his room and to Dominic's bed by the window where his brother's swimming trunks and goggles had left a quickly drying damp patch on the sheet. It took a couple of seconds for his eyes to adjust to the book in his hands. The letters materialised out of the grey and then the white of the page like soldier ants falling into order. He couldn't concentrate on what he was reading.

Dominic had gone swimming in the morning and Sebastian had declined to join him, wanting to have the bedroom to himself for a while. And then Dominic had returned, got changed and agreed to accompany their mother in her search for painters' panoramas.

Yesterday, that task had fallen to Sebastian. After some exploring in a rather spooky tunnel in the heart of the village, in which, Dominic claimed, an old woman lived, and a swim with

Dominic and some German boys Dominic's age, he'd followed his mother willingly from panoramic viewpoint to secluded glade, carrying her easel under his arm while she carried her paints over her shoulder. They had searched for the ideal place at which to stand the easel and to paint but, of course, the spot changed with the time of day. He knew his mother's methods. The easel would be carted around for a couple of days and never once extended. She'd spend three or four days pencil-sketching on paper and then a couple of days with watercolours on board, only then having deployed the easel. And then, only if she were sufficiently happy with her work to that point, would she take out the oils. He and Dominic would grumble about lugging the easel around but she'd insist, saying she wouldn't feel like a real painter otherwise. In truth, he didn't mind and he liked their time together. He particularly liked it when passers-by would stop to look at her work and show their surprise at its quality. She would say rather modestly that she was a Sunday painter who happened to paint on weekdays but he (and she, he believed) knew she was better than that. Besides, she had a dealer and her paintings sold at art fairs.

Sebastian and his mother had walked around the village's periphery, hugging its fortress-like walls and ducking in between fig, cherry and olive trees. The figs and cherries were ripening nicely; his mother had recalled the fig and cherry jams at breakfast. The olives wouldn't be ready for picking until November, she'd explained, when the village and its neighbours would hold their annual olive festival. They'd passed locals whom Mrs Kentish had addressed warmly and spoken to in passable Italian – her French helped. And they had passed other holidaymakers whom she had snubbed or, at least to Sebastian, appeared to. She'd ignored them and held a pencil or a drawing pad up in one hand while holding a straw sun hat with the other and addressed Sebastian loudly, mentioning perspective, composition, the quality of light and the choice of media – watercolour or oils? Crayon or chalk?

Sebastian suspected his mother of being a snob but he wasn't sure. She was very good at talking down to people and quite happy to tell him who he should or shouldn't have as friends based on – what? Some obscure social code or what their fathers did for a living. Sebastian suspected that her strong sense of social hierarchy and her place within it – close to the very top – came from her father having been in the French military all his life, from her having grown up in a world in which rank, status and social standing was visible in virtually every salutation, item of clothing and barracks home.

Having rounded the village once, Sebastian and his mother had ducked into an opening and up a steep cobbled path with close stone walls and brightly painted red, green and turquoise doors on either side. Paths led off it and steps – one set seemed to go on forever and Sebastian had looked up the outdoor stairwell to a blue sky as if from the bottom of a sea.

'Ooh, I must see where that takes me,' Mrs Kentish had said enthusiastically.

'I know. I went up there earlier with Dominic. It takes you to the very top, to a flat roof, the highest point in the village. I'll wait for you here.' Sebastian hadn't fancied struggling up the steep, narrow steps with the easel. 'Just here, in fact,' he'd shouted after her, taking a few steps along another path into a patch of sunlight.

He'd stood against the pale stone walls feeling the heat of the sun on his face and the warmth of the stone on his back when a green-painted door had opened and Rosetta had stepped out carrying a mop, a bucket and a basket of cleaning products. He'd caught sight of washing machines and piles of sheets before she'd closed the door behind her. She'd squinted and held her hand above her eyes and turned her back against the sun and faced him. Her sullen expression had been replaced with a smile.

'You're an artist!' she'd said, observing the easel.

For a reason Sebastian couldn't explain to himself, he'd been embarrassed to have been caught standing there with an easel. 'Well,' he'd replied and had been momentarily lost for words. 'Yes.' As a matter of fact, he did consider himself something of an artist but, clearly, what she'd meant was that she considered the easel his, so he'd felt obliged to mumble, 'No,' and then he'd looked down at his feet and kicked a stone along the path.

There was something about Rosetta that confounded him. There was an absence of care, of grooming, of make-up, of jewellery; her dark hair was unbrushed and her eyebrows bushy and there was a manner to her, an indifference, that made her appear savage. And yet bare legs and arms and a slim waist and a cleavage contained by a simple black dress announced her to be very much a young woman.

Sebastian had raised his eyes to hers and wondered if hers were naturally green or if what he was seeing was the reflected greens of the mountains and he felt himself falling. 'Well,' he'd repeated and shuffled his feet to regain his balance and adjusted his grip on the easel, 'I draw and paint sometimes but my mother's the real artist.' A trickle of perspiration had run down his cheek and dried there.

'So, what kind of things do you paint?' she'd asked, her head to one side, and she'd stepped closer, as though she'd find the answer written on his face.

Sebastian had immediately become aware of her smell. It was neither strong nor unpleasant but it was there, the smell of a person who did menial work in a hot country, of a woman who washed but wore neither perfume nor deodorant – it was a fresh smell, dark, heady, human and intoxicating. The sun had been almost directly behind Rosetta. It had lit some fine hairs on her arm and above her lip and minute beads of perspiration by her ear. He had imagined the world reflected in miniature in them and feared succumbing to a strange desire to lick them.

He'd begun perspiring again.

When Rosetta had tucked her hair behind her ears with her free hand, he'd wiped his face with his.

'Ah, the cleaning girl.'

Sebastian hadn't heard his mother descend.

'We mustn't keep you from your work. You can run along.' Mrs Kentish had stood with her arms across her waist, an elbow cupped in each hand, as though expecting to be obeyed instantly.

Rosetta had gathered her mop and bucket and, with one expressionless backward glance at Sebastian, had indeed run along.

'I'm sure you can find plenty of children of your age to consort with,' had said Mrs Kentish, as they'd watched Rosetta turn the corner to the *piazzetta*.

'But there aren't any,' Sebastian had said, resisting the temptation to stamp his foot like a child as he'd added, 'and I wish you wouldn't say, "children". And I wasn't "consorting", I was –' but his mother had moved on, one hand clasped to the hat on her head as she continued to look up and around her.

Sebastian realised that he'd been gazing at his book for an hour and had yet to turn a page. He looked at the chess board on which he and Dominic had started a game. It was his move but he'd wait for Dominic's return to make it. He felt too lethargic to go for a swim. He thought of tracking his father down for an early lunch but he knew he couldn't interrupt his interview with the American. His father had been a bit miffed when, yesterday, the American had requested a day's adjournment before the interviews had even begun. His father had said, 'I hope he's not getting cold feet.' That expression always amused Sebastian. He looked down the length of his legs and wiggled his toes.

Sebastian heard the front door open and there stood Rosetta, with a broom and her mop and her basket again. He saw her through the open bedroom doorway. She stood straight, framed by the open door with sunlight streaming in from behind her. Against the light, she resembled an Amazon, clutching spears and a shield.

'Hello,' he said, deciding it best to announce his presence rather than wait to be discovered. He resisted the impulse to stand, recalling his mother's instruction that one stands for a lady but not for a servant.

'I've come to clean,' she said.

That's pretty obvious, he thought. 'You didn't clean yesterday,' he said.

'That's because I don't clean every apartment every day,' she replied, her head to one side, as though *that* were obvious.

She wore shorts – short shorts, cut-off jeans – and a blue and white striped men's shirt rolled up at the arms and tied around her waist. If she got any closer, thought Sebastian, he'd see her navel.

She leant the mop and the basket against the frame of the open door and began to sweep around the sitting area and then around the breakfast table. Motes of dust she disturbed drifted excitedly in the sunlight around her legs. She removed a pan and brush from her basket and when she knelt, she was just out of Sebastian's field of vision; he could only see, if he leant forward, the small of her back, the fabric of the jeans stretched tight across her bottom, her heels, the dirty soles of her feet and of her red flip-flops. She rinsed a kitchen cloth, squeezed it and wiped the kitchen surfaces, the sink, the oven and the fridge. Had this been the Kentish home with Mrs Kentish supervising, she would have told the girl to start with the kitchen tops and save the floor till last. The girl entered his parents' bedroom where Sebastian heard her plumping up pillows, smacking them loudly for his benefit, he imagined. He tried to picture the action behind every sound.

Rosetta stood in the doorway to his and Dominic's room and leant on her broom. 'You're holding it upside down,' she said, indicating his book with a nod.

Furiously embarrassed, Sebastian turned the book the other way only to find that he'd been holding it the right way up to begin with.

'Very funny,' he said righting the book immediately, now just furious.

Rosetta laughed, showing her teeth. 'So,' she said and ran her tongue across her top lip, 'your mother is an artist, your father is a writer and you're a reader.'

'What do you know about my father?' asked Sebastian, suddenly interested to know.

Rosetta shrugged. 'I saw him yesterday. In the room downstairs from the bar. Everyone is by the pool and he's there with his typewriter. And you're here with your book.'

That had been said rather contemptuously, Sebastian felt. 'And what do you do? When you're not – working?' He'd intended to say *cleaning* but he'd been afraid he'd sound like his mother and felt a little ashamed that the put-down had occurred to him.

She shrugged again.

'Don't you have any hobbies?'

'Hobbies?'

'You know, things you like to do when you're not working.'

'I fight.' That was said nonchalantly.

'You fight?' Sebastian couldn't keep the note of astonishment from his voice.

'Yes, you know, judo. I go to lessons.'

'Judo! That's not real fighting,' said Sebastian, regaining his composure. 'That's just people rolling around hugging each other.'

'Not real fighting?' Rosetta arched an eyebrow.

'Anyway, what on earth do you need to learn to fight for?'

'When you are one sister and have brothers, you need to learn to fight, believe me.'

'You don't fight your brothers!' Sebastian found it all rather amusing.

'Certainly I do.'

Sebastian laughed. 'Sorry, I just don't see you beating a boy in a fight.'

Again, she shrugged. 'Please get off the bed. I need to make it. And clean your room.' There was an unspoken slur that she only had to do it because he was incapable of it.

'Make me,' said Sebastian.

'Make you?'

'Yeah, make me,' said Sebastian momentarily afraid that she might have confused making the bed with making him, whatever that could mean. 'Make me get off the bed. I'm sure that if you can beat your brothers in a fight, you can get me off the bed. Unless you can't, of course.'

Sebastian was uncertain as to how it happened but in the next moment, he'd lost his book and found himself with his back to the cupboard by the bed. His legs were shaky, he had a pain in his pelvis and his head was only a little sore from having hit the cupboard door. One arm, where it was held in two vice-like grips, didn't hurt so much as smart.

'Hey, that was unfair,' he protested weakly. And in the full knowledge that he would regret it as soon as he said it, he added, 'I bet you couldn't do that again.'

She did. Not letting go of him, she fell onto the bed pulling his arm after her with her falling weight and, using both her momentum and his and all the strength in her legs, lifted him with the tops of her feet on his thighs so that he flew over the bed and landed on his feet between his bed and Dominic's.

'Bloody hell!' Surprise, indignation and humiliation competed to overwhelm Sebastian. He couldn't believe it.

'Again?' Rosetta asked, eyebrows raised, as though she were offering a child another go on a merry-go-round.

Sebastian could tell she was enjoying this. She had yet to let go of his arm and, were she to throw him again, he feared it would come out of its socket. He saw her eyes narrow and felt her arms go tense and her grip tighten but, on this occasion, he was readier than he had been. He deflected one foot from his thigh with his free arm and stepped aside from the other, so that, no longer having any purchase on his body, Rosetta only managed to pull him onto the bed on top of her. He suddenly realised that he, momentarily at least, had the upper hand, and his anger and desperate need to regain some dignity and reverse his humiliation to that point gave him strength. He tried to wrench his arm free from her and succeeded only partially when he prised the fingers of one hand off, but she still held him by the wrist with the other. The realisation that she thought it was only a game while for him his honour was at stake increased his fury. With his free hand, he tried to grab her but managed to catch only the front of her shirt. He couldn't free his other hand and resorted to pulling violently at her shirt and the buttons down its front popped. He saw anger come into her eyes and delighted in it. He sat on her with all his weight while she writhed and tried to scratch his face, or so he thought, so he rolled his wrist out of her grip and caught her wrists and held her hands down on the pillow above her head and pressed hard. She bucked and struggled and kicked her legs out ineffectively behind him and he looked down in satisfaction at her face only inches from his and he waited for her to acknowledge defeat. Her dark hair lay on the pillow like storm clouds about her head. Her breasts, barely contained in a purple bra, heaved before him. And her eyes were dark wells of fury or, if not that, some other intense emotion. And all of a sudden she stopped moving and she and Sebastian stared at each other intently and just at that moment that all of Sebastian's life had been leading up to, in the intense heat of the day and of their exertion, in the hot air that was charged with possibility, at the very moment when Sebastian became aware of the warmth of Rosetta's thighs under his legs and noted the rise and fall of her heavy breathing, just when gravity had pulled his lips to only an inch away from hers, he heard his mother say, '*Mon dieu! Mais, qu'est-ce qui se passe?*'

SEVEN

Bravo left Francesca and the *ufficio* with a wave of one hand and, with the other, holding the key she had given him, indicated to Mr Kentish the way they should follow. They walked up the gravel path towards the church before turning right and down a wider, gentle grass track. Above them was the car park; below them and to their left, the office and storage rooms, built into the mountainside so that only one long, glass wall interrupted by glass doors indicated their presence. In front of them lay the amphitheatre, a stream and a view of Colletta with the mid-morning sun behind it. Immediately by the guest office front door, in a little garden behind a wrought iron gate and a hedge of hydrangeas, were a wrought iron table and two chairs.

Bravo unlocked the door, entered the office and re-appeared with two cushions. 'I think this will do,' he said, although he thought they might get too hot. Besides the shrill sound of cicadas, it was perfectly quiet. They stood little chance of being disturbed. He handed Kentish a cushion and both men sat down.

Kentish turned from the view to his satchel from which he extracted some notebooks, a black Sony TCM portable cassette recorder and a microphone. He crossed his legs and, an unopened notebook on his lap, said, 'Shall I tell you when this all began for me?'

'Please do,' said Bravo.

Kentish turned his gaze to the grove of olive trees ahead. 'In February 1976. When New York's *The Village Voice* published the leaked Otis Pike Committee Report that the House of Representatives, having voted to create a House Select Intelligence Committee as recently as February 1975, attempted to suppress only a year later. Representative Pike and his Committee had set about examining the cost of U.S. intelligence, its effectiveness and who controlled it. Of its many findings, one really stood out – the extent of the United States' interference in Italian state elections.'

Bravo only nodded. He'd read the Pike Committee report too.

'The C.I.A. admitted to having paid over 65 million dollars between 1948 and 1968 to Italy's Christian Democrats and to other right-wing parties, as well as an undisclosed amount to Italian right-wing newspapers and media. As recently as the 1972 Italian general election, the C.I.A. paid ten million dollars to twenty-one Italian right-wing election candidates.'

Again, Bravo nodded. 1972 – that was just six years ago.

'I must admit, I was staggered.'

'Well, it *is* staggering,' said Bravo

'I dug around and called what contacts I had. I was shown a facsimile copy of U.S. Army Field Manual 30-31, upon which "NATO" had been stamped.'

'Ah, so you saw that, did you?'

'In it was detailed a "Strategy of Tension", a strategy to combat communism by perpetrating crimes and then blaming them on the Left. It contained appendices purportedly co-authored by the Pentagon that gave detailed instructions on acts of terrorism, such as kidnapping, torture and public bombings and guidance on how to use the media and communications channels to implicate the Left in those crimes. I wasn't allowed to keep the document and was later told it was a forgery even though it contained the truth.'

'I was going to say,' said Bravo.

'Anyway, that is when I first heard mention of Operation Gladio. In 1977 – last year – I tried to research it but I could find no-one to speak to me on the record. One potential lead led to another and, finally, your name came up and we corresponded by letter but you too deferred.'

'I admit I did.'

'But then on 9 May this year – just a month and three days ago – President Aldo Moro was assassinated and the following day I received a fax from you saying that you would speak to me after all. For which, thank you,' added Kentish as an afterthought. He retained his notepad in one hand and removed a pencil from his satchel with the other. He looked directly at Bravo. 'Are we ready?' he asked.

'We are,' said Bravo.

Kentish placed the microphone on its stand, equidistant between Bravo and him, and pressed the play and record buttons of the cassette recorder simultaneously. 'Monday, 12 June, 1978. Colletta di Castelbianco. Interview,' he said and stopped there. 'I'm not used to not using names,' he said. 'I find it awkward.'

Bravo shrugged apologetically.

'Very well,' said Kentish and sat up straight. 'Interview of a former member of the Central Intelligence Agency, now retired, by Peter Kentish.' He raised his eyebrows as if to say, *Will that do?*

Bravo shrugged, this time as if to say that it would. He pressed a thumb and index finger to his eyes. He could feel beads of sweat forming at his temples. He stood. He leant on the wrought iron gate and looked out over the valley immediately before him and the village to his right. Kentish had done his research. But where *exactly* to begin?

Allow me to begin before the beginning. Let me give you the big picture stuff. I was born in New Jersey. My parents were of Sicilian descent. Teachers. Hard-working. They were deeply grateful to the U.S. that had given them a shot at a new life and they made a point of christening me Robert, not Roberto. They were happy for me to consider myself American, you see, and delighted to hear my friends call me Bobby or Bob. They were proud when I gained admission to the University of Pennsylvania but unhappy when I chose to study philosophy; they didn't see where it could lead. And I wouldn't have guessed where it *would* lead: to the U.S. Navy, where I had been recruited by naval intelligence. My first posting was to Indochina to help provide what assistance the U.S. could to the French under the Japanese occupation there. And then, in 1942, I was assigned to the Office of Strategic Services upon its formation. The O.S.S. was the precursor to the C.I.A., by the way. I was despatched back home, to Catoctin Mountain Park, for training, so I could participate in the Allied invasion of Sicily in 1943.

But I'm running away with myself.

If I had to choose three words to explain the driving motivation behind the politics of the U.S., they would be *fear of communism*. Everything – all of my country's foreign policy decisions during and after World War Two – can be explained by those three words. The fear was such that when the Nazis sent messengers via the Vatican to plead a separate peace with the U.S., we actually entertained the idea. For the Germans, such a peace would have allowed them to focus on their Eastern front. For us, we would have had a strong Germany act as a bulwark against Bolshevism. We knew of Germany's pogroms and we had some inkling of the Nazi's concentration camps, of course, but we considered that the Soviets had committed acts of genocide that were even more savage – decossackization; the Jewish genocide during the Russian White Terror; the Kazakh genocide; Holomodor, the famine in the Ukraine; the purges in Poland and Latvia... Tens of millions of people killed, starved and displaced in the name of communism.

The Soviets, you see, have a godless ideology. They call for the collapse of capitalism. For the building of a state based on common ownership. For a world revolution beginning with a take-over of Western Europe. We were – and remain – afraid of them.

The Nazis, on the other hand... They were Christians who believed in capitalism and in the right to private property. Even Vatican City sheltered Nazis. Because the Vatican was terrified of communism, the Pope was determined to do everything in his worldly power to prevent the godless forces of communism from taking control of Rome. 'Godless communism versus the free world.' I lost count of the number of times I heard that. There was this idea of a Christian fascist new world order. The Pope even helped us create the rat lines we used to help Nazis and German scientists escape Europe.

The Allies' victory never felt as certain as it appears now, with the benefit of hindsight. So, during the war, we prepared for the possibility of a German victory by creating *stay-behind* guerrilla warfare units. They were intended to attack enemy supply routes in each of the occupied countries, working with local partisans to destroy infrastructure and harass troop movements. We trained volunteers in handling explosives and in living rough among the local populations, in espionage and in reconnaissance that would have to be conducted in dangerous environments.

But then we won the war.

And we chose not to disband those units. On the contrary, we strengthened and expanded them, with two objectives. One – deploying the same wartime guerrilla and espionage tactics against the Soviets, should they invade, and – two – of weakening Italy's Communist Party in any event. Today, our clandestine sleeping soldiers can incite acts of terror at will. Should they uncover plots, well, we can just allow them to happen, we can sit on our hands and look the other way. The beauty is that, either way, we can fix the blame on the communists. We can destroy the communists – or help them destroy themselves. Well, that's the thinking.

One goal: to generate anti-communist sentiment. To polarise popular opinion so we can save the nation. In dull moments we pursue a debate about whether it is more efficient to do so by means of blind terrorism or of selective terrorism. The difference? *Blind* is the committing of massacres indiscriminately – actions that risk having a large number of victims and that will feed the country's indignation. *Selective* is assassination – the elimination of chosen persons, actions that raise the fear index. Unable to reach a definitive conclusion, we've used both. Most units have continued to receive generalist, military training but some have specialised – in explosives, in assassination, in driving, in hand-to-hand combat, in sabotage. Each country was assigned a code name for its stay-behind soldiers.

In Italy it is Gladio.

Kentish stopped writing. 'So that's Gladio,' he said.

'Yes,' said Bravo. He felt sweat trickling down his back that he had presented to the late morning sun. But now the sun was beating down on his left cheek and his ear felt hot and, thinking ahead to lunch time, he suddenly felt hungry but, above all, he felt relieved, elated even, now that he'd begun talking. He had so much to say. He had to get his thoughts in order. He had to have answers ready for the questions of why he was doing what he was doing, why he was lifting the lid of a box of secrets, why he was bringing into the light a forty-year career that had been pursued in the shadows.

Kentish said nothing.

'From *gladius*, the Latin word for sword, the type Roman foot solders carried,' Bravo felt compelled to add. 'Shall I carry on?'

Kentish held a finger up as he checked to see how long his cassette had to run. 'Yes,' he said.

Gladio is divided into forty groups, each specialising in sabotage, propaganda or guerrilla activities. It has a training camp in Sardinia. I visited it on many occasions. I wrote some of the training manuals.

Of course, most Gladio members were Italian but not all of

them. We recruited from amongst the Nazis in Fort Hunt – that's the interrogation centre in Virginia where high-ranking captured Nazi officers were taken to. They – these senior S.S. personnel – and members of the Soviet anti-communist spy network – the Russian czarists – returned to Europe to join the stay-behind armies. And some of them evolved into the Agency's European subsidiary.

But not only did we befriend and employ Nazis, we befriended and employed the Mafia too. The U.S. was prepared to prevent Italy from falling into the clutches of the Soviets at any cost. If this involved a pact with organised crime, well, it was a price we'd pay. But that came later. At the time, the O.S.S. was charged with implementing plans for the invasion of Sicily. The plans centred on the establishment of contact with the Mafia and giving them every possible assistance. And the principal reason that I – and others – were chosen was that, besides our intelligence background, we were of Sicilian descent. I spoke the dialect, as my parents spoke it at home.

I and other O.S.S. operatives landed in Sicily in secret before the invasion to prevent Mussolini's forces from sabotaging the ports and to establish supply lines, to organise support from locals for our troops. And then, July 1943: Operation Husky. It took you Brits and the Canadians six weeks and thousands of casualties to reach your objectives while it took us one week and at only a very small cost to our soldiers. It was 'our' *blitzkrieg*. You see, the Sicilians had always been anti-Fascist and anti-Italian. By then, two million Americans of Sicilian origin were living in the U.S. Maybe one half of the island. First and second generations. We lived in a degree of prosperity that was unimaginable by the people back in Sicily, many of whom had become totally dependent on the money sent to them by their now American relations. We saw to it that the Sicilian component of our invading force was as high as possible; maybe one fifth of it was. Anyway, because of that, over half of Mussolini's soldiers on the west of the island deserted. So we had relatively little opposition.

To my frustration at the time, being in Intelligence, I saw no action. Well, not at first hand. We set up base in Licata and stayed there for some weeks, managing logistics and, well, intelligence, but I spent the rest of the war and some time after it traveling around Sicily.

I was shocked by what I saw.

Everywhere, there were buildings in ruins and funerals and shrieking women and beggars and cripples and mutilated former soldiers. Criminals had been let out of jail and the lunatics out of the asylums. Worst, was the smell. Smallpox, typhoid and malaria were rife – and venereal diseases; prostitution was ubiquitous, and much of it child prostitution, distressingly. Every town had a street in which women stood facing a wall ready to hitch their skirts above their hips in exchange for cans of meat that soldiers would place at their feet. The contrast between the white of their buttocks and thighs and the dark tan of their calves always struck me as obscene, more than the act itself, for some reason.

Everything was for sale in the black market. The shops were empty; they had no food, no soap. Whole families would be out along roadsides and in fields searching for edible plants. Landowners retained bandits to keep the peasants in order. Sicilian peasants who'd returned from the First World War had spoken of the Northern Italians they'd met and of their revolt against feudalism and servitude. But back home, in Sicily, those ideas had fallen on ears as deaf as Sicily's soil was barren. Like everyone but the Sicilian aristocracy, my parents, despite having received an education of sorts and gone on to become school teachers, were poor – or had been, until they'd emigrated. They would recall sermons preached on the blessedness of poverty – you know, the Lazarus parable – and of rendering unto Caesar the things that are Caesar's. In other words, you paid your tithes, your taxes, whether to the Church, the State, the Mafia or the landlord – no matter, you paid and sought your reward in heaven. Thirty years later, by the time of the Second World War, nothing had changed. Life in Sicily had barely changed in decades. Nearly half of Sicilians were illiterate. Only half the houses had sanitation. For Sicilians, it had been a feudal, subsistence level life that became even harsher in the aftermath of the war. What labour that had been given them on the feudal estates had been poorly paid and infrequent, providing barely enough food to keep body and soul together. When they had tried to stand up for their rights, they had been beaten down by the Mafia, whose senior members were of the Sicilian aristocracy and owned the land.

The war over, nearly all Italians despised the Mussolini régime for having dragged the country into disaster and, consequently, they hated the fascists and their collaborators who put themselves forward as candidates for democratic election. The only political parties that could lay claim to harbouring no damaged reputations or political turncoats were those of the Left. Indeed, many socialist and communist leaders could boast of the years they'd spent in fascist prisons. And so there was a rise in the support for Left-wing parties in Italy just at a moment when we felt it was necessary to confront the communist Eastern bloc with an undivided anti-communist West. The swing to the Left at the polls seemed especially likely in Sicily, where the Left's appeal was based on the redistribution of property. The Sicilians were very hungry for their own land, literally – they were starving. They were very receptive to the new parties that were promising to turn Sicily's uncultivated estates over to them and to this new idea of trade unions that the Left campaigned with – at least the peasants were. However, the landowners regarded trade unionists with a sort of amazed contempt and some fear. There seemed something basically un-Christian in the way they corrupted ordinary, decent labourers, put ideas into their heads, induced them to extort grossly unfair rewards for their labour by the threat of withholding it altogether. The Right floated the idea of detaching Sicily from Italy, with some senior members of the Mafia in favour of the Sicily's becoming either a British colony or an American state. Others wanted it to become a Catholic monarchy. Some even argued for two kingdoms: the south of Italy and Sicily, both for a long time a colony of the industrialised north and a source of cheap labour and foods. We encouraged the separatists, on the principle that should Italy take a disastrous plunge to the Left, it might not be a bad thing to know that Sicily, with its excellent naval bases, remained in friendly hands. That never happened, as we know, but the Mafia aligned itself with the political Right anyway and set about the quiet elimination of trade union leaders. It was a surprise to see the Mafia lining up with the fascists; initially, they'd hated them, as only Mussolini had ever stood up to them. In fact, he would have eliminated them had he been victorious. But he wasn't. We were and we liberated them from the prisons and had them appointed as mayors across Sicily.

Of course, the irony is that we had fought with the communists against the Germans during the war. The partisans we supplied and supported were communist. And it was they who forced the Germans out of northern Italy and who captured Mussolini. And hanged him. The thing is, though, that they could do it because Italy was the home of the largest and most powerful communist party in Europe. We had nightmares that communists might win power in Italy. It was deemed the essential rampart of European defences against the Soviet Union. The Italian Communist Party therefore had to be destroyed and we did it by all means possible, by fostering an imagined communist subversion in Europe, by rigging elections, by subterfuge, by buying influence, by murder even.

There was a *clunk*, as the cassette came to its end. Kentish didn't move to turn it over. He spoke slowly. 'You're telling me that the U.S. used the O.S.S. – that became the C.I.A. – and NATO and the Nazis and the Vatican and the Mafia in the fight against communism.'

Bravo wasn't sure if that was a question and said nothing. It didn't sound believable to him, sometimes. He had been standing with his back to the gate and now found himself in the shade and his legs were tired. The perspiration had dried on his cheek and on the back of his neck.

'To think I came here with questions and now have more than I started the day with,' said Kentish, flicking back through his pages of notes.

'We should have brought some water,' said Bravo.

Kentish concurred. 'I think I should keep my new questions for later.' He stopped turning the pages of his notepad. 'I must admit, it's a lot to take in.'

The American nodded as he put away the cushions. He locked the office door and said, 'Forgive me for confusing you. I haven't rehearsed any of this.'

'There's nothing to forgive,' said Kentish hurriedly, 'It's not how you're telling me, it's what you're telling me.'

'When we meet tomorrow, I'll tell you about the 1948

Italian national election and about the Portella della Ginestra massacre.'

They looked out over the amphitheatre and in the middle distance Bravo could see Dominic struggling uphill with his mother's easel.

EIGHT

'Hello, Dad,' said Sebastian.

'Hello, Seb,' said Mr Kentish, looking up from his type-writer. 'Blimey!' What happened to you?'

'Oh, just playing,' said Sebastian sheepishly, lifting his hand to the scratch on his cheek. 'Mum and Dom are waiting upstairs. Outside. She said you're to come up for lunch.'

'Lunch already!' was more of an exclamation than a question. 'Let me just put these things down. Dario said I could leave my typewriter here.'

They took the stairs up through the bar and out into the square and made their way to Mrs Kentish and Dominic on the terrace.

Mrs Kentish's large black sunglasses hid a still angry expression. Sebastian could tell from the crimson slash of her mouth. He had seen it all through his mother's eyes. The disarranged beds. The strewn flip-flops, book and swimming goggles. Chess pieces on the floor. Rosetta's ripped shirt. Their tousled hair and dishevelled states. Her son astride the cleaning girl. Behind her had stood Dominic, wide-eyed.

He'd tried to explain, of course. Rosetta, in as dignified a manner as she was capable of under the circumstances had tried to tidy herself up and then the room but had been asked to leave by Mrs Kentish in a trembling but terrible voice. He'd taken refuge from his mother's admonishment in the shower until the water had turned cold.

'Have you told him?' asked Mrs Kentish.

'Told me what?' asked Mr Kentish.

Sebastian shook his head.

'Sebastian and Rosetta had a fight!' said Dominic.

'What?' said Mr Kentish incredulously.

'At least Dominic believes me,' said Sebastian, not daring to look at his mother.

His mother choked. 'What do you take me for?' She spoke through the tightest of lips. 'From now on, you stay well away from that girl.' She accepted a menu from Francesca that she used to shoo her away. 'Do you understand me? You don't so much as speak to her. Have you understood?' With her stretched lips and big black sunglasses and her hair bunched up under her straw hat she looked more like an alien than a mother, thought Sebastian.

'Steady on,' said a bemused Mr Kentish, 'what's all this about?'

'And you, you too,' said Mrs Kentish. 'You can stop making eyes at that Francesca girl, for a start. What kind of example do you think you're setting? Now, before everyone looks at us, let's just keep quiet and look at the menu.'

Sebastian felt bad for having dragged his father into this. And yet he too was uncomfortable with the way in which his father followed Francesca with his eyes. He glanced up from beneath his fringe. Shame, Anger, Astonishment and Bemusement have just sat down to lunch, he thought to himself. He avoided his father's eye.

Sebastian sulked around the village, feeling a little annoyed that the charm of the place could only dampen his mood for so long – he had been quite enjoying his feeling of being the victim of unjust persecution, his having been misunderstood and ill-judged by his mother. 'But nothing happened! We didn't do anything!' he'd protested. Of course, had his mother burst into the bedroom just a minute later, he might no longer have had that defence to hand.

He wandered along the service road and then up to the church where he took the step to the door, in the expectation of finding some relief from the heat. It was locked. At least the front of the church was in the shade. He put his face up against a window and both hands either side of his face but the contrast between the sunlight and the unlit interior was too great for him to make anything out. It was more of a chapel than a church, he thought.

'Are you wanting to confess yourself?'

Sebastian started and spun around.

The driver of the Lancia ran a hand through his hair and said, 'The church, she is only open on the Sundays.' He stood with his back to the door and looked out over the village. He adjusted his shirt collar. 'In Italy, the churches they have many arts. And they are much stolen. For money, you know? And *sfortunatamente – come si dice?* – they are then must be closed.' He pronounced closed, clo-*zed* . 'You like?' He cast his hand over the village that lay curled like a sleeping cat before them. 'Is quiet, no? Everyone is making the siesta.' He took his sunglasses, that had been hanging from the bottom buttonhole of his blue polo shirt and put them on. 'Your father, he is a nice man. He is a journalist, no?'

'I think so,' said Sebastian, resting his hand on the windowsill.

'Ah, you think so!' said the driver. He put his finger to the side of his nose and laughed and winked as though he and Sebastian were sharing a joke.

'I mean, he's not affiliated to one newspaper or anything,' said Sebastian, wondering if he was saying the right thing. 'I don't think so, anyway.'

'He is friends with the American? You are friends? Family friends?'

'Oh, no,' said Sebastian.

'So is work?'

'Yes.'

'He is a colleague.' The driver bent down and adjusted the crease of his blue jeans, so Sebastian couldn't see his face.

'No, they're not colleagues.' Sebastian hastened to correct the misapprehension. He looked at a sweat patch on the small of the driver's back. 'Dad is interviewing him.'

'About what?' The driver stood and leant against the door, his head back against it and his arms crossed. His eyes were invisible behind dark glasses.

'I don't know. Politics, I expect. That's what Dad does, mainly. He interviews people. And then writes about them. I think.'

'*Bene*,' said the driver. He put one foot up against the church door and stood on just one leg, leaning against the door. He took a keyring with the Lancia insignia out of his pocket and twirled it around one finger and caught it, twirled it and caught it. With his free hand he patted Sebastian on the shoulder and repeated, '*Bene*.'

Sebastian took that as a signal he should go. He was happy to leave the driver there twirling and catching his keyring and skirted the side of the village above the amphitheatre. He strolled amongst fig and cherry trees with no particular objective in mind. He exchanged hellos with a couple of walkers and, a moment later, having heard them laugh, he looked back in time to see an embarrassed Dominic give up his hiding place behind a tree, betrayed by the friendliness of strangers.

'You cheeky rotter!' he called. 'Been following me, have you? I'm going to get you for this!' Sebastian might have struggled to get the better of Rosetta but Dominic would be a less formidable opponent. Sebastian was too quick for the ten-year old. When he caught him, he put him in a gentle headlock and ruffled his hair and tickled him.

'What did the driver want?' asked Dominic after he'd squealed and wriggled away from his brother.

'Nothing. He was just being nosy. Fancy a fig?' Sebastian plucked one, rubbed it on his T-shirt and ate it.

Dominic reached for one and then pulled his hand back quickly. 'Urgh!' He shuddered and pointed.

The boys brought their heads together and looked closely at a large pendulous fig that seemed to be moving and shaking of its own accord. It resembled a dark, purple scrotum that, stretched and already torn near the stalk, threatened to fall to the ground at any moment. A black fly was motionless on one side of it, its proboscis inserted in it. The fig revolved slowly, and the boys edged around to better see the other side. They saw a large fleshy hole, the edges of it a pinkish red and oozing yellow seeds and in the middle of which a bright emerald green beetle not much smaller than the fig itself was consuming it from within.

Sebastian thought he'd never seen such a brilliant green. 'I think those are its wings,' he said. They flashed blue and gold in the sunlight. 'It's funny, isn't it, how something so beautiful can be so, well, bad.'

'The fig is beautiful,' said Dominic, 'but it's not bad.' He prodded the fig with a twig and the fly flew away.

'No,' said Sebastian, 'What I meant was the beetle, it eats and makes its home in the fig and yet destroys it.'

'You mean it's like biting the hand that feeds you?'

'Yes, something like that.' Sebastian looked at his brother approvingly. Dominic surprised him sometimes. 'Come on,' he said.

They stood and moved on, Dominic swinging a stick as they went, whacking the weeds and grasses that bordered the beaten earth path. They reached the path of large steps hewn into bedrock that led into the village from the back. Dominic stopped, so Sebastian stopped. Higher up, at the very top of the path, were Rosetta and the passenger from the Lancia they had seen on the drive to Colletta in what appeared to be a heated exchange of words. The passenger was waving his arms animatedly, the sun catching his gold necklace and bracelets, while Rosetta just stood there, her arms crossed, a basket of laundry at her feet. The boys were too far from them to hear what they were saying. Rosetta took a step back as the passenger took a step forward and then he turned abruptly and walked off. She watched him go, then picked the basket up, shouldered it, and walked in the other direction.

'It was that man again, wasn't it?' asked Dominic, excitedly.

'Yes,' replied Sebastian. He realised his fists were clenched. If the passenger hadn't left, he would have run up and been ready to defend Rosetta. He formed the intention to disobey his mother's prohibition to spend time with her. 'Tell me,' he asked Dominic as they resumed their walk up the uneven rocky path that would lead them into the heart of the village, 'is there any part of Colletta you haven't explored yet?'

Dominic stopped to reflect. 'Well, I haven't been up there yet,' he said, pointing to some stairs ahead of them. 'They probably lead to another flat roof, like the other ones. You know.'

'Let's find out,' said Sebastian. The convoluted and uneven staircase, formed by arches and right angles lit by shafts of sunlight, reminded Sebastian of the black and white prints he'd seen in one of his mother's art books.

The boys climbed the twisting and turning stone steps and reached a terrace bordered by a stone parapet on three sides and sliding glass patio doors on the other. On it were two sunbeds, two white plastic garden chairs and a table next to a furled green parasol. Geraniums and other flowers and plants that Sebastian couldn't name grew in pots and discoloured buckets on old dinner plates.

'I think this is private,' said Sebastian. 'We should probably go back.'

They were about to start on their way down when they heard, *'Ciao, ragazzi!'* for the second time that holiday. Francesca stepped out of the room behind the doors and stood on the terrace drying her hair with one towel while wearing another wide enough to reach her thighs and tucked in on itself above her breasts.

'Oh, sorry!' said Sebastian, turning again to go. For a moment, Sebastian hadn't known whether to be terrified or hopeful that the towel would slip.

'No. Please, come. Welcome, welcome to the servants' quarters!' Francesca laughed.

Dominic took the last step up to the terrace and Sebastian had no choice but to follow.

'Is this where you live, then?' asked Dominic and tucked his hands in his pockets.

Sebastian envied Dominic's ability to remain unflustered around beautiful, nearly naked women and guessed that would change once Dominic reached puberty. He'd tried to remember what he'd been like when he'd been Dominic's age but couldn't.

'Yes, me and Rosetta,' replied Francesca, leaning her head to one side to better towel her hair. Wet, it appeared black. 'This is our hiding place!' She laughed again.

'It's nice,' said Dominic. 'Do you live here all the time?'

'No. Only in the summer. When we're working here.'

Sebastian looked out over the low stone walls to the inter-locking spurs he'd seen on the drive in, behind which the sun would soon be setting. In the other direction, above the village and in the direction of the sea, he knew, the sky was so pale that it appeared almost white. The views were magnificent and the terrace, while overlooking, was not overlooked at all.

'I am forgetting! We don't often have visitors – would you like a drink?'

'Oh, no thank you,' said Sebastian, not wanting to disturb and feeling that, really, they shouldn't be there.

'Yes please,' said Dominic, sitting on a plastic chair, 'What have you got?'

Well, he's got a cheek, thought his brother and made eyes at him, while Francesca listed juices and fizzy drinks.

'Please. Sit down,' said Francesca to Sebastian, indicating the vacant chair. 'I'll be back in one moment.'

Sebastian sat, facing the open, sliding patio glass doors with his and his brother's double reflections to one side and, to the other, the single room that seemed to comprise the apartment. There was a kitchen at the far end and a door that, no doubt, would lead to a bathroom. While Dominic rambled on about something, Sebastian watched Francesca toss the towel with which she'd been drying her hair onto a bed, open and close a refrigerator door, pour the pear juice Dominic had opted for into a glass, drop the towel she stood in to the floor and, quite unwittingly, Sebastian was sure, present herself fully naked to him from the back. Five minutes ago, if asked, he'd have said the most delicious moment in his life was the moment in which he'd sat astride Rosetta just before his mother had interrupted them. Now he was no longer so certain. Francesca stretched and ran her fingers through her hair, from the top of her head to the small of her back. She stepped to one side, so that now Sebastian saw her through the glass, and she leant and picked up a pair of knickers from the bed. As she did so, she crossed Sebastian's reflection so that, to him, as he raised his hand to his face, it brushed her hanging breast while the other hand, open on his lap, cupped her buttocks.

'You're not listening,' said Dominic.

Francesca stepped into a dark blue summer dress that she zipped up at the back and then she appeared on the terrace with the pear juice in one hand and a hairbrush in the other. '*Prego.*' She placed the juice on the table next to Dominic and asked him to finish zipping her up, which he did as though it were the most natural thing in the world. She then brushed her hair using the glass patio doors in place of a mirror. 'Well,' she said, having slid the doors shut, buckled a pair of sandals on and draped a dark cardigan over her shoulder. 'I must go for the dinner, but you can stay as long as you want. And do come again, whenever you want. See you at dinner!'

'Thank you,' said Sebastian, thinking that she should be thanked for her hospitality and blushing to think what he was really thanking her for. 'Will you be showing the football this evening?' He didn't care but he didn't want the moment to end

– the beauty and charm of the young woman, the quality of the last light of day, the vision he'd been presented with, the contentedness of his brother as he slurped his pear juice and, underlying it all, the morning's sensation of Rosetta's body beneath his.

'There's no football being played today,' said Dominic before Francesca could answer. 'Tomorrow there's Austria v Holland and Italy v West Germany from Group A, and Brazil v Peru and Argentina v Poland from Group B. They're all at 4:45 except for Argentina's game which is at 10:15. In the evening, of course. Everyone's saying it's a bit dodgy that the Argies get to play their game after the Brazil Peru game. They're all second-round matches. Holland, Italy, Argentina and Brazil are the favourites to go through.' Dominic swirled his pear juice, in the manner in which Sebastian had seen adults swirling wine.

Sebastian looked at his brother. How did he know all that? And how did he remember it? And he didn't even look smug.

NINE

'You know, my taking off like that on our first day... Well, I'm sorry. It's just that this brings back many memories and I thought it best I go for a long walk and order things – in my mind – you know.'

'Yes, of course. And what you said was very ordered.'

'I'm glad you think so. I walked along the beach from Alassio to Laigueglia and back. You know, I've stayed away from beaches. Since 1943.' Bravo laughed. 'I suppose that's why you find me in the mountains or deep inland when I'm not here. That's never really occurred to me before – not consciously,' he added.

'I understand,' said Kentish. He looked enquiringly at Bravo, pressed the play and record buttons on his cassette player simultaneously and spoke the day and date. 'So. The 1948 election.'

Bravo nodded. 'To make sense of it, we have to go back a couple of years.

'Italy had its first post-war general election in June 1946. The Christian Democrats were only able to form a government with the help of some smaller right-wing parties, as the Communists and Socialists together had run them close. The Left had fielded separate candidates so had only ministerial posts under De Gasperi but, all the same, this put the fear of communism into the Truman administration. Truman froze the loans Italy had been promised and summoned De Gasperi to Washington when it was made clear to him that Italians who did not fully share our ideology should not be allowed to participate in government. It was only then that Truman resumed generous aid flows and, additionally, cancelled Italy's one-billion-dollar debt.

'I had been stationed in Rome where, incidentally, my job included briefing sympathetic reporters on stories that the Communist Party was being funded by bags of money doled out from the back doors of the Soviet embassy, but I returned to Sicily ahead of the regional election in 1947, in April. It was a big thing for the Sicilians; they'd always been ruled from Rome so this would be the first ever election for a Sicilian parliament. The Christian Democrats were supported by the church and by the landowners and were considered certain to win. I must admit to having been shocked by the atmosphere of political intimidation, the cajolery and coercion both. On the Sundays prior to the election, I listened to priests delivering sermons in praise of the Right while warning the flock against the evils of the Left. During the week, I witnessed nuns bribing voters with one-kilo bags of pasta and with one-thousand lira notes. Political meetings of Left-wing parties were disallowed. Hundreds of certificates of blindness were issued to the elderly whom I watched being accompanied by the Mafia into polling booths to ensure that they voted Christian Democrat, while armed Mafia thugs stood outside the voting booths to intimidate the other voters.

'And yet, despite all of this, astonishingly, the Christian Democrats lost: the Left's was a resounding victory. In retrospect, the idea that the Sicilians who voted communist *were* communist is fanciful. They weren't voting *for* communism but for the distribution of feudal land holdings to the peasants who worked the land and against the continuation of a government they considered, at best, useless and, at worst, evil; against a conspiracy of corrupt politicians abetted by criminals who conspired to keep the fruits of the land from them, from the people who worked it. Communism – and socialism – were just empty terms that meant nothing to them. And yet this election raised the very real spectre of a Communist government in Italy spreading from the south.

'Of course, the politicians – in Rome, in Washington – were concerned but the Sicilians – well, the landowners, the Church and the Mafia – were furious. The Right decided to give the peasants a lesson and on May Day, just twelve days after the election, they exacted their revenge.'

'The Portella della Ginestra massacre?'

'Yes. It had been intended to be a big celebration, a parade, with addresses given by leading communists and trade unionists.'

Kentish consulted his notes. 'Eleven people killed and twenty-seven wounded, by one account, and eight killed and thirty-three wounded, by another. Including four children. Indiscriminate machine gun fire into the May Day parade followed by fleeing civilians being shot at by gunmen on horseback. One girl had her jaw blown off. American machine guns and spent ammunition were found on the scene, apparently. Was the C.I.A. involved?'

'The C.I.A. had yet to be formed.' Bravo scowled. 'It was created four months later,' he added in a mumble.

'Alright then, the O.S.S.'

'The O.S.S. had been disbanded. Two years earlier.' Bravo shuffled his feet.

'Very well then, American intelligence. Was American intelligence, whatever name it went by at the time, involved?'

Bravo held up his hands. 'No! But did we know that things were going to heat up ahead of the next election? Yes. People in Washington spoke of turning back the *red tide* so, from our perspective, we couldn't allow the risk of the country going communist. And did we think the Mafia would let this vote go "unpunished"? No. However, we never thought they would act so soon.'

'So it was the Mafia? The newspapers blamed it on bandits, on outlaws, on the ones tried and convicted in Palermo three years later.' Kentish considered his notes. 'One bandit said at the trial, "We were a single body – bandits, police and Mafia, like the Father, the Son and the Holy Ghost." Was *bandits* a euphemism for American intelligence?'

'No! The clue's in the name, *intelligence*. At the time we were only there to gather intelligence.' Bravo regretted having betrayed his irritation with Kentish's persistence.

'My research,' said Kentish, 'supports evidence that nearly 500 left-wing politicians were assassinated in Sicily in 1948 alone by the Mafia. Might the C.I.A. have been complicit in those murders?'

Bravo sighed. 'Look, had it not been for the Mafia, the communists would by now be in control of Italy.' He found himself sitting with his shoulders hunched and his hands open, palms upward.

'That doesn't really answer my question. In the town of Corleone – just the town of Corleone – over 150 murders took place between 1944 and 1948,' said Kentish looking up from his notes. 'Are you saying that these were committed by a Mafia that, having been hand in pocket with American intelligence since, it would appear, 1943, suddenly started acting unilaterally?'

Bravo placed his hands on the table. 'I can't speak in such generalisations. Have you forgotten the communist takeover of Czechoslovakia in 1948? How alarmed we became about the Soviets' intentions? What that did to us?'

'Alarmed or paranoid?'

'Your country too. If a leftist coalition had been allowed to win an election in Italy the country would undoubtedly have been drawn into the Soviet Union's sphere of influence.'

Kentish sat back and asked quietly, 'So the end justifies the means?'

Bravo sighed. 'That is precisely how we thought.'

Kentish nodded. 'I've seen copies of the newspapers of the time. Time Magazine warned that a leftist victory would take Europe to "the brink of catastrophe". It said that the U.S. was prepared to use force to prevent Italy turning communist.'

Bravo laughed. 'Of course we were! It was precisely the fear that that might happen that led to the creation of the Office of Policy Coordination, which gave us the legal authority to undertake covert political, propaganda and paramilitary operations. We warned Italians that, under a Communist government, the nation's factories would be dismantled and shipped off to Russia and that millions of Italian workers would be turned into slave labourers. And Truman accused the U.S.S.R. of plotting the total subjugation of Western Europe.'

'Which was reason enough to burn down eleven Communist Party branch offices and to make four attempts on the life of the leader of the Communist Party? The 1948 election referenced in the Pike Committee report – talk me through it.'

'It's simple. We were prepared to do anything to prevent a repetition of the regional elections at the national level.'

'So what did the C.I.A. do? Exactly.'

'What did we not do?' Bravo began enumerating what the C.I.A. had done on his fingers. 'We organised a nationwide letter-writing campaign from Americans of Italian extraction to their relatives and friends in Italy begging them to vote for the Christian Democrats. We produced radio broadcasts, urging Italians to vote for freedom and not for dictatorship. We printed millions of leaflets and made T.V. documentaries with the same messages. *The fate of Italy depends upon the forthcoming election and the conflict between communism and Christianity, between slavery and freedom.* That kind of thing. We had "friendship trains" painted in the colours of Italian and American flags run the length of the country handing out "gifts of the American people" at every station. We promised Italians the recovery of their lost colonies in Ethiopia and Libya, not that any of them cared. We signed a treaty with Italy promoting friendship, commerce and navigation. Just a month before the election, Truman made a "gift" of twenty-nine merchant ships to the Italians as a "gesture of friendship and confidence in a democratic Italy" that were, in fact, Italian vessels seized by the United States during the war.'

'So Truman was just returning them.'

'Yes. And just six days before the election, we announced that Italy would receive over three million dollars in gold in return for gold looted by the Nazis.'

'Even though Italy had been Nazi allies.'

'Yes. And the House Appropriations Committee approved nineteen million dollars in interim aid funds. And shortly after, we gave Italy over a million dollars as the first payment on wages due to Italian war prisoners who had worked voluntarily for the Allied cause.'

'Even though the peace treaty said that Italy was liable.'

'Yes. We authorised shipments of food – one alone for eight million dollars of grains.'

'These were all bribes; what about the threats?'

'Oh, we had those. The Justice Department announced that Italians who joined the Communist Party would be unable to emigrate to the U.S. And, of course, we had a very slick disinformation department that distributed sordid personal details about the candidates on the Left that were mostly made up.'

'And what about the violence?'

'Oh, there was plenty of that. We had hundreds of Italians – you could call them *mafiosi* – transported to Italy from New York to help address the communist problem. They beat up communist candidates, smashed left-wing gatherings and generally intimidated voters.'

'And the money? Where did it come from?'

'Our administration had already sent 350 million dollars to Vatican City for economic relief and political payments. Ten million dollars for the Christian Democrats came from us –'

'The C.I.A?'

'The C.I.A. via our Office of Policy Coordination. And the Vatican Bank, that was our bank, really. The Vatican used thirty million dollars from Truman's aid package to create Catholic Action, an organisation to generate propaganda against communists and to, well, hire the mob muscle to do its dirty work.'

'The Pike Committee report mentioned a total of sixty-five million dollars. Did that all go through the Vatican Bank?'

'Yes. Most of it taken in cash in large suitcases by the Mafia and by priests.'

'How did you feel? You know, when the results of the election came through?'

'Good! We felt good! The Christian Democrats got half the vote, more than the Communists and Socialists combined. The C.I.A. had achieved its task of stopping the Italian Left from winning the first national elections after the war. We felt really good. Mission accomplished!'

Bravo had spoken with the ardour he'd felt at the time, thirty years ago, before his enthusiasm and energy had lessened and become, passing through indifference and detachment, disillusion and self-doubt. He regretted that he hadn't been able to keep a tone of triumph out of his voice, because he no longer considered the C.I.A.'s accomplishments favourably. Looking back, he felt not so much ashamed as soiled. Looking ahead, he didn't dare think any further than his evening drinks.

TEN

Sebastian felt guilty. He'd refused to carry his mother's easel around after her, grumbling that he'd signed up for a holiday and not for a porter's job. 'Artists don't have lackeys,' he'd said, peevishly. And he felt foolish, recognising that he was punishing himself as much as her: he quite enjoyed his mother's company when she wasn't telling him off, which, to be fair, was not that often. She'd left the apartment with his father, he with his cassette recorder and notebooks and she with just her sketchpad and pencils.

Sebastian and Dominic drifted to the pool and selected sun beds in the shade of the olive trees where they read, interrupting their reading for dips in the pool and trips to the bar for a *panino* at lunchtime and a *gelato* in the afternoon and on both occasions, in the case of Sebastian, with the hope of bumping into Rosetta.

There had been a crescendo of anticipation in the square ahead of the late afternoon's two football games and, as the brothers gathered their things and walked up from the pool to the busy bar shortly before kick-off, Dominic asked, 'Which game do you think they'll have on T.V?'

'What do you mean, *which game*?'

'Austria v Holland or Italy v West Germany?'

'Oh, I see. I don't know,' said Sebastian. 'I'm not that bothered really. Italy v West Germany, I suppose. After all, we are in Italy.'

'Hello, Mr Better,' said Sebastian as he and Dominic stepped into the small square that was already buzzing with people.

'Oh, call me Clifford, please. Listen to this! Hilarious!' He carried his jacket over his shoulder.

Kees, wearing only swimming trunks and flip-flops and a towel over one shoulder, had his arm around Dario. 'Come on, you're going to show the Holland game, aren't you?'

Dario rolled his eyes. 'You're crazy! Why I would want to show the Holland game when Italy is playing?'

'Because it's going to be so much more exciting. There will be goals. Italy only play defensively, and West Germany is boring, it's a boring team.'

Godehard also had his arm around Dario. He wore only military boots, shorts and sunglasses and his hair long. Sebastian had seen him at the pool but only now noticed how tall he was, how tall both he and Kees were. And blond. And tanned. Dario appeared uncomfortable being the tug of war between the taller men. 'Of course,' said Godehard, 'you want to show the two best teams in the tournament. It's only natural. Holland – Holland couldn't even beat Scotland!' He released his hair from its ponytail and scratched his bare chest with his free hand.

'Oh, you're *here*,' said Kees, turning his attention from Dario to Godehard. 'That's funny, I thought you were by the pool –

but no! It's your *towels* that are by the pool and not you – so silly of me!'

Godehard said something to Kees in a language that wasn't Italian.

'Kees!' Clifford slapped him on the shoulder before he could reply. 'Relax! This is Italy! There's no way we're not going to watch the Italy game.' This was said to the broader audience in the square, to the Italians who, Sebastian could sense, had become irritated by Kees' insistence.

'The *West Germany* game,' said Godehard, clearly smarting from Kees' comment.

'The Italy game, the West Germany game – same game!' said Clifford, playing at peace-maker. '*Guardiamo la partita dell'Italia, sì?*' And the Italians shouted their assent.

Dario disengaged himself from the Dutch and German embraces, swept his hair back and patted it down. He straightened his shirt collar, hunched his shoulders and showed his palms as though to say, *Really? Was there any question of our not watching the Italy game?* Or, *You see? It's out of my hands.* Or, *You see what I have to put up with?* Sebastian was coming to understand that this second Italian language, gesticulation, had a large and ambiguous vocabulary.

The German smirked and the Dutchman rocked on the balls of his feet.

'Come,' said Dario, taking Kees by the arm, as though recognising that he had to do something to deflate the competitive tension that, Sebastian sensed, had arisen, 'Come and help me carry the T.V. out.'

Kees planted his legs firmly where he was. 'I'm not carrying it out to show the West Germany game,' he said resolutely.

'Oh really!' exclaimed Godehard, exaggeratedly exasperated. 'I'll help you, Dario,' was said virtuously and pointedly.

'Must we show football at all?' said the witch who had materialised amongst them. The effect of her bright red lipstick on her brown and wrinkled face was shocking. Sebastian recalled the incongruity of the beetle in the fig. In her leopard print sarong, she resembled an animal carcass. Hers was a ridiculous question that was ignored by everyone.

'Look, there's Dad,' said Dominic.

Sebastian looked. His father and the American stood at the top of the path that led from the square to the church and car park beyond it. The church was in sunlight and its little steel cross shone as if in appeal and encouragement. There must have been something comforting for the peasants in the Middle Ages, Sebastian thought, to have beheld the church there, a benevolent church that looked over and out for you, your walk up the path to the church and its priest really a reassuring premonition of your ultimate ascent to heaven and God. Thoughts of God had begun to discomfit Sebastian, especially thoughts of God reading his mind at times. He'd decided it would probably suit him best if God didn't exist – unless He happened to be a very forgiving God who understood and forgave the thoughts of teenagers.

Mr Kentish and the American turned their heads as if watching and expecting someone and, sure enough, the passenger stepped into view.

'Oh, him,' said Dominic.

Introductions were made by the American and the three men stood talking for a short time before the American handed something to Mr Kentish who took it in one hand while hoisting his satchel onto a shoulder with the other. Then the three men waved goodbyes, the American and the passenger walking off in the direction of the car park and Mr Kentish beginning his descent into the village.

Sebastian was at the point of waving at his father but Mr Kentish turned and darted into the open *ufficio* door.

'*Spostati!* Out of the way!'

Sebastian and Dominic stepped aside to allow Dario and Godehard to pass with the television. It was plugged into an extension cord and switched on. A channel was selected, its aerial was adjusted, and a colour image of the Estadio Monumental in Buenos Aires materialised.

'*Forza Italia!*' cried the Italians.

'Oh, hello Mum,' said Dominic. He leant back into his mother who put her arms around him.

Sebastian hadn't heard her approaching and when he turned he was surprised to see the little square so much fuller with people than it had been the other night. The Germans would be in a very small minority.

'Hello,' said Mrs Kentish. 'Have you had a nice day? You've caught the sun. Have you seen Dad?'

'He's there,' said Sebastian pointing, just as Mr Kentish and Francesca stepped out of the office chatting, Mr Kentish watching while Francesca locked the green *ufficio* door. They descended the path together, laughing.

'Oh, hello,' said Mr Kentish.

'Hello,' said his wife, coolly.

'*Bene,*' said Francesca brushing her hair behind her head and showing shaved armpits through her raised T-shirt sleeves. 'I now have my two hours break before I come to serve all you lovely people dinner. I go to make the *siesta* before *la festa*! She caressed Dominic's cheek. 'Come up and see me for more *succo* any time you want to, *caro.*'

'Cool,' said Dominic casually.

Sebastian thought that of the four of them, Dominic was the only one who was.

The Kentishes were unable to continue their conversation. The football match kicked off and the Betters stood by them and asked after them, Clifford holding his beige linen jacket over his shoulder with one hand and a bottle of beer in the other. Then a tall Italian-looking couple both with big, black hair and sunglasses, he in white trousers, shirt and loafers and she in a white dress and high heels that appeared perilous on Colletta's cobbles, descended the path from the church. Sebastian recognised them as some of the people his mother and he had passed on their first expedition around the village.

Mrs Better made the introductions.

'Ah, you are the artist!' said Anna Pompeo to Mrs Kentish.

'It's our honour,' said Michele Pompeo.

His mother was flattered, Sebastian could see.

'Have you found our little village inspiring?' asked Mrs Pompeo. She held on to her husband as she wobbled on her heels.

'How could one not?' said Mrs Kentish, charmed.

'I hope that you will show to us the fruits of your work before you leave,' said Mr Pompeo.

'Oh,' Mrs Kentish flapped a hand. 'You'll only conclude that I'm incapable of doing this fairy tale of a village justice.'

The Pompeos pooh-poohed the notion, as manners dictated they do, and turned their attention to the television.

Sebastian had little interest in the game. He felt lethargic and in need of a wash before dinner. 'Mum, do you have the key to the apartment?'

'I'll come with you,' she said, and they walked the rocky path to the apartment. 'I want you to keep an eye on your father and that Francesca.'

'Mum! Whatever for?'

'I don't like her.'

'But she's nice!'

'It's the nice ones that are the dangerous ones.' She looked at him out of the corners of her eyes.

Sebastian said nothing. He wished his mother would show a little more composure and less jealousy whenever his father noticed an attractive woman. It wasn't his father's fault that there were pretty women around. They entered and exited the short tunnel hewn out of the rock and made an abrupt turn. Sebastian followed his mother's legs with his eyes as she climbed the stone stairs. Anyway, his mother was as pretty as – if not prettier than – all the women here, Sebastian thought with a degree of filial loyalty. But a little older, admittedly.

'I mean it,' said Mrs Kentish, opening the door to the apartment. 'Keep an eye on her for me, please. And on him. We don't want him going and ruining things, do we?'

'Mum!' Sebastian was acutely embarrassed. 'You can't go asking me to spy on Dad! And, anyway, what for? You're imagining things. And it's so unbecoming. Undignified. That's what it is.'

'I'm sorry.' She ruffled his hair. 'Actually, I do like her. It's just that I don't want your father making a fool of himself.'

'So, how was the game?' Mrs Kentish asked Dominic, smoothing her skirt from behind as she took the chair Mr Kentish had pulled out for her.

Mr Kentish regained his seat, smiling at everybody. His satchel and cassette recorder were slung over its back. He hadn't gone back to change for dinner but had been seduced into staying in the square for the match by cold beer and the passion of the locals for their national team.

'Oh, it was alright,' said Dominic, who'd been seated at the table and waiting for his mother and brother long enough to finish the *grissini*.

'I fell asleep,' said Sebastian by way of apology for having kept his brother and father waiting.

'Nil all. A bit boring, really.'

'We spent our time chatting, didn't we, Dom?' said his father. 'To the Betters and, well, to everyone. Everyone's very sociable here.'

'And who's playing now?' Mrs Kentish asked Dominic.

'Brazil and Peru.'

The television set remained in the square, the picture on but the sound off.

'Sebastian told me you had a nice day by the pool.' Sebastian began to feel that his mother was addressing his brother and ignoring his father rather pointedly when she turned to her husband abruptly. 'And what about you, darling? How was your day? Did you spend it working hard in Francesca's office?'

'No,' sighed Mr Kentish, 'I was just returning the key to the guest office below the car park. That's where I've been, in the guest office.'

'I wondered what the American had given you,' said Sebastian, a willing ally.

'Oh, you saw us?' said his father.

'Yes. He seems to be friends with the passenger – you know, from the car. What's he like? What did you talk about?'

'Not much. Just some introductions and then they were off. Yes, they do seem chummy, come to think of it. I think he said he was Argentinian.'

'Who? The passenger?' asked Sebastian.

'That's what your father just said,' said his mother.

'Argentina is playing next,' said Dominic. 'Against Poland.'

'Great,' said Sebastian with a scowl. 'We'll probably have him skulking around the square for the rest of the evening then.'

Francesca walked past carrying dishes. She seemed not to be serving their table that evening.

'How's it going with the American, you know, with your work?' Sebastian thought to ask.

'Well, I'd say,' said his father, appearing as though he wished to say more but then deciding against it. 'But have you seen your mother's drawings from yesterday? They're wonderful! How did you get on today, darling?'

Mrs Kentish flapped her hand at him.

'I just realised that they don't give you menus here, they just bring food out, don't they?' said Sebastian as one course followed another. They'd been served *farinata*, that was described to them as chickpea and rosemary pancake, followed by stuffed cabbage leaves and a fish stew with mussels and then lemon cake and raspberries for dessert. 'I don't think I've ever eaten so much or so well.' He leant back in his chair to look up at the stars. He'd been staring at the candle on the table so he knew to wait for his eyes to adjust. He imagined his pupils widening and after some moments of looking up he felt he could no longer tell if he was looking up or down and felt he was falling, falling down or up into beckoning, winking pinpricks of light, as though drawn to eavesdrop on their murmur that was, really, the hum of the other sated diners' conversations. He heard Italian and some German. He heard Clifford laugh. He heard Godehard mention Kees.

'Five one.' That was Kees. He'd descended the path into the village and stopped at the terrace. 'Five one,' he said, holding up one open hand and one index finger. '*Fünf eins*,' he sang, now pointing that finger at the Germans' table.

'*Ja, Ja*, so Holland won their game,' said Godehard.

'And what was the score in your game? Zero zero – boring! The Holland game? Exciting! We were *so* good!'

'Austria were so bad, you mean,' said Godehard.

'Did you find a bar to watch it in then?' asked Clifford from another table.

'No.'

'I didn't think you would!'

'He went to Albenga in the hope of finding a bar that would show it,' explained Mrs Better to Mrs Kentish, tossing her hair behind her ears and leaning back in her chair to speak to her.

'I listened to it on my car radio,' said Kees. He removed his cap from his head, ran a hand through his hair and pulled his cap firmly back on.

Dominic slid from his chair and joined the others who had drifted from the terrace to the square that was lit by the flickering television set, by candles on two wine barrel halves and, most strongly, on one side by the electric light that emanated from the open bar.

'*Chiaroscuro,*' observed Sebastian looking from his brother to his mother who had learnt the word when they had looked at a book of Italian paintings together.

Sebastian joined Dominic on the stone bench to one side of the bar. His mind drifted from the match. Leaning back against the rough stone wall, he was surprised to find it warm, that it had retained so much of the day's heat despite the cooling night. Some people had put shirts on over their T-shirts and others hung jumpers over their shoulders. There was less intensity and tension about the Argentina Poland game than there had been about the Italy West Germany game or even the Holland Scotland one. Some people, the women mainly, stood with their backs to the television set while others, though watching it, were quite happy to talk. The English and the Italians, Sebastian noted, had changed for dinner – not into formal dress but into slacks or summer suits and dresses – while the Dutch and Germans still dressed as if for the pool. Sebastian observed the little community of holidaymakers in front of him. Lit mainly from one side by the light from the bar, they resembled masks in profile congregating on a stage, reminding him of paintings of carnivals. They held beers and *digestivi* – after-dinner drinks that tasted to Sebastian of either sugar or cough medicine – served to them by Rosetta and Francesca. Children swam in from the darkness and out again, competing to feed and befriend a one-eyed cat. Above them and alone in the distance, candles in vases flickered around the Virgin Mary in the alcove in the church.

Argentina scored.

While the crowd in Rosario celebrated raucously and threw toilet rolls on to the pitch in celebration, there were only murmurs of appreciation from the small crowd in Colletta's *piazzetta*. It was late and the day's sun and earlier match had sapped the Collettiani's energy. Sebastian watched the replay and admired the movement, the long pass and the header.

'Good goal,' said Kees loudly. He drained his beer and, sidling over to Sebastian, winked. 'I might need your help later,' he said mysteriously.

In turning to acknowledge Kees, Sebastian noticed the passenger – an Argentinian, apparently – leaning against a wall and watching the game impassively. He wore jeans and a jeans jacket over a grey T-shirt and a red handkerchief knotted loosely around his neck, obscured, at the collar, by his jet black, combed-back oily hair. A gold chain hung to halfway down his chest. His cowboy boots looked old but polished, and their pointed steel toecaps were bright. He never moved, like the toothpick that remained fixed in one corner of his mouth.

Sebastian's attention was back on the game until half-time. He'd forgotten about the Argentinian when Dominic nudged him and said, 'Look.' The Argentinian was seated too, now, with a beer to hand on a barrel top but focused on, it seemed, cleaning his fingernails with a pocket knife so large he had to hold it by the flat of the blade to manoeuvre it safely below the nail.

'Opinel,' said Dominic, impressed.

Sebastian and Dominic had a boys' veneration for the Opinel pocket knife, the wooden-handled, carbon steel-bladed pocket knife that they'd always beg to be allowed to buy when on holiday with their grandparents in Savoie in France, where the knives were made. The blades were hard and sharper than sharp and locked into place by a swivelling ferrule and they'd cut your eye if you so much as looked at them too closely.

'Wow!' said Dominic. 'I bet that's a Number Twelve!' The knives came in different sizes; Dominic had a Number Two, the smallest size and the only one his parents would allow him to have, while Sebastian had a Number Eight that Dominic coveted. Dominic stood and ran to his mother to tell her about the knife.

The Argentinian never looked up but meticulously cleaned one fingernail after another. When the Polish and Argentinian teams appeared for the second half, he folded his knife and inserted it in the breast pocket of his jeans jacket, drank some beer and resumed watching the game. He spoke to no-one and no-one spoke to him. With the exception of Rosetta, whom he'd follow with his eyes as she exited and entered the bar with drinks and empty glasses, he looked at no-one.

Sebastian turned his attention back to the match and was

only vaguely aware of Kees and Godehard having an animated discussion in either Dutch or German, he wasn't sure which. Maybe both. He was at a loss as to how to reply when Kees sat next to him and said, 'Well, what do you think?'

'About what?'

And then Argentina scored again.

Sebastian watched the replay then looked at the Argentinian. He hadn't so much as moved. His face registered no emotion. Maybe he's not Argentinian, thought Sebastian.

'Now's the time. Come on,' said Kees furtively and Sebastian, intrigued, followed him out of the square and down the dimly lit path that led to the pool. Around the first corner, the light and hubbub suddenly dimmed. Surrounded by tall stone walls in darkness and silence, it was not only as if an invisible hand had turned the lights off and volume down but as though, too, it had waved a magic wand and sent them back in time.

'Where are we going?' Sebastian asked Kees' back. He could only just make Kees' orange cap out in the gloom ahead of him.

'We're going to teach them a lesson.'

'Who?' He lost Kees momentarily every time they turned a corner.

'The Germans.'

'The Germans! But why?'

'If they can't take over the world by one way, they find another.'

Their footsteps were loud on the cobbles, the staccato slap of Kees' flip-flops announcing his progress in a steady Morse. Sebastian passed an open window through which he saw an elderly Italian man in a string vest and cardigan reading a book in the yellow light of a lamp. A fine mesh over the window kept the mosquitoes out.

Sebastian followed Kees down the steps that led to the

swimming pool and stopped when he stopped. The pool was lit by half-domes at each corner just below the water level that cast their light on the nearer olive trees' lower branches. The whole scene was further illuminated by the weak light of the moon and the brighter light emanating from two large globe-bearing lamp-posts that stood sentry at the two entrances to the pool area. Amidst the olive trees and around the pool were the sun beds, cleaned and neatly aligned, ready for the following day.

'Every morning I come down here to find that the best sun beds have been reserved by that German,' said Kees, 'even if he doesn't use them until later, a lot later.'

'So, what do you intend to do?' asked Sebastian.

'We are going to discourage him,' said Kees, 'from ever doing it again.' He grinned and rubbed his hands. 'We are going to deliver to him a message.'

'We?' said Sebastian weakly.

'Well, I,' said Kees kindly, 'and you are going to help me. Come on.'

Twenty minutes later, Sebastian made his way into the relative light of the square to find that the match was over and that his family had returned to the apartment.

'Where were you?' asked his mother when he joined them. 'I was worried.'

'Oh, I just went for a walk,' he said and, announcing he was tired, he got changed for bed and lay in it, staring at the ceiling.

'How come you're not reading this evening?' asked Dominic. Through the open window by his bed came the cicadas' loud rasp.

'Oh, I'm too tired to read this evening.' But, really, his heart was beating too quickly.

'I heard Mum tell Dad she didn't know whether to worry for you more or less when she saw that Rosetta was still in the square,' said Dominic.

'Thanks,' said Sebastian. He liked that his brother looked out for him.

ELEVEN

Bravo felt something moving deep within him. It was as though a boulder that he'd never consciously acknowledged was slowly shifting and being leveraged off his heart and being transported up on its way out of him. And then, Atlas-like, he'd balance it on his shoulders for a moment, before, with a shrug and a heave and one final interview with Peter Kentish, he would free himself from it forever.

He filled the bottom half of his moka pot with water up to the safety valve and added ground coffee to the funnel basket that he dropped into the pot before screwing the top half on. He placed the assembled whole on his smallest gas ring and looked out of his kitchen window onto the forested hillside, into a morning sun that had only just cleared the immediate horizon of mountain tops. He knew that when he opened the window, he'd hear the gentle gush of the stream out of sight below. He only looked down when the moka pot's cough and gurgle announced that his coffee was ready.

Bravo knew what Kentish's agenda was – he wanted to know about Operation Gladio and about the C.I.A.'s financing and manipulation of Italian political life – but what was his own now that he had to take Kentish's family into consideration? He knew that he'd had one – that he'd had a motive – but he'd thought little of the consequences of his intended disclosures and certainly not at all of what they might mean for the journalist's family. He poured his coffee and tied his dressing gown around him but then paused by his front door. He rolled an empty bottle of grappa that lay on the floor out of the way with his foot. Was his to be a selfish act, whereby he'd gain some form of redemption and, one day far away, depart from his life with a clear conscience, much as a repentant Catholic trips in sprightly fashion from the confessional into the sunlight? Or was it a selfless one that, once committed, risked placing his and now the Kentish's lives in immediate danger as a penalty for his having exposed the West's darkest secrets to the glare of the lights of the world's media? He sighed. As he'd said to Kentish, no names, so no revelations of others' misdemeanours but absolution for himself. He'd have to satisfy himself with that. He had once envisioned television images of politicians and former colleagues being led into waiting cars in handcuffs but that would have to come later. He would now simply sow the seeds.

Stepping out of his ground floor apartment and up the uneven stone stairs to the patio by the swimming pool, Bravo dropped his coffee cup and saucer. He missed the top step, stubbed his toe and jarred his back. He looked around for something to hold on to – a tree, a post, a lamppost – but nothing was at hand, only a low hedge and a low swing gate, so he had to manage the few steps to the low stone wall where he sat down heavily and jarred his back for the second time. His mouth and his dressing gown hung open.

Bravo couldn't believe his eyes. Really, Kees had gone too far. He closed and opened his eyes again, as though to give what lay before them a chance to disappear. It didn't. He doubted that the German would be leaving his towels on the sun beds that day. Or any other day.

The sun beds had been arranged around the pool in the shape of a swastika.

Bravo had his first coffee of the day at the bar. He hadn't wanted to be at the pool when Godehard arrived with his towels. He liked Germans, generally, and Godehard particularly.

He stood at the bar for his coffee like he had done so many times in his life, in the French cafés in Saigon, first, then in Licata, in Rome, in Naples and in Milan, drinking his first and second *espressi* of the day. He'd been intrigued by the manner in which coffee changed in taste in Italy as one travelled north, from bitter and rough to sweet and smooth. He'd been impressed by the Italians' pricing policies, with the espresso consumed standing at the bar costing less than the same consumed at a table that, in turn, was cheaper than the one drunk on the terrace. He had once flicked coffee beans off a coffee counter at a bar in Venice, as he drank strong coffee after coffee on his way through a hangover, to find that some beans sprouted legs and beetled off to dark corners at the other end of the counter. He'd looked again at the huge coffee bean vats that lined the wall behind the bar and realised he might have been drinking ground beetle juice, for all he knew. He'd marvelled at the evolutionary short cut he believed the beetles must have taken to grow to resemble roasted coffee beans. At the back of his mind was the idea that he might simply have still been very, very drunk.

Claudia was busy with pastries and coffee cups. He watched her at work. She was *di bell'aspetto*, as the Italians would say, handsome, agreeable. Locals would tease her about her never having married and Dario once suggested to Bravo that he consider proposing but, of course, he hadn't. For one thing, he liked her too much to impose someone on her who was so much older than her. And then he didn't love her enough to do so, either. She wore her long black hair piled high on her head, and gold bangles as earrings. If one looked closely, one would observe that they had distended her ear lobes a little. He watched over his coffee cup rim as she leant to align the pastries on the bottom shelf behind the glass counter and, not for the first time, admired her bosom in its tight, figure-hugging summer dress. She was, he would say, beautiful and fun – he had enjoyed her sense of mischief when she had begged him that morning to allow Kentish to try to negotiate his way through his phrase book again – but, he would add, she was not his type, despite his not wanting to admit to himself quite what his type was.

He hadn't yet quite figured Kentish out. Kentish was intelligent and diligent, courteous and friendly. On occasions he impressed Bravo with what he knew, then, on others, he surprised him with what he didn't. Professionally, Kentish was on top of his game. Socially, Bravo thought, there were times, principally when he wrestled with his Italian phrase book, when he appeared a naïf. Ah, there he was. He looked at Kentish through the open bar door. Satchel and cassette recorder slung over one shoulder and looking up to Dario, Kentish looked as though he were on his way to school.

Kentish scribbled on a cassette in pencil, inserted it in the cassette recorder and pressed the play and record buttons. 'Am I right in believing,' he asked, 'that the Allies expected a Soviet invasion in the immediate aftermath of the war?'

'Yes. The possibility of a Soviet attack on Western Europe seemed real enough to warrant preparations of an extremely secretive nature.'

'Did it never occur to anybody that politically – militarily – the Soviet Union was on its knees and in no ready state for another war?'

'No. Anyway, I'm not sure that's true.'

'So those arms dumps that had been amassed during the war, that were scattered around Europe, that this secret army could have recourse to, have just been left in situ, just "in case", as it were?'

'Yes.'

'How many of them are there?'

'We have 139 in Italy. Mainly around Gorizia, north of Trieste. What we call "The Gorizia Gap".'

'139,' repeated Kentish dully. 'In what kind of places are they?'

'Secret places. In caves, forests, cemeteries, basements of government offices, freight yards of railway stations, abandoned fortifications... they hold abundant supplies of munitions and explosives.'

'139 arms caches,' said Kentish. 'For how many men? I mean, how many people are in on Operation Gladio?'

'In terms of men on the ground, well, you can figure it out: there are 622 stay-behind units and each one consists of twelve to fifteen men.'

Kentish did some calculations in his notebook. 'So maybe about 10,000 people in Italy alone must be in on this "secret" army. It must feel like the world's best-kept secret.'

'Not really. Our gladiators – that's what some of them call

themselves – became ordinary men after the war, men who now go about their ordinary lives but who occasionally get together for training and briefings.'

'Where do they do that?'

'We run a training camp in Sardinia.'

'Oh yes. I remember. When the invasion failed to materialise, did it not occur to anybody that it was never likely to?'

'We would never say never. It still may. You have to understand there has been a massive investment in the possibility. A political, financial and psychological investment. We have created an enormous infrastructure in order to nourish and support the secret armies that have come to be seen as, well, just another kind of investment for the future.'

'For a non-communist future?'

'Yes.'

'The document I saw was stamped "NATO".'

'The Gladio units fall immediately under NATO's direct control, yes. It has carefully established departments of clandestine warfare, each of which manages the secret armies and allocates their tasks. Don't believe the common narrative that NATO was established to preserve and nourish genuine liberal democracies. It was the start of a mission to join Western Europe to a United States empire committed to the destruction of communism.'

'Doesn't every action have a consequence?' asked Kentish pensively. 'The Soviets were so worried about NATO and about the Marshall Plan that they founded the Council for Mutual Economic Assistance in order to prevent countries in their sphere of influence from moving to that of the Americans.'

Bravo laughed drily. 'Yes, Comecon. And that had a consequence too. Comecon worried us so much that we chose to extend our support for the Christian Democrats and the stay-behind units with more millions of dollars. We were giving the Christian Democrats up to twenty million dollars a year.'

'All via the Vatican Bank?'

'Yes. And paid out to groups that met with the Pope's approval through other Catholic banks.' Bravo laughed humourlessly again. 'The Pope issued a solemn decree ex-communicating members of the Holy Mother Church who joined the Communist Party, as well as Catholics who read or published or disseminated communist ideology. But, of course, this was insufficient to guarantee the crushing of the forces of godlessness, hence the money.'

'Was there no dissenting voice in the Church?'

'If there was, it never reached our ears. Thousands of priests and bishops trained willingly for the ideological war against communism. And hundreds of Italian clerics even joined the Mafia in support of Operation Gladio. And the Church, that had condemned freemasonry and threatened its members who participated in masonic rites with excommunication, now even appeared to endorse it, enabling Italian Masons to raise the money they needed to fight the commies from American Masons.'

'I heard that the C.I.A. even planted microphones throughout the papal apartments.'

'Of course we did.'

Kentish rubbed his chin. 'How did the Italians feel about this? I mean, come to think of it, hasn't there been a renunciation of sovereignty? Could the C.I.A. really be influencing Italian domestic politics and, potentially, Italy's foreign policy and face so little opposition from Italy's politicians?'

Bravo shrugged. 'I never saw it that way. In fact, Italy's stay-behind army – Gladio – is run and directed by the Italian intelligence services but, yes, all their personnel have to be vetted and approved by us. So I suppose you're right. Maybe it's that fear of communism goes a long way. Or simply that money does.'

'And yet, in the subsequent election, in 1953, the Christian Democrats lost seats to both Socialist and Communist parties. And the result of the '58 election was not much better; if anything, it was a little worse from the Right's point of view, with a still weak centrist coalition. What went wrong?'

Bravo reflected. 'Perhaps we'd grown complacent. We'd let it be known that no U.S. department of defence procurement contracts would be awarded to Italian firms whose employees had voted to be represented by communist-controlled labour unions and we could see those unions' share of the vote falling dramatically. Maybe we thought that between us, the Mafia and the Church, we'd done enough. Maybe we were distracted.'

'By what?'

'Iran. Korea. There was a lot going on. And the Mafia, closer to home.'

'Yes?'

'The Mafia back home – in the U.S., that is – was now being led by younger, rebellious men. They'd come through the theatre of war, if you'll pardon the cliché, that had done so much to disrupt traditional hierarchies, and had become indifferent to violence. They had also begun to question why they had to return so much of the money from the heroin business to Italy. They even threatened to do business with the Corsicans through Marseilles. This was heresy. The Mafia heads, the *capi*, here in Italy wanted them dealt with and summoned us to a mob meeting at the Grand Hotel des Palmes in Palermo and, well, instructed us to deal with it.'

'When was that?'

'In 1957.'

'So now we have the Mafia dictating terms to the C.I.A?'

'Well, it wasn't exactly like that. Let's call ours a symbiotic relationship.'

'What hold could the Mafia have had over the C.I.A?'

'It wasn't a hold so much as the recognition and exploitation of a need. By uniting our interests we'd in fact be helping each other and ourselves simultaneously. For example, we used Mafia money and C.I.A. funds to establish a Lichtenstein holding company. In turn it purchased the Banca Privata Finanziaria that then served for the conduit transfer of funds into Italy. Diversification from the Vatican, if you will.'

Kentish flicked a page back from his notebook and read it. 'Did I hear you correctly? If I did, I must conclude that the C.I.A. willingly and knowingly facilitated the Mafia in their heroin business.'

'Oh, it wasn't like that exactly,' said Bravo. 'You see, we consider it *our* business.'

Kentish pushed his chair back and stood. He took the few steps to the gate and low privet hedge and looked out over the tops of the olive trees. 'I think I've seen too much sun,' he said. 'I'm feeling a little sick.'

'You were sitting in the shade,' said Bravo. 'Here.' He poured them both some water and handed Kentish a glass.

'Thank you. I had thought we could follow some sort of order, a chronological order,' said Kentish, his back to him again, 'but I find I'm being pulled in all manner of directions.'

'Would you like to adjourn?'

Kentish appeared not to have heard and turned to face Bravo. 'Could we talk about you for a moment?'

Bravo found he was nodding and pushing his lower lip out, as though to say that of course they could.

'And then I'd like to understand more about the business with the drugs.'

Again, he nodded. 'May I suggest we order some lunch?' Bravo felt hungry, his morning routine having been upset. When Kentish gave his assent, he entered the guest office and, once his eyes had become accustomed to the relative darkness, located the telephone and called the bar. When he came out, he didn't sit down but stood next to Kentish and the two of them said nothing for a moment until the cassette recorder went *glock* as the play and record buttons popped up to announce the end of one side of the cassette.

Having inserted a new cassette, Kentish said, 'You said you were summoned from Indochina to Italy because you are of Sicilian descent.'

'That's correct,' said Bravo.

'Why were you in Indochina in the first place?'

'It had been felt, for some time, that we had missed a trick in neglecting South East Asia to the extent that we had. Out of nowhere, it seems, the French had successfully exploited their territories. Tea, rice, coffee, pepper, coal, tobacco, zinc and tin all provided the French with considerable revenue. Rubber plantations supplied France's automobile industry – and ours too, but to a lesser extent. We looked on from afar, thinking we had missed the boat, as it were. When the Japanese occupied Vietnam in 1940 I'd be surprised if there were as many as a hundred Americans in the country and they were mainly missionaries. We had one consul, in Saigon.'

'Japan was at war with China.'

'That was the pretext for the invasion, that Japan hoped to close off China's southern border and halt its supply of weapons and materials. But we knew that Japan had long-term imperial plans to place themselves at the head of an economic coalition of Asian nations that would kick Western interests out of the region and keep its resources and commodities for themselves – well, for Japan, really. China, Korea and Vietnam would be ruled by puppet governments. They would provide cheap land, labour and resources for Japanese industries. It was Japanese imperialism cloaked in a veil of Asian nationalism. Anyway, Japan took advantage of the German invasion of France and, the French surrender at home having weakened the French colonial government in Vietnam, Japan acted quickly.

'I was one of a small group of Americans assigned to naval intelligence, initially to the French to offer what help we could to them and then tasked with building relationships with the Kuomintang – we wanted neither a Japanese nor a communist Chinese empire. That was when we were subsumed into the Office of Strategic Services.'

'What was the O.S.S. exactly?'

'Think of it as the precursor to the C.I.A. During the war, the O.S.S. had multiple activities and missions, including collecting intelligence by spying, performing acts of sabotage, waging propaganda war, organizing and coordinating anti-Nazi resistance groups in Europe, and providing military training for anti-Japanese guerrilla movements in Asia. Later, the O.S.S. trained Kuomintang troops in China and Burma. That's when we noted that Chiang Kai-shek raised money for the Kuomintang for their war against Mao Zedong's communists by selling opium to Chinese addicts. We took this idea home to the guys in Washington who loved it and, later, when the C.I.A. was formed without the necessary budget for the covert operations it wished to undertake, borrowed it. The Truman administration had set aside no funds for covert post-war operations so here was our dilemma – how could we raise the necessary funds from congress for covert operations and yet have them remain covert? We couldn't. So we found our answer in drugs, drugs that could reduce the count of America's undesirables and help America against the commies at the same time.'

'America's undesirables?'

'The low-lives that use drugs.' Bravo shrugged apologetically. 'Initially, we funnelled money from the Nazi gold we sold and from arms sales for the opiates we brought in from Chiang Kai-shek and that became the pipeline of funds for secret operations. We created the Civil Air Transport from surplus aircraft and delivered guns in exchange for opiates. This became Air America – the C.I.A. fleet of planes that transported cocaine and heroin during the Vietnam conflict. World War Two had disrupted international shipping and imposed tight waterfront security making heroin smuggling virtually impossible. Of course, the C.I.A. wouldn't have that trouble.'

Kentish sat down. 'How do you know all of this? I mean, where were you in all this?'

'I was everywhere. I was in the middle of it. I considered myself lucky!' Bravo shook his head. 'I'd come from naval intelligence. I'd joined the O.S.S. I was of Italian descent. It all came together for me. Look, we needed funds and had decided our best bet was by importing heroin into the U.S. At the same time, we also needed help for the Sicily landings. By a stroke of luck, the one person who could best help us with both of those problems was a certain Charles Luciano, a Mafia hood who'd been jailed in 1936 for running a prostitution racket across 200 or so brothels that, incidentally, provided a ready outlet for what was then only a small amount of heroin importation. He was serving his time in the state penitentiary at Dannemara, a maximum-security prison that the crims called "Siberia", so we had him moved to the Great Meadow Penitentiary, where he was more conveniently accessible to naval intelligence. The thing is,

Luciano wasn't just any hood. He was probably the most powerful Mafia boss and pretty much controlled the Longshoremen's Union. At the time –'

'When was this?'

'1942, '43 – at the time, the US Navy was paranoid about security at the New York waterfront and worried about the possibility that German U-boats might gain access and destroy U.S. shipping. So the office of naval intelligence sought the help of union officials and were told that only Luciano could guarantee security. Not everyone in the White House was enamoured with the idea of springing a criminal of Luciano's calibre from prison but they were given a nudge by Luciano's pals: they set fire to the Normandie – a French steam ship, an ocean liner converted to a transport ship – and sank it. This was blamed on Nazi spies, and so Luciano would get his release and a pardon in exchange for which he provided us with a list of mafiosi who supported the U.S. when it landed in Sicily.'

'And a drug distribution network for you to exploit.'

'Yes. With Luciano effectively working for us we could make use of his network of narcotic distribution in inner city America. And, you know, it averred that Luciano's and the Kuomintang's networks had been in contact about distribution into the U.S. in the 1930s, so it was like the closing of a circle. The deportation of Luciano to Sicily in 1946 was followed by that of more than sixty other American mafiosi and they ensured the election of Christian Democrats.'

'So, the drugs providing the financing; the Sicily landings; the political manipulation... it's astonishing, really, the Mafia and the American government, hand in glove. When did the first shipments of heroin take place?'

'In the summer of 1947. We established a shell financial firm in Miami and appointed a lawyer who, it was agreed by both sides, would handle legal disputes between the Mafia and the C.I.A. We performed a 200-kilo test run, shipping it in crates of oranges, cans of sardines, wheels of cheese and barrels of olive oil to Cuba, where it was cut before being sent on to New York, New Orleans and Miami. One sweet factory produced chocolates filled with heroin; another was a fruit export business. The heroin was cut in Cuba and then delivered to New Orleans, Miami and New York using routes protected by the Longshoremen's and Teamsters' unions.'

The two men stood side by side, looking out over the olive trees and woods beyond them, their extended fingers loosely holding onto the low, black railing. At a small distance from them, Giulio, the gardener, was repairing a stone wall; a wheelbarrow beside him carried tools and plants. Bravo was aware of the smells of the hydrangeas – a sweet aroma, not unlike honey – and of Kentish's cologne – an odour of stale lemons and lavender.

'I thought we were going to talk about you,' said Kentish.

'Didn't we?' asked Bravo, surprised. 'I thought we had.' He reflected. 'Well, you did also say you wanted to talk about the drugs.'

They watched Giulio crossing the olive tree orchard, pushing the wheelbarrow steadily uphill.

Bravo envied Giulio – he was young, tanned and muscular – and he was jealous all of a sudden of the seeming simplicity of his work – its seasonal regularity, with the steady, periodic demands of seeding, weeding and feeding and of pruning, cutting and burning – and of the absence of duplicity, judgment and malign calculation. From where he stood, level with the top of the tallest of the olive trees, the former C.I.A. agent looked down on the gardener whose world was so clearly delineated by the borders of his garden that he had so magnificently cultivated. He hadn't run from country to country to save the world from one ideology while replacing it with another, but had created and maintained a natural harmony and beauty in just one very small part of it. To be candid, thought Bravo, if everyone minded their own business as Giulio had maintained Colletta's gardens, the world would in all probability be a far better place.

Pushing his wheelbarrow, Giulio passed Claudia carrying a wicker basket and, like Pavlov's dogs on hearing their dinner bell, Bravo felt immediately hungry on seeing the basket. 'Ah,' he said. 'There's our lunch.'

TWELVE

'I'm bored,' said Sebastian and flicked his brother's ear.

Dominic looked up from an Astérix book.

The brothers had read all the Astérix books – in French – countless times. Sebastian's favourite was *La grande traversée* in which Astérix and Obélix sailed to the new world of North America where none of the continent's new immigrants were able to communicate with each other but whose dogs could. The brothers had discovered Corsica, Switzerland, Spain and Greece thanks to author Gosciny and illustrator Uderzo so that Sebastian felt he knew those countries despite never having visited them. It had become a matter of national esteem to have had one's country lampooned by Gosciny and Uderzo and Sebastian wondered how, say, the Belgians and the Dutch felt about not having been honoured with an Astérix comic book set in their countries. England had featured, of course, and the brothers had been tickled by the portrayal of the English in *Astérix chez les Bretons*. They were always amused by *Le générale* waving it about his head while exclaiming, 'But no! This is not a comic book. It is a guide book. The English really are as described in it!' But then, quite seriously, he'd draw attention to the authors' note stating that they weren't intending to insult the English but to make fun of stereotypes, adding 'You won't find that in any other volume.' Their grandfather, Sebastian knew, had a deep respect for the British. Sebastian liked to hear the stories about when, on meeting the young Peter Kentish for the first time, his grandfather had shaken him by the hand and thanked him, as a representative of his nation, for Britain's great sacrifice undertaken to render France back to the French. When his future son-in-law had asked him for his daughter's hand in marriage, the old French soldier had embraced the young Englishman and wept and declared it an honour to have the friendship of their two nations consummated in the marriage of his daughter to an Englishman.

'We could go for a swim,' said Dominic.

'Nah. Done that.'

'We could go and find Mum,' said Dominic. 'Or we could go and spy on Dad.'

'What do you mean?' asked Sebastian. That hadn't occurred to him. 'What would you want to go and do that for? He's working.'

'Well, he's just listening and writing while the American is talking. Is that working?'

'So you know where they're meeting? Exactly?' Sebastian only had a vague idea.

Dominic nodded. 'I went for a wander yesterday. You know, when you wanted to stay by the pool. I was by the car park when I heard voices and went to see who it was.'

'And it was them? In the car park?'

'Yes. Well, no, not in the car park. Just below it. I could hear them but I couldn't hear what they were saying. Anyway, I didn't stay. The driver was there. I didn't want him to see me.'

'The driver! What was he doing?'

'I think he was concentrating.'

'Concentrating? On what? One doesn't just *concentrate!*' Sebastian flicked his brother's ear.

'He was sitting by the front of his car by the little hedge things so I nearly didn't see him.' Dominic rubbed his ear.

'Hiding behind his car, more like. I bet he was eavesdropping. I don't like the idea of eavesdropping,' said Sebastian. 'You know that Dad's work is off limits.'

'Fine,' said Dominic in a resigned grown-up kind of voice, leaving Sebastian wondering if he was joking. 'Let's go and find Mum, then. And get an ice cream on the way.'

The bright sun, a bronze, heavy disc that hung directly above and threatened to bring the sky crashing down onto their heads, had beaten the holidaymakers back indoors and the locals had known better than to venture out after lunch in the first place. In an hour or two, siestas would conclude, and people would emerge from their homes for a swim or some essential shopping but, for the moment, the village was quiet.

The brothers took the longer path through the cooler, spookier tunnel pausing only for their eyes to get accustomed to the gloom. They entered the bar through the lower restaurant door and made their way upstairs where they found Claudia and Rosetta.

Claudia was leaning on the counter; she smiled at them. Sweat patches formed dark semi circles on her summer dress around her armpits and strands of her hair had escaped from its precarious bun. Rosetta sat on a bar stool fanning herself with her skirt, her face flushed with the heat. A rotating electric fan placed on the countertop between them redistributed warm air evenly, first to one and then the other, lifting their hair alternately as it did so.

'We've come for an ice cream,' announced Dominic, making his way to the counter.

Sebastian wished he hadn't said yes to the ice cream. He feared he'd appear childish and immediately rebuked himself for his insecurity. 'And then we're going to look for our mother,' he said, as though an ice cream were permissible in that case.

'A good idea,' said Rosetta, 'I think I'll have one too,' and when Dominic passed her one she pressed it still in its wrapper to her forehead, her cheeks and her chest. '*Mamma mia, che caldo,*' she said to no-one in particular. 'I saw her earlier,' she said. 'She was walking in the direction of the stream. You know, where is the little bridge.' She removed an empty laundry basket from the bar stool beside her so that Sebastian felt it would have been rude of him not to sit down. Its plastic red top stuck to his thighs.

'Thank you,' said Sebastian. He had the sensation of having had a certain feeling before, a *déjà pensée*, a feeling of saying Thank you seemingly for one thing while meaning for another. He was grateful to Rosetta for having an ice cream. He wondered if she'd read his mind. Licking an ice cream alongside his little brother in front of a girl he was hoping to impress was made all the easier if she licked one too.

'If I was you, I'd stay inside,' said Rosetta. 'By this heat...'

Claudia opened a ledger and Sebastian watched as she entered their names, the date and the price of two ice creams and then closed it decisively. Maybe Rosetta was allowed free ice creams.

Rosetta addressed a few words to Claudia in Italian and got off the stool and held the empty basket to her hip with one hand and the unfinished ice cream with the other. It was melting more quickly than she was eating it; she licked some cream off her knuckles and got some on the tip of her nose. She looked like a cat and, not wanting to laugh, Sebastian looked down. Small puddles of perspiration had gathered in the slight indentations Rosetta's thighs had left on the bar stool. '*Allora*. I am going,' she said and then, turning around as she stood in the doorway, 'Hey, Francesca said you visited us. Next time, you visit when I am there, okay?' and she flashed Dominic a warm smile that Sebastian chose to believe had been intended for him.

As Sebastian and Dominic made their way down the path to the stream, Sebastian reflected that Rosetta hadn't appeared at all discomfited by the bedroom incident. In any case, she'd made no reference to it. He was grateful to her for that too. And that she'd given him an open invitation to visit her.

The path down was steep, unpaved, earthy and rocky. It followed a stone wall down on their left and an amphitheatre, now a terraced field of wild grasses, on their right.

'I don't think flip-flops were a good idea,' said Sebastian as he slipped.

Dominic put his fingers to his lips and pointed upwards. Above the zizzing din of the cicadas, Sebastian could just about make out the drone of the American's monologue. He shrugged and they moved on.

The path dropped into a wood where it was immediately cooler, darker and quieter. Insects scudded from leaf to leaf or hovered momentarily immobile in shafts of sunlight that penetrated the treetops and lit ferns and wild flowers.

Sebastian stopped. He grabbed Dominic by the shoulder. To their right in a clearing barely visible through the trees' lower branches was the motionless outline of a man.

The boys left the path. They beat their way through the undergrowth to the clearing where they gazed in wonder at a dozen thick sheets of glass eight feet tall fixed, it would appear, deep into the ground and upon which had been etched, life-size, the cross-sections of a body. Beyond it, after a bit of a drop, was a pond. The effigy presented a three-dimensional ochre-coloured silhouette of a man looking out over the water. It changed in outline as the viewer walked around it. The front sheet had etched and painted onto it only the man's protruding belly. The back sheet, the wings of his shoulder blades and a bit of his buttocks. It was as though a man had been lain on a bed and then sliced horizontally before being righted and entombed in glass. Seen from the side, he was invisible. From any other angle he was massively present, his outline resembling the geographic contours of hills on an ordinance survey map. Sebastian felt he was in the presence of something profound. He knew that the artist had intended a statement about man and nature or man *in* nature, but he couldn't put his finger on it. His racing heart slowed. He placed his hand on Dominic's shoulder and the two of them stood there admiring the unexpected discovery.

'Pretty cool,' said Sebastian.

'It makes me feel sad,' said Dominic. 'He must feel lonely just standing there.'

The ochre, sliced figure had stood there for years, Sebastian could tell from the weathered glass, dirty where rain drops had spattered mud around his feet and ankles, and would in all probability remain there for many more. The ochre paint, he now saw, had peeled off in places. He looked from the figure to his brother. Again his brother had surprised him: he wasn't looking *at* the glass-encased man but looking *out* from *within* him. While he, Sebastian, grasped for some big statement, his brother was drawn to the immediately personal. His brother, he thought, had empathy.

The brothers left the clearing by the one path leading into and out of it and came immediately upon a stone bridge where a stream met the pond and filled it. The arched, low-sided bridge was lit as though by a spotlight – the trees' canopy didn't quite protect it from the sun. It was only just wide enough for two adults abreast and was maybe a dozen feet across. Just the other side, in the shade to one side of the path by the stream, stood their mother by her easel.

Dominic waved at her and she waved back.

His mother, Sebastian had come to know, painted two types of scene and had two kinds of style. The first was of clear, defined urban views, with buildings clearly delineated first in pencil and then in Indian ink. What her cityscapes lacked in ambiguity they made up for in precision. They banished doubt. They announced that the world could be known, captured and measured. The second was of landscapes, the vanishing points of which led to places of obscurity or, simply, a lack of detail, that had the viewer wanting to step closer, to wonder what lay at the end of the country road, the river, the bridge or in the clearing *exactly*. And the closer you approached the more clearly you only saw paint.

Sebastian looked over his mother's shoulder. There was the bridge, the path and the clearing and then nothing. Trees, branches and foliage – just strokes and daubs of watercolour, inviting you to look for something that wasn't there or, perhaps, something that lay within yourself. Sebastian's grand-parents had one of their daughter's paintings, a bright water-colour of a French landscape, hung over a Vietnamese teak console in their entrance hall, and surrounded by smaller framed black and white photographs of Indochina where it appeared incongruous. As the photographs faded, so the painting increased in prominence every time the family visited, as though the daughter were insisting she not be forgotten. Or so it appeared to Sebastian. It had never occurred to him to ask his brother what he thought of their mother's work; perhaps he would.

Dominic, who had slid down the bank where his flip-flops now lay in order to paddle in the stream, squealed. 'It's cold!'

'It's mountain water,' said his mother.

'Tadpoles and things,' observed Dominic, squatting and looking into the rock pools around his feet closely.

'Are you bored, darling?' asked Jacqueline Kentish, not looking from her painting.

'A little,' said Sebastian. 'But it's alright.' He didn't want his mother to feel guilty for having taken him on what was a pleasant enough holiday. 'It's just that there's no-one here my age. Except Rosetta,' he added, thinking his mother could feel a little guilty for forbidding him from hanging out with Rosetta during her time off work.

'There are girls and there are girls,' said Mrs Kentish, looking closely at her painting and they left it at that.

Jacqueline Kentish stepped back from her easel and wiped her brow with the back of a hand. 'I think I've finished for the day,' she said. She joined her sons splashing in the stream where she tucked her dress about her thighs and crouched to clean her brushes. The moment she had finished and stood she heard Dominic exclaim, 'Watch out, Mum!' and she turned around to see him pointing excitedly at a dark grey-green snake in a rock-pool close to her.

'Mum!' shouted Sebastian who, stepping back, caught his heel on a rock and sat down in a shallow pool.

'Don't worry. Don't panic.' The American stood on the bank of the stream looking down on them. 'It's completely harmless.

It's a grass snake. A male, at a guess. It prefers frogs and mice to people.'

When the Kentishes, who'd looked up, looked back down, the snake had gone. All the same, they scrambled out of the stream and up the bank.

Sebastian gallantly shouldered the easel, pulling, with his free hand, at the seat of his wet shorts. Dominic carried the paints. Mrs Kentish placed the painting between sheets of blotting paper in a folder. The American now stood on the other side of the bridge.

He waved. 'After you, please.' He stepped back and indicated the way across the bridge with both hands, an action Sebastian considered unnecessary. He wore beige shorts and walking boots with thick grey socks around his ankles. Sweat had dried on his faded red polo shirt, leaving white patches like a map on his chest. His hair and his legs were white but his forearms were tanned and his face was the pale red of his shirt.

'Thank you,' said Mrs Kentish, 'for having re-assured us.'

'If I had only arrived just a few moments earlier, I'd have had the good fortune to have admired your work,' said the American politely.

'Oh, you haven't missed much,' said Mrs Kentish.

'I'm sure you're just being modest.'

'Do you know much about snakes, then?' asked Dominic.

'As a matter of fact, I do,' said the American and then, 'it's very good of you to help your mother.' He ran his forearm across his brow. 'And how are you, Mrs Kentish? Are you enjoying this little paradise of ours? Me, I'm just off for my late afternoon constitutional. I am inclined, when the day is cooler, to wander off to Veravo' – and he waved his hand in the general direction of the village on the other side of the mountain from Colletta – 'to have a little *aperitivo* there. If I don't do it very often it's because the locals tell me that I must not surprise the wild boar that root and forage along this path because, surprised, they may charge, to protect their young – and they're fierce little creatures, you know – and so, when I go, I must sing, so that they can hear me coming and have the time to make themselves scarce, taking their young with them out of harm's way, and my problem is that I can't sing in tune and I'm afraid that that could enrage the boars. I understand from your husband that you were born in Saigon. I was stationed there for some time. In the early '40s.' The American panted. He hadn't drawn breath.

Sebastian, to one side of him, regarded him closely. Presented with his mother, he was different to the taciturn bear of a man he appeared in the village square. He could only take his eyes off his mother to look at him, it would seem. Where the three of them stood, at the end of the bridge, their fair hair shone bright in the sun. Dominic, dark and small of stature and standing to one side laden with the paints, was indistinct in the contrasting shade.

'Yes,' said Mrs Kentish, 'but my family left soon after I was born. I don't remember much about it.'

'Ah,' said the American, 'your parents returned to France.'

'No. We went to Algeria. And from there to France. As my father would say, there were no more wars for us to lose.'

'I see,' said the American and looked in the direction of Veravo and then of Colletta. 'Perhaps I'll forego my walk this evening,' he said, 'and return with you. If you don't mind, that is.'

Mrs Kentish and the American walked slowly up the path, out of the wood and alongside the amphitheatre's long grasses into the last light of the afternoon, Sebastian and Dominic following with the easel and the paints.

. . .

'You told him I was born in Saigon,' said Mrs Kentish.

'Did I? Maybe I did,' said Mr Kentish. 'This is delicious!' he exclaimed, his mouth full.

'How, in the context of your interviewing him, did I come up?' Mrs Kentish twirled spaghetti about her fork without eating it.

'He was telling me about his life. A little. Over lunch. I haven't got him to open up. Not yet. Not exactly. I mean, about why he's telling me what he's telling me. Anyway, I'm in no hurry. I've got another week with him. Don't you want your clams?'

Mrs Kentish pushed her plate towards her husband. 'Well, he seemed very interested. In where my father was stationed. In what my mother did. Of course, I couldn't tell him anything.'

'Well, he is a military man, I suppose. Or was.'

'I realise I have my father's reticence to talk about such things.'

'What things?'

'Vietnam. Algeria. Normally, I'm the one who's there silent, watching my father squirm as he deals with questions about France's military history and his place in it but this time it was me. It felt strange to me to feel like my father for a time.'

'That's understandable. You didn't exactly cover yourselves in glory.'

'Dad!' Sebastian groaned. The recitation of the French and British empires' relative triumphs and failings was not something he wanted to sit through again.

His father placed his hand on his wife's and gave it a squeeze.

'And he told me what *you* did!' said Mrs Kentish rounding on Sebastian. 'It's shocking!'

'What?' said Sebastian.

'What you did with the sun beds. Around the pool. I told your father. You agree, don't you, Peter?'

'Oh that,' said Sebastian. He pushed a clam around his plate.

'You should apologise to him. To that German.'

'It wasn't me, it was Kees,' said Sebastian defensively. 'I just moved them around like he told me to. It was only after, when I looked back, that I realised.'

'You were only following orders,' said Dominic.

'Oh be quiet,' said Sebastian peevishly.

It had been a long, energy-sapping day. The crowd that gathered around the television set in the piazza was smaller than it had been and the cheer, when Italy scored against Austria, sounded perfunctory. Godehard being exceptionally forgiving, the German and the Dutch families had formed a truce and, taking the English with them, gone to Albenga in order to watch the Holland West Germany game, to a bar where Kees had negotiated the viewing of that game in place of the Italy one in exchange for the promise of a crowd and a large beer tab.

Francesca came to clear the first course, her action in leaning across the table to remove the plates reminding Sebastian of her movement when she'd picked her knickers up from her bed. Rosetta came to carry the empty serving bowls away and her face, momentarily, was inches from his again.

'Dad,' said Sebastian, wishing for distraction. 'Is your work off limits or not? I mean, can we ask you questions about it? As Mum just did?'

'You can ask me all you like,' said his father, 'but I won't necessarily answer.'

'Why not?' asked Dominic.

'Because a lot of what I'm told is confidential.'

'But then you write it up in an article that gets published in a newspaper.'

'Or a magazine or book,' added Dominic.

Mr Kentish sighed. 'It's not that simple.'

'You know his name?' said Dominic.

'Yes,' said his father.

'A good journalist never reveals his sauces,' ribbed Sebastian, moving his shins beneath his chair so that Dominic couldn't kick them, as, the first time Dominic had heard his father state that, he'd asked after ketchup and mayonnaise.

Dominic just narrowed his eyes.

Francesca returned with clean plates and said, indicating the dish Rosetta had followed her with, 'Chicken. From Tigullio. Cooked in white wine.' Mr Kentish nodded assent to his wine glass being topped up.

Sebastian felt that the two beers he'd had, the second under a reproachful look from his mother, had gone straight to his head. 'Do you like him, Dad?' he asked.

'Liking someone is not a prerequisite for interviewing someone but, yes. I'd say he's a likeable person.'

'Why has he chosen to live here?'

'I don't know. I don't think he lives here all the year around.'

'I mean, it's very nice and all that but a bit cut off.'

'It's lovely,' said Mrs Kentish.

'What kind of things are you interviewing him about?' asked Dominic, emboldened, Sebastian thought, by his questions. 'Can't you even give us a clue?'

'No.'

'So what will you do with all that information? He's been talking to you for three days! Will you be writing a book?' asked Sebastian.

Mr Kentish looked down at the napkin on his lap and ran

his fingers across it as if to smooth it. He stared intently at it as though the answer were written there. 'Maybe,' he said.

For dessert they were served something called *panna cotta*, a pale, almost translucent, lavender-scented cream jelly that barely resisted their spoons' excavations. It had the family in raptures.

'How does Claudia do it?' Mrs Kentish asked Dario, whose chest swelled with pride.

Dario stood at the end of the table in his stripy matelot's shirt and lit a cigarette. 'We say, to work here, you have to have one of two things. You must be able to cook – for the Italians – or to speak English – for the tourists. Because we know there is no-one who can cook *and* speak English – I know, because I went to England! Once.' Dario lifted an index finger. '*Mamma mia!*' He waved his hand and whistled. 'The longest year of my life!'

'That's what we say in France too – about English cooking,' said Mrs Kentish to Dario, as though wishing to remind him that she was, actually, French.

Dario appeared unimpressed. 'French cooking.' He shrugged. 'You know you have us to thank?' He pointed at himself and nodded as though he were delivering an unequivocal fact. 'It was Catherine de Medici who took Italian cuisine with her to Paris when she married, er, one of your kings.'

'*Henri deux*,' said Mrs Kentish.

'A *digestivo*, Peter?' proposed Dario.

'Maybe a small one. What I had the other night. What was that?'

'One *grappa*,' said Dario, 'and for Mrs?'

Sebastian noticed the slide to informality, as his father would refer to it, or familiarity, as his mother would call it. His father had been *Mr Kentish* to begin with but somehow, some time, maybe after one too many *digestivi* the other evening, a switch had been pulled and he'd become *Peter*. His mother remained and would remain, Sebastian was willing to bet, *Mrs Kentish*. She wore her pride or her inherited military bearing – Sebastian wasn't sure which – like a suit of armour that certain people, people like Dario or Rosetta, would never be allowed to penetrate.

Mrs Kentish opted for a *limoncello*.

The hippy with the guitar they had seen on the evening of their arrival appeared, pulled gently by the hand into the square by a tall lady with straight blond hair that hung to the small of her back and was garlanded with wildflowers. She wore a long gold and white tie-dyed dress, leather sandals and necklaces fashioned from driftwood and beads. With her other hand, she led a young girl, no more than eleven years old, who was also blond but barefoot and clutching a flute. The hippy, whose guitar had been slung over his back on a thick bandolier, now sat on the wall with his guitar on a crossed knee. Dominic left the table to listen more closely to the music. Dario switched a spotlight on. It was fixed to the wall and had a weak light, clearly only intended for these occasional outdoor performances. The odd couple played a succession of tender, moving melodies, the hippy's hair obscuring his face as he leant over his acoustic guitar, and the bangles on his wrists flashing as he plucked the guitar strings and the bangles caught the light. In between pieces, the diners on the terrace and the drinkers in the square applauded and the girl curtsied.

Sebastian, lulled into a torpor by the food, the alcohol and the music, felt himself to be cocooned in the night's warm blanket and was on the point of nodding off when he heard Dominic run back and say, 'Look.'

Down from the terrace and across the square, past the bar

and in the alleyway just beyond it, in the yellow light of a solitary lamp, Rosetta and the Argentinian stood arguing. Sebastian could tell from Rosetta's frown and the shaking of her head that she was in disagreement with whatever the Argentinian was saying. She made to move away, towards the square, but he extended his arm, hand against the wall, and barred her way. She remonstrated some more, it seemed, and he relented, following her slowly to the square but not crossing it, sidling along the wall, past the open bar door and to a seat against the wall that gave him a good view of the television.

'He seems to want something from her,' said Mr Kentish.

'I don't like him,' said Sebastian, wide awake and gripping his chair.

'I don't want you getting involved,' said Mrs Kentish.

'Have you seen his knife?' asked Dominic excitedly.

'His knife?' said Mrs Kentish.

'He's got the biggest Opinel knife I've ever seen,' said Dominic with his hands apart and pushing his chair back so he could better demonstrate just how big it was. 'It's this big!'

'It's not that big,' said Sebastian.

'What does he need a knife that big for?' said Mrs Kentish. 'What does anyone need a knife that big for?'

'For hunting. Or whittling,' said Dominic.

'He cleans his fingernails with it,' said Sebastian.

'One thing's for sure, you don't need a knife that big to clean your fingernails with,' said Mrs Kentish, looking at her nails from which she'd removed all trace of her oil paints.

'He's the manager of the quarry,' said Mr Kentish.

'How do you know that?' asked his wife.

'The American told me. They know each other. Though I don't think they're friends exactly.'

There was the sound of car engines gunning up the hill and then headlights swept the car park.

'That'll be the Dutch and the Germans returning,' said Mr Kentish, 'I wonder what the score was.

'Two all,' said Dominic. 'I heard someone saying.'

'Oh good,' said his father, 'a draw. So World War Three won't be breaking out in a small village in Liguria then.'

'Why does he come here then? Of all places?' asked Mrs Kentish.

'Who?'

'The Argentinian.'

Dominic rolled his eyes. 'To watch the football, of course. It's Argentina Brazil now.' And he too went to watch.

THIRTEEN

People came and went in waves. The square was empty until all of a sudden it wasn't. And then it was again.

The Cespuglios and the Romanos met for coffee that Claudia brought out to them on round polished wood trays. They drank their coffee standing, saucers in one hand and cups in the other, eyes on the weather and on the sheer mountain face across the valley while debating the merits of the yellow, orange and red walking routes. It was always the same: Giorgio Cespuglio only had to suggest one route for Emilio Romano to propose another. Giorgio wore a bright green vest, tight pink shorts, grey walking stockings that he pulled above the knee and the latest in footwear technology for him and for Giorgia, or so he liked to boast. She was similarly glaringly outfitted. Emilio and Emilia, who both dressed in khaki and carried backpacks as though ready to disappear into the *boschi* for weeks, couldn't beat their friends for style but, it couldn't be denied, they had the best walking sticks. These had been hewn and fashioned from Roman chestnut wood, steamed and peeled, and fitted with decorative, beaded hand grips made by Emilia. The only thing the two couples had in common, it had struck Bravo, was their love of walking, and so they holidayed together every year. Giorgio consulted his watch while his wife made the last necessary adjustments to her make-up. The Pompeos arrived late, as usual, arguing about Mrs Pompeo's choice of footwear, and were officiously told that there was no time for coffee if they were going to stand a chance of completing their walk before dying from heat exhaustion. And off they strode, down past the bar, past the water troughs and down out of the village, Giorgio and Emilio leading the way and still arguing about which route to follow, Giorgia and Emilia following and talking over one another and the Pompeos lagging behind before they had even left the village, still arguing.

For a time, the square was quiet again, the shadows on the terrace cast by the chairs and tables shortening and moving slowly in their day's progression eastward.

Godehard came without bread and went with it.

Clifford, Kees and Renzo appeared for their post-swim coffee and pastries. They sat on the stone bench in swimming trunks, towels and bath robes and watched as Claudia laid their breakfast out on the barrel halves that served as tables. They waved to Bravo and he waved back and the four of them waved again when the swimmers departed.

From his position on the terrace Bravo could see down two of the paths that led to the bar, the two either side of Colletta's tallest construction – and maybe even the first built, 700 or so years ago – the one with, at the base of its wall, the stone bench the swimmers had been sitting on. Along the path nearest the bar came Rosetta, carrying a red plastic bucket that, judging from the angle of her shoulders, was full and heavy. She had been cleaning windows, he knew, choosing to start early before it grew too hot for outdoor work. Along the other, came the elder Kentish boy. Bravo sat up in his chair. He took an interest in seeing Sebastian and he took an aesthetic pleasure in the symmetry of the two young people's approaches. He sat forward, as Rosetta stumbled but regained her balance and staggered on. She turned a corner. So did Sebastian. Sebastian raised his hand in greeting. Rosetta lurched forward. Sebastian took some steps towards her and held his arms out. She dropped the bucket and fell, and Sebastian caught her, just. Unaware that he'd even formulated the intention, Bravo found that he was on his feet and running from the terrace to the square where Sebastian was on his knees with Rosetta unconscious in his lap.

'Rosetta!' Sebastian called her name repeatedly, his voice rising with every repetition. 'Rosetta!' Sebastian shouted.

Having reached them, Bravo was at a loss as to what to do. Rosetta's head lolled back in the boy's arms. Her eyes seemed to have travelled to the back of her head; only the whites showed, barely, through her long eyelashes. Her arms lay limp at her side. Sebastian's hurried catch had been in time but only just, and the thrust of one hand and the weight of her had meant that Sebastian had inadvertently caught the back of her dress when reaching for her, so that the front of her dark blue cotton dress was twisted and stretched with one breast threatening to break free should the buttons that lined the front of it pop.

Rosetta's cries had brought Claudia to the door of the bar. She stood with her hands to her mouth.

'Help me!' pleaded Sebastian. His eyes were wide open in terror.

Bravo realised he'd been standing in a trance. He shook himself together. 'Fetch the doctor,' he barked at Claudia and was surprised at how suddenly and quickly she moved, turning the corner Rosetta had come from and disappearing from view in a second.

Mr and Mrs Kentish rounded the other corner. And stopped. At their feet lay their elder son and the cleaning girl in a barely decent embrace. Above them stood the American. Mrs Kentish clutched her husband's arm, her mouth and her sunglasses forming three dark Os.

'Dad!' shouted Sebastian, 'Fetch some water!'

'Don't tell me what to do,' said Kentish without much conviction. It was a reflex for Bravo to note that Kentish wasn't any good in crisis.

Mrs Kentish regained the power of speech. '*Mon dieu!* What is going on? Get up! Get up right now!'

Rosetta's legs lay outstretched and splayed in a Y on the cobbles. Her torso was in Sebastian's arms, her head back and her black hair clouding Sebastian's arms and the roughly hewn stones beneath her head.

'Mum! Don't be ridiculous!' shouted Sebastian. 'Can't you see she's fainted? Something's happened to her! Dad, get her some water!'

'How do you know it's water she needs?' asked Mr Kentish uncertainly, stepping forward and looking at the girl more closely.

Claudia arrived with the doctor still in his pyjamas, his dressing gown flapping open behind him. Dario was immediately behind them. Sebastian recognised the doctor as the old man he'd seen reading, the evening he'd gone to the swimming pool with Kees. The doctor pulled his pyjama trousers up at the knees and knelt. He held two fingers to Rosetta's wrist and then placed them by her throat. He turned to the person closest to hand, who happened to be Mr Kentish, and said, '*Un bicchiere d'acqua, presto.'* Kentish looked dumbfounded. 'A glass of water, quickly.'

Kentish moved slowly but Claudia raced to the bar and returned within seconds and handed a full glass to Mr Kentish who handed it to the doctor.

Eva and Clifford Better arrived and Clifford exclaimed, 'Blimey! What happened?' and stood with his arm around his wife.

Dario wrung his hands and lifted them imploringly, repeatedly.

'Please to lift her head,' the doctor instructed Sebastian calmly. 'Let's see if she will take some water.' He brought the glass to her lips, parted them and, when he saw the swallowing reflex, repeated the action. 'What happened?' he asked Sebastian. 'Did you see what happened?'

The walkers returned and joined the small crowd around the prostrate Rosetta.

Francesca appeared and knelt by Rosetta, the other side from Sebastian.

Bravo felt himself jostled. Behind him he could hear the Pompeos still arguing, now about what might have happened to Rosetta, and he could smell Giorgia Cespuglio's perfume that followed her like a banner. He reached to move the bucket, that had not spilled when it had been dropped, to one side before someone tripped over it and was hit, as he leant over it, by the stronger, competing stink of ammonia.

'Dario!' Bravo had a way of speaking, at times, that commanded authority. He had pronounced Dario's name quietly and yet so distinctly and definitively that everyone who had been talking stopped.

'*Si,*' said Dario, wide-eyed and as though ready to deny that anything was his fault.

'Rosetta was cleaning the windows this morning, right?'

'Right. Is her job.' Dario looked pleadingly at the jury gathered around the victim.

'For that, she uses ammonia, right?'

'For sure.'

'Do you tell her to dilute it?'

'Of course! Of course! Fill the bucket with water first and then one cup ammonia.' Dario leant towards the bucket and then withdrew his head sharply, his face a mixture of pain and disgust, the back of his hand going to his nose. 'Ai! *Che cosa ha fatto?* No! This is not dilute like I tell her to!'

The doctor patted Sebastian on the shoulder and said, '*Bravo.* You did good!' He kept his hand on Sebastian's shoulder, returned the glass to Kentish, and, using the boy as a support, stood slowly and tied his dressing gown around him. He approached the bucket and inhaled, from a distance. He nodded. 'So, this is what happened. Is insufficiently dilute so she faints. But she will be alright.' He looked at Dario. 'Take her to her room. Give her lots of water and lots of hair. Make sure her room is well ventilate.'

Dario, in Italian, gesticulating with the thumbs and fingers of each hand pressed together as if in supplication, asked the doctor why he was speaking to him in English, a question that the small crowd that had gathered around Rosetta took for what it was, a signal that everything was going to be alright.

The doctor shrugged and raised his hands and eyebrows.

Francesca reappeared with a yellow cotton blanket.

'*Aiuto*', said Emilio Romano and so did Giorgio Cespuglio.

'Me too, I'll help,' said Clifford.

The men lifted Rosetta from Sebastian's arms onto the blanket, Francesca adjusting Rosetta's dress before wrapping the blanket around her. They stood and looked down at the yellow cotton chrysalis at their feet. Then the men lifted her and, walking carefully and slowly, followed Francesca down the cobbled path and out of sight around the corner.

The square had filled with people and now with chatter. Claudia would be busy making coffees for the next hour. She headed for the bar, and Dario made as if to follow when Bravo caught him by the arm and suggested he call Rosetta's father.

Bravo had long noted that the Italians, once a crisis and their excited response to it was over, forgot all about it, while the English, rarely ever openly acknowledging a trauma, carried it about with them to the point of it making them ill. So he sought out the Kentishes and inquired after them. Kentish, he'd noted, had bridled at having been told what do by his son and had been peeved to have received the same instruction from the doctor. But Kentish said he was fine, quite fine. Sebastian, on the other hand, had behaved admirably; he'd saved the girl from smashing her face on the stone floor and he too said he was fine, standing next to his mother with his arms limp by his side, not wanting to show, Bravo surmised, how much they ached from having held the girl for so long. Bravo had a harder time figuring Mrs Kentish out. He was drawn to her as a father might be, he knew, but he wasn't sure he liked her. For a reason he couldn't put his finger on, she seemed angry with her son and, perhaps, angry with her husband for not being as angry with her son as she was. She had stood with her arms crossed; when she had finally unfolded them, he had noticed the half-moons her fingernails had left on her upper arms. The image he was forming of her as a wife and a mother was at odds with the favourable image he had of her as an artist. Of course, she wasn't English but French and, of the French, Bravo had only had that one experience many years ago. Now, she had her son by the arm and was admonishing him in hushed, urgent tones.

Bravo regarded Kentish with raised eyebrows. 'Shall we? Before it gets even hotter?'

They walked up, up towards the church and to the *ufficio*. Bravo popped in and, Francesca being absent, helped himself to the key to the guest office Kentish and he would use. They passed Godehard's family waiting by the church for Godehard to fetch the car; laden with rubber rings, parasol and towels, the German family was off to the beach. They ducked down by the olive trees and up the steps to the office and sat, as they were becoming used to doing, at the wrought iron table in the shade.

Kentish had no agenda for the day – at least, he didn't declare one and seemed happy for Bravo to just talk. Maybe, despite his denials, he had been unsettled by the morning's excitement. And, so, Bravo talked, attentive not to revisit old ground and aware that they had last discussed the 1958 election. He found he could answer questions sitting down but was happier delivering a monologue – if that was what was required of him – pacing the office's little front garden.

'By the early '60s, the Communist Party in Italy had a membership of nearly one and a half million – and did you know that it received support from the Soviet Union in the form of some forty to fifty million dollars every year?'

'So you weren't the only ideologues buying influence.'

'My point precisely. However, what worried us more than the money was the Vatican's stance. The new pope, John XXIII who had succeeded Pius XII, did not condemn this increase in Communist Party membership and instead even attempted a rapprochement between Catholicism and communism. Can you believe it? So, when John XXIII died, we, not wanting another *pink* pope, ensured the appointment of our man. Paul VI had served in the O.S.S. during the war and had then been placed in charge of a Vatican charity that provided protection for anti-communist

German soldiers and Nazi sympathisers; he had been an ardent supporter of Catholic Gladio and had received and disbursed millions of dollars from us for his charitable work as Archbishop of Milan. We did what we had to do to ensure his election.'

'Are there no limits,' began Kentish and shook his head. He looked directly at Bravo. 'Was that really necessary?'

'Yes. Absolutely. You see, for the first time, the Italian bishops' conference, under John XXIII, had failed to endorse the Christian Democrats. Consequently, in the election that year – 1963 – the Christian Democrats lost a third of their share of the vote, with the Communists increasing theirs by the same amount. And the Socialists did better than expected. For us, it was a disaster. It was only by giving socialists government posts that Moro could form a soft centre right government. But that didn't appease the communists – they – well, the Communist Party fronted by the construction workers' union – held a demonstration in Rome. Of course, we were alarmed, we had to do something.

'First, we assembled the largest number of members of Gladio we could and, with some of them disguised as police and others dressed simply as civilians, we smashed the demonstration. They never knew what happened. It was brutal. It left more than 200 people injured.

'Second, we worked for the election of Paul VI.

'And third, we stepped up the creation of a state within the Italian state, the creation of an organisation that could control the government by whatever means. You must understand, this compromise with the socialists was a serious setback, one that, potentially, could have been the end of the free world as we knew it. It was the justification for our conducting intensive surveillance of Italian political, religious and business leaders in order to identify communist sympathisers. It was on a massive scale. Within a few years, the C.I.A. had files on more than 157,000 people of prominence and, in these files, we had tape recordings or photos or witness statements that could be used for blackmail or coercion, many of them false and completely made up, of course.'

Bravo stood by the iron gate, his back to Kentish. At times, when he heard himself speaking, he disgusted himself. He would try to push the disgust to one side, attempting to believe that someone else, an earlier version of him, had been responsible for his past actions; he was only responsible for what he did today and what he'd do tomorrow. He wondered, without really caring, what Kentish thought of him. Kentish, in his years as a journalist, had come across worse, he assumed. He wondered, too, whether he'd have said anything different to a psychologist or a psychotherapist – he never had been quite sure of the distinction – but had revolted against the idea of the safe purgation, the confession without consequences. He had seen Mafia hoods walk in and out of confessionals and despised the Catholic church for the ease with which it forgave. Was he seeking forgiveness? If so, from whom? From himself? Surely not from Kentish, to whom he'd said as little as possible about his own, personal involvement, speaking as much in generalities as possible. But what would Kentish do with the information he was giving him? Without corroborating evidence? Could his act of gross self-indulgence be putting Kentish and his family at risk? He assumed not, if he kept to the broad outline of the thing. Others would follow Kentish and others would follow them until, one day, this particular onion would be peeled. But not yet. Bravo gripped the iron gate with both hands and hung his head. A centipede crawled from a stone by one of his boots and away. Sweat from above his ears trickled down and stung his eyes.

Behind him, Kentish changed the cassette over. His iron chair scraped on the stone as he pushed it back and stood. He joined Bravo in looking out over the amphitheatre and the olive and fruit trees below, where Kees Langemensen and his family were picking figs off the trees.

'That Dutchman is a nice chap,' said Kentish. 'An unusual sense of humour. I asked him when he would be going home, and he replied when they'd finished the potatoes they've brought from home.'

'He wasn't joking,' said Bravo.

They watched as Kees summoned his family and four blond heads came together over a fig he held in the palm of his hand.

'I feel, sometimes,' said Kentish looking straight ahead, 'that there are parallel worlds and we move between them daily, sometimes inhabiting more than one at a time. It's a discomfiting experience. It happens at many levels. I see it in my wife's art, there's this schism that she can't explain. I see it in my domestic and professional lives. Domestically, I'm called upon to share my wife's concern that my son is infatuated with a cleaning girl. Professionally, I have been learning that the world is like a rotten fruit, that everything we believe or are told to hold important is a lie perpetrated by the people who tell us to hold it important, the very people we elect to help us maintain those beliefs.'

'But it's not a lie,' said Bravo quietly. 'Liberty and democracy, freedom of thought and of speech, the right to vote and to representation – these aren't lies.'

'No, of course not,' said Kentish hastily, 'but we are being lied *to*.' He arched his eyebrows. 'You see, I have believed everything you've told me.' He shook his head, as though to clear his thoughts. 'Those early '60s – those were tumultuous years. The Berlin Wall. Cuba. Kennedy. I suppose you recall Eisenhower's farewell address? When was that? 1961? I can remember some of it verbatim. *We must guard against the acquisition of unwarranted influence, whether sought or unsought, by the military-industrial complex. The potential for the disastrous rise of misplaced power exists and will persist. We must never let the weight of this combination endanger our liberties or democratic processes...*'

Bravo held his hand up. '...*We should take nothing for granted. Only an alert and knowledgeable citizenry can compel the proper meshing of the huge industrial and military machinery of defence with our peaceful methods and goals, so that security and liberty may prosper together.*'

The two men looked at each other. It felt to Bravo as though they had shared the delivery of a liturgy.

'You spoke of the creation of a state within the Italian state but a state already existed within the U.S. state, it would seem,' said Kentish. Kentish sat down. 'Was Eisenhower warning us or playing us?'

Bravo leaned back on the gate, his back to the view, and shrugged. 'Probably both. I mean, he knew some things but not *every* thing. I mean, even one of yours, Keynes, noted that the U.S. would find it difficult to sustain lasting economic prosperity without maintaining a large war machine and that was well before.'

'So, tell me something Eisenhower didn't know.'

Bravo inhaled deeply. 'I can tell you something you won't believe.'

'Go on then,' said Kentish.

'You mentioned Cuba. And Kennedy. In the eyes of the Agency, Kennedy revealed weakness by bowing to the Soviets during the Cuba missile crisis in 1962. He risked becoming a liability. He was nicknamed The Closet Communist. The Agency decided on a project that, if successful, would garner sufficient international support to justify a full-scale U.S. invasion of Cuba. It was a detailed plan designed to wreak mayhem across America. We were to hire snipers, well, Mafia hoods, to shoot Cuban refugees in Florida and pin the blame on Cuban saboteurs, on Castro. But then why stop at Cubans and why stop at Florida? How long would the Americans tolerate the assassination in broad daylight of American citizens by Cuban subversives? Castro would have declared the war; we'd just be finishing it.'

'But that's crazy,' said Kentish. 'You're talking of Americans murdering Americans for – what? A twisted ideological end!'

'Acts of terror to be performed under the American flag on the orders of the highest military commanders in the land.' Bravo nodded. 'But the end wasn't considered ideological in the sense of an ideology as something that remains purely theoretical. There was a profound conviction in the Agency that it was acting in the interests of a free and better world. *The end may justify the means as long as there is something that justifies the end.* How ironic that Trotsky was quoted without irony by our leaders! It was a sacrifice of the few for the good of the greater number. Of course, that logic pervaded the Agency. One saw it in the mutation of NATO and of Gladio, this sanctioning of a, well, prefabricated violence because the Agency believed the benefits gained by the state counts for more than any injustice against individuals.'

'It's ironic in the extreme. The country that represents individual freedoms against totalitarianism behaving like a totalitarian state with a callow disregard for civil liberties – for human life! Was Kennedy ever made aware of this – this grotesque plan?'

'Operation Northwoods. Yes. He quashed it.'

Kentish nodded his approval.

'But the cat was out of the bag. Things began to get really twisted. Gladio bombed the Christian Democrats' headquarters and some right-wing newspaper offices and blamed the Left. And NATO – NATO even rolled tanks into Rome to intimidate the government and it worked: Moro had the socialists abandon their ministerial posts.'

'But things didn't really go your way, did they?' Kentish pulled some papers and a notebook out of his satchel. 'Didn't the communists do well in the 1968 election?'

'Yes, but at the expense of the socialists.'

'Still, together they had more votes than the Christian Democrats. And the communists gained control of a large number of cities and regions, didn't they?'

'Yes, yes, but don't forget the times. We were over ten years into the Vietnam War. The anti-war sentiment was strong. Emotions were running high. Flower power dominated the streets.' Bravo waved his arms in the air and scowled. 'Che Guevara and Chairman Mao were folk heroes, for Christ's sake.'

Kentish nodded. He fanned himself with a sheaf of paper. 'Do you think the Left was actually ever as powerful as you feared? Was there a risk that the Right believed its own propaganda?'

'That's a fair question.' Bravo considered it. 'One could answer yes to both of them without contradiction. Don't forget, there was huge industrial unrest. There still is. All the strikes.'

'But you made something ideological out of it.' Kentish waved a sheaf of newspaper cuttings at him. 'Well, the Christian Democrats did. The Right chose to blame Left-wing radicals and Marxist intellectuals rather than address low wages, high inflation and poor working conditions. Is it true that the Fiat factories in Turin were infected by intellectual radicals proselytising on factory floors, by agitators taking orders from Moscow?'

'Yes, there is some truth in that.'

'But was there anything to justify the fear of a nationwide workers' revolution? I am developing a sense, listening to you, that the full-blown political crisis that Italy slipped into was, at its roots, largely artificial. Or manufactured.'

'Well, of course. A climate of fear that would force the Italian government to proclaim a state of emergency. A *soft* coup, enabling the authorities to end the wave of strikes by means of a draconian clampdown that would permanently marginalise the Left.'

'How far up the chain of command did this go?'

'Pretty much all the way. One person who was extremely concerned about the Communists' gains was Kissinger.'

'And by then he was –'

'National Security Advisor to Nixon. He ordered we step up the intensity.'

'Of what?'

'Terror attacks. Coups attempts.'

'Such as,' said Kentish coyly, his eyes on his papers, 'the bomb in the Banca Nazionale dell'Agricoltura?'

Bravo hung his head. 'In retrospect,' he said, 'I think that was the beginning of the end for me.'

'The twelfth of December 1969.' Kentish read from his notebook. 'In the Piazza Fontana in Milan. A bomb in the lobby explodes killing sixteen people and injuring eighty. Another report gave the numbers as seventeen and eighty-eight but let's not quibble. They are farmers, mostly, in town to deposit their earnings. Three more bombs explode in Rome that day, injuring fourteen. The blame is pinned instantly on the Left, on the agitators, on the radicals provoking unrest in Italy's industries.' He looked up. 'Of course, a bank in Italy's financial centre would be an ideal target for Marxist militants. But, really, it was Gladio?'

'Yes.' Bravo felt there was not much for him to say after that but, as Kentish said nothing, he added, 'One of our agents attached to the NATO command in Verona planned the attacks and led the attack with Gladio troops on the bank in Milan. We had fallen so far that we had come to consider the murder of non-combatants to be a legitimate political act.'

Kentish put his notebook and papers down on the table slowly. He said quietly, 'Why did you say it was the beginning of the end for you?'

Bravo heard a noise behind him and looked around. It was the younger Kentish boy, at the foot of the steps, looking up at him.

'Francesca said,' said Dominic, 'that she thought you might like some lunch. She was going to bring it to you but then Mum thought that perhaps I should, because Francesca is very busy helping in the bar.'

'Sure. Thank you,' said Bravo and stepped back, opening the gate as he did so.

Dominic climbed the worn stone steps and deposited a wicker basket covered with a tea towel on the wrought iron table.

'Thank you very much,' said Mr Kentish, 'and please thank Francesca very much too.' He considered his son affectionately. 'Not too hot for you?'

Dominic shook his head. 'We had lunch in the shade and Mum said Seb and I can go for a swim once we've digested.'

Dominic stood still, not a little self-importantly and expectantly, as though waiting for a tip for having run the errand.

Bravo opened the gate wide. 'Yes, thank you,' he said. 'And Francesca.'

'I'll see you later,' said Kentish gently to his son.

Bravo watched Dominic take the big steps down. 'By the way,' he called after him, 'how is Rosetta?'

Dominic turned and raised his shoulders as though to say he didn't know.

'Has her father been, do you know?'

'I don't know,' said Dominic.

The *click* of the gate shutting was accompanied by the *glock* of the cassette player's play and record buttons popping up. Kentish made no move to change the cassette but lifted the tea towel from the basket and withdrew a bottle of water, two bottles of beer, a bottle opener, two napkins and two plates on which were bread, sliced salamis, hams, cheese and fig jam.

'Just looking at this makes me hungry!' exclaimed Kentish.

'Me too,' said Bravo and felt suddenly so hungry that he regained his seat quickly for fear of fainting.

Bravo knew that Kentish hadn't forgotten his question. He wondered if the fact that he was no longer being recorded would change his answer and, he had to admit to himself, he didn't know. He had always had the tendency to choose his words carefully – at least, he thought he'd always had it – he had this predilection for pedantry that formed, in part, how he thought of himself. He had said 'non-combatants' and not *innocent* people – how he hated that phrase! How could one know if a person, now dead, had been innocent or not? And innocent of what? And he had said 'murder' and not *killing* because that was what it was. He too was, he'd come to recognise, guilty of murder, as implicated in all of the Agency's activities as those who had detonated bombs, pulled triggers, cut throats and cudgelled heads. 'I will answer your question,' he said.

They drank the beer straight from the bottle. The Englishman made sandwiches out of the assortment of foods on his plate. The American picked at his and tore his bread, like an Italian, and ate with his fingers.

The war had interrupted his philosophy major, Bravo said, but the University of Pennsylvania had allowed him to complete it by correspondence and with only a few short periods of attendance for exams. He'd returned for his graduation to please his parents who had hoped he'd study further to become a university professor, a profession they considered more exalted than theirs of school teacher. As Kentish knew, he'd declined the opportunity to return to a full civilian life but had spent the next dozen years in Italy and in the Far East, playing a role in the formalising of the C.I.A.'s businesses there – the money-laundering in Rome, the Gladio training in Sardinia and the heroin supply routes from out of the Far East. Ironically, his name within the Agency was *the Professor*: he was the man of ideas, not of action, the man who decided that something should be so and then had the satisfaction of seeing that it was through the agency of others. He had never taken a life directly but, looking back, he concluded that it was the war – the bodies, the pain, the filth, the poverty that followed it – that had numbed him. It had numbed everybody without their realising it, it had removed their capacity to think as well as to feel. Anything could be justified by the unconditional need to avoid ever revisiting such inhumanity. In the war, any military action would be justified by a measure of lives saved versus lives lost. Life was a numbers game. On the battlefield, do you risk ten lives in a frontal assault to save fifty? Of course you do. It's a no-brainer. The war had made everybody an adherent of the lesser evil theory, the belief that any evil so long as there is a greater can be justified. The war had made utilitarians out of everybody.

When he'd joined the C.I.A., he'd been filled with a sense of purpose, of mission, not merely at the national, patriotic level. He'd believed the Agency would be a force for good across a new, free world. When twenty years later the C.I.A. had proposed to commit acts of terrorism against American military and civilian targets and blame Cuba in order to justify a war, that's when it occurred to him that something was broken. He had ignored the sentiment for a while. And then he just learned to live with it. It was not unlike living with the tinnitus he'd developed after an explosions demonstration in the Gladio training camp in Sardinia that had been found to contain more explosives than it should have done. That, though, for him, had been the end of the beginning. And the beginning of the end, as he'd said, was the bomb in the Banca Nazionale dell'Agricoltura. The murder of nearly twenty farmers. For what? The sacrifice of the individual in the fight for the freedom of the individual – it no longer made sense. The ideological spectrum, he'd come to realise, ran not in a straight line but in a circle, both sides having come to regard terror as an instrument of cleansing and of renewal.

Kentish pushed his empty plate away from him and wiped his mouth with his napkin. Bravo did the same. They finished the beers that had already become warm.

The day after that bomb, Bravo continued, he'd had an idea. The Agency and Italian intelligence had grown worried about the perceived radicalisation and politicisation of Italian universities. These were increasingly considered hotbeds of hotheads, reds, communists, socialists, Marxists, Leninists, Trotskyites – whichever, they needed watching. He proposed he enrol in a university as a mature student studying for a doctorate. He was a philosophy major and had lived in mufti, as it were, for so long that he'd have no concerns for his cover. The Agency had liked the idea. It would be a reward for his twenty-seven years of service, a formal informal last posting prior to retirement.

But which university? Trento, that had started life with Italy's first faculty of sociology, and Milan, that had recently established a new school of social and political sciences, were subject to a high degree of leftist agitation, but he chose Bologna, that had been held continuously since the war by the Communist Party. It was a shame, because he preferred the wines of the Piedmont and the North East to those of Tuscany and further South. His thesis was on Marx's conception of freedom as man's ability to exercise control over his natural environment and over his own social forces. It took him five years to complete his doctorate, all the while identifying and reporting those young men and women who, he assessed, posted a threat to society at large, passionate politicos who may have been contemplating some sort of violent action, who may have wanted to walk the talk rather than just talk it. Occasionally, he wouldn't see those students again, their seats in the lecture halls vacant and their friends assuming they'd dropped out and returned home. He had attended lectures increasingly rarely, discomfited by the spurious moral justification for communism his fellow students proposed which too closely resembled his country's rationale for state-sponsored violence. He read other philosophers, besides Marx, and revisited old philosophers and discovered new ones. One in particular accounted for why he now found himself talking to Kentish.

Bravo stopped talking and regarded Kentish closely. Kentish was listening with his eyes closed. He'd fallen asleep still clutching his napkin in one hand.

Bravo wasn't offended. He sympathised. He was perspiring slightly, even in the shade doing nothing more energetic than talking. They'd had a full lunch and a beer not followed by a coffee. He understood completely. He was suddenly very desirous of an afternoon nap himself. He didn't want to sleep there, though, at the office's garden table with Kentish and he didn't want to wake him, either. And he fancied a little *digestivo*. Looking behind him, out over the little valley, he saw and heard no-one – the whole world would be asleep now. He locked the office door and replaced the plates and bottles in the picnic basket with the tea towel and his napkin; he wouldn't risk trying to ease Kentish's napkin from his grasp for fear of waking him. Quietly, he opened and closed the gate and walked back to the village under a sun that seemed to be getting bigger and hotter by the day. Francesca's *ufficio* was locked, so he kept the office key in his pocket. The bar was closed, so he placed the basket on the bench next to it. He walked home past the swimming pool that had no-one swimming in it but around which, on sunbeds that had been pulled into the shade cast by the olive trees, holidaymakers were sleeping or reading. On two of them, he recognised the Kentish boys, both reading. He looked around for their mother but couldn't see her. He thought of their father, asleep in the office garden on his own, and regretted that he wouldn't be there to see him wake up.

FOURTEEN

Sebastian slipped into the swimming pool's cool water and allowed himself to sink slowly to the bottom. The quality of the silence in the water was different to that out of it, where even children slept on their sunbeds in the shade and the cicadas had stopped their percussive chirrup, such was the heat. Underwater, the throb of the swimming pool's water filter motor was translated into a steady hum. He sat cross-legged, palming water upwards so as not to float to the top. He expelled air through pursed lips, producing bubbles that, when he leant forward, split either side of his nostrils and streamed up past his ears. He'd felt guilty when Dominic had risen to the challenge of trying to breathe underwater by inhaling his own expelled breath through his nose and had only succeeded in inhaling the chlorinated water and getting brain freeze, or so he'd called it. Sebastian tilted his head back, his mouth shaped as though to impart a kiss, and he watched a stream of bubbles percolating upwards, each bubble containing a word, a name, and each string of bubbles containing a sentence, a three-letter sentence repeated like a mantra. If one blew kisses underwater, on whom would they land? He flexed his knees and rose slowly to the water's surface.

Sebastian clung to the side of the pool. He considered Dominic, asleep on a sunbed with his mouth open. They had had to promise their mother that of course they wouldn't swim within three hours of having lunch, when so much of one's blood was diverted from the brain and from muscle tissue to the stomach for the digestive process. One risked fainting or cramp or both and, ultimately, drowning. Their father had questioned that theory, in a dispute long won by their mother and her family who recounted the story of a maid – or was it a manservant? – to a French military family in Indochina – or was it Algeria? – who'd had the nerve to go swimming in the family's pool after lunch and had died. The anecdote trumped the science every time. Generally, the Mediterraneans and the Anglo-Saxons differed on the question of whether it was safe to swim after a meal, he'd come to realise. He flicked water onto Dominic, whose *Tintin en Amérique* had fallen by his side. 'Oi, sleepy head,' he hissed. He didn't want to disturb the Dutch family occupying sunbeds near theirs.

'I wasn't asleep,' mumbled Dominic.

'There's no shame in being asleep like all the other children,' said Sebastian, knowing that that was an unfair dig, given that all the adults seemed asleep too.

'I wasn't.'

'Swim-chess?' Sebastian knew his brother would say yes. He knew that his kid brother was, actually, a good sport, a young friend who would always go along with his proposals, and he loved him for it.

Swim-chess was a game their father had invented. One holiday, on a day on which Sebastian had wanted to swim rather than play chess and his father had favoured chess over swimming, Mr Kentish had taken the chess set to the swimming pool and laid the pieces out on the board on a table at one end of the pool between two sunbeds. The rules were straightforward. Whoever is Black swims one length of the pool and back while White makes their move; as soon as Black is out of the water, White must dive in and swim the two lengths while Black plays. A player who hasn't made their move by the time their opponent leaves the water forfeits the game. Sebastian enjoyed swimchess because he found both swimming lengths and playing chess uninterruptedly rather tedious, and their combination just the opposite: neither activity had the time to become boring. The game provided stimulation for both mind and body. The stronger swimmer, in principle, had the advantage because their opponent would have relatively less time to consider their move.

Sebastian and Dominic were about twenty moves and forty lengths into the game when Sebastian realised that Dominic was likely to beat him for the first time. He hadn't been concentrating on the game. And so he felt sorry for Dominic when the young German boys Dominic had met on their second day of the holiday asked him to join them to make up even numbers for their two water polo teams. Dominic was torn, Sebastian could see, and so Sebastian said that of course it was quite up to him and, yes, perhaps he should join the new friends he'd made and, no, he didn't mind if they abandoned the game.

Sebastian knocked his king over. 'You can have the victory, Dom.' He felt magnanimous.

Sebastian dried himself and put his T-shirt and flip-flops on. He hung his towel around his neck and put the chess pieces away. It had come to that time of late afternoon and early evening when one could sit at one end of the pool and watch the swifts dive-bombing the pool in search of insects. There was something elegant and thrilling in the way in which they'd wheel about above them all and then break off and swoop down and skim the water's surface.

'I'll see you back at the apartment,' said Sebastian to his brother, tucking the chess set and his book under one arm.

Sebastian waved to the holidaymakers he'd come to know by sight as he wove his way between the sunbeds and olive trees. He thought he'd take the circuitous way back and, strangely enough, it took him past the stairs that led to Rosetta's and Francesca's studio apartment. He stood at their foot and looked up. The criss-cross of the stone staircases that turned back on themselves, now in sunlight, now in shadow, presented a kaleidoscope of muted tones of beige and grey. Rosetta had been taken ill and might be in need of another glass of water or, simply, company. And Francesca *had* invited him to visit at any time. It would be rude *not* to call in on them, he reasoned, and so he did.

Turn after turn, into the sun and to the top of the world – well, of the village. Turning a corner for the last flight of stairs to the terrace he saw the end of a sunbed, then a pair of legs by a chair, then the soles of two feet on the sunbed and, finally, as he stepped up and onto the terrace, Rosetta reclining in a chair, her face to the sun, her eyes closed, and Francesca asleep in a bikini on the sunbed, her eyes obscured behind sunglasses. Clearly, they hadn't heard him. He had, should he want it, the opportunity of turning around and descending the way he had come without their ever knowing he'd visited. Instead, he said, 'Hello.'

Rosetta opened her eyes and smiled weakly. 'Hello,' she said.

'*Ciao!*' Francesca raised a hand and let it drop. She made no effort to get up. With Rosetta present, perhaps she felt no obligation to play the host. Or perhaps she'd divined that Sebastian had really come to visit Rosetta. She seemed to fall straight asleep again.

'I just came to see how you were,' said Sebastian.

Rosetta took his hand and squeezed it. 'I'm alright, thanks to you,' she said and she motioned him to the garden chair next to hers.

She wore a purple bra for a bikini top and cut-off jeans in a hot-pants style. Her hair was unbrushed and fell in cascades down both shoulders, and her face and fingernails were completely free of make-up and nail polish. The sun, now getting low in the sky, painted her top lip with a faint down and her tummy and thighs with fine, black hairs. There was something savage and artless about her that Sebastian found intoxicating. Her head, if she were to lean back, would get lost in the wild green fronds of the plants and tall grasses that grew in terracotta pots behind and around her. She hadn't let go of his hand.

'You're not going to throw me again, are you?' he asked. 'I'm just checking.'

Rosetta laughed and for the second time Sebastian got lost down the back of that pink and fleshy deep throat. 'Not today. Not unless you provoke me again.'

'So, how are you feeling? You seem better.'

'Well, thanks God I'm not seeming worse. To begin with I was feeling terrible. It's like the smell goes to the back of the head, to the back of the eyes, into the brain, and the eyes and the brain hurt and you can't breathe – it's terrible. But now I'm okay. Better.' She stretched her freckled, sun-tanned legs and placed them on the sunbed. Slipping down in her chair a little, she managed to wiggle her toes against her friends' legs. 'Nurse Francesca has been looking after me very well.'

Nurse Francesca gave the faintest of smiles.

'She's tired, poor thing. She has had to do my work as well as hers. And she has to do my dinner service too.' Rosetta took an empty water glass in one hand and made as if to get up.

Sebastian stopped her. 'What do you need? More water? I'll get it for you.' He walked to the sink in the kitchen unit at the back of the studio and ran the tap for a moment before filling Rosetta's glass and, being thirsty himself, drinking from it. He refilled it and handed it to her and said, 'Perhaps I could water the flowers?' He filled a pink plastic watering can and did so, imagining he was restoring colour to the real world in the way in which an artist applies it to a canvas. He resumed his seat and extended his hand for hers.

There was something delicious in the moment he was experiencing. He'd been out with a group of friends not long ago when a girl, complaining about some of the boys' immature behaviour, had asked him when a boy becomes a man. Sebastian, after a little reflection, had answered that it was when he no longer cares whether he's called a boy or a man. The answer had gone down very well and had been repeated admiringly by the girl to the other girls in the group so that he'd felt rather smug and then bothered by feeling smug because, he'd thought, a man, as opposed to a boy, wouldn't have felt so self-congratulatory. But at that actual moment, there on the terrace among the rooftops in a remote Ligurian village, in the company of two beautiful older women who were accepting of him and behaved naturally in front of him, he had a feeling of having arrived, of having turned a corner, of being no longer a boy, of having come of age.

Until his mother arrived and destroyed that sentiment completely.

Sebastian couldn't believe his eyes. They had been drawn to movement, to where the stairs came up to meet the terrace and his heart had beaten just that little bit faster. Was it a rat? Was it a cat? No, it was his mother's head. And she was making eyes at him, eyebrows raised beneath that blond busby of hair. And now she was mouthing something to him and one hand, like a pink paw, was beckoning him.

Sebastian's 'Mum!' was a strangled croak.

He estimated that she could see him, Rosetta's legs and the soles of Francesca's feet. He neither wanted nor knew how to let go of Rosetta's hand. He made eyes at his mother in return. 'Go away!' he mouthed. He lifted his free hand but didn't quite dare shoo her away.

Mrs Kentish renewed the intensity of her supplication and, Sebastian could tell, was moving up the anger gears.

Sebastian was startled by Francesca's loud exclamation of, 'Is that the time!' and her sitting up suddenly, one hand holding her watch and the other on her bikini top, the strap of which, he could now see, was unfastened at the back. 'Why, Mrs Kentish!' said Francesca to Sebastian's mother's head, 'You've come to visit!' and she stood, wearing just her bikini and a welcoming smile.

Mrs Kentish had no choice other than to finish climbing the stairs to the terrace.

Sebastian wondered which he'd find more humiliating, his mother's coming to fetch her naughty boy home and away from the dangers of nubile women or her making a lame excuse for being there, such as having got lost. On occasion, however, his mother surprised him. By the time she stepped onto the terrace she was completely composed. She walked to the terrace's edge and looked out over the parapet.

'What a lovely place you have here! What views!' She turned to face them. 'And here, it's so homely. It's a garden! Angel's Trumpet, Jasmine and Dianthus.' She pointed at plants in turn. She rubbed a leaf between her fingers and smelled it. She was coiffed and dressed for dinner – or any other eventuality; like that, Sebastian knew, she could take on the world. She looked solicitously at Rosetta. 'And how are *you?*' she asked as sincerely as she could manage. 'You gave us all such a scare this morning.'

'I'm better enough to be out of bed, thank you,' said Rosetta who had taken her feet off the sunbed and let go of Sebastian's hand.

'Oh good,' said Mrs Kentish and then, to Sebastian, 'Shall we, darling? Daddy and Dom are waiting for us in the square. Drinks before dinner and all that. Dom's disappointed because the football is tomorrow and not today. And I think you'll want to get changed.'

Of course, the charm had been an act. Mrs Kentish harangued her son all the way to their apartment. If she'd pulled Sebastian there by the ears, his ears couldn't have been any redder. The man he'd felt himself to be all too briefly was now reduced to the boy he had been and would remain a little longer. If his mother's admonishments were to be summed up in one sentence, it was that he was too young to be consorting unsupervised with members of the opposite sex and of a lower class. Actually, the first, Sebastian recognised, was unfair: his mother had always despised the all-male boarding school his father had chosen for him and would go to some lengths, when he was home from school for the holidays, to ensure that she invited friends of hers with daughters his age to visit. So what remained was a class thing. It wouldn't do to have one of *them* fall pregnant. *They* were scheming and calculating. Sebastian was young and gullible. He'd fall in lust at the drop of one item of clothing and confuse it with love. While he found the lecture, that didn't stop while he showered and dressed, mortifying, he was to find the dinner that followed equally so.

Jacqueline Kentish and Sebastian followed the uneven, roughly hewn foot tunnel and then the rocky path bordered by a rock face and stone cottages. A couple of steps, a left turn and they were into the busy square that fell silent when they'd been noticed. Sebastian's first impression was that there were more people than usual in it. He had little time for a second before there arose a cheer. Those people without a glass in their hands clapped.

'Bravo!'

'L'eroe!'

Sebastian blushed to receive pats on the back.

Dominic stood by him as though to receive plaudits too or to provide him with moral support. 'I wish I'd been there,' he said to his older brother admiringly. 'I'd have helped you, you know I would have.'

Sebastian heard his father tell someone that he'd brought Rosetta a glass of water.

An Italian in a khaki uniform stepped forward and said something that Sebastian didn't understand. He shook Sebastian's hand before putting his arm around a similarly dressed woman and looking at him admiringly.

Clifford strode out of the bar and handed Sebastian a bottle of beer. 'The right man in the right place at the right time,' he said.

'Thanks,' said Sebastian, feeling rather fraudulent to be accepting the bottle, 'but it was nothing, nothing,' he mumbled.

'Shall we go to our table?' proposed Mrs Kentish.

Claudia left the kitchen to bring the Kentishes their *antipasti*. She placed them on the table and crossed her hands on her chest and thanked Sebastian in Italian that no-one at the table actually understood while understanding that Rosetta was like family to her and that Sebastian had done a wonderful thing. And then she was saying something else and laughing and looking at Sebastian and moving her hands to her heart while mentioning Rosetta so that Mr Kentish eagerly pulled his phrase book out of a pocket.

'Oh, Dad,' said Sebastian, rolling his eyes, 'please put that away.'

'Why?' enquired his father, appearing hurt.

'They make fun of you because of it,' said Sebastian urgently, embarrassed to be telling his father this.

'Oh, really,' said Mr Kentish, 'Claudia has been saying *amore* which means love, doesn't it?' He turned some pages of the phrase book.

Dario placed the bottle of wine he'd been holding on the table and took the book gently from Mr Kentish, as one might take something from a child. 'Please. With me here, you don't need.' He flicked through the loose pages with difficulty. 'What is this? *Ha della mutandine celesti per signora?*' he read out loud to all the diners within earshot.

The Italians roared with laughter.

'"Have you any ladies' vests and knickers in light blue?"' Dario asked Mr Kentish. '*Favorisca foderare le tasche con pelle scamosciata,*' he announced to the Italians. '"Please line the pockets with chamois leather,"' he instructed Dominic.

Sebastian's father took it all in good humour and held his hands in the air as though to say that, although the phrase book was his, he hadn't written it. His mother, Sebastian knew, was seething behind her smile. No doubt she'd accuse Dario to his back of being familiar.

'Now,' said Dario, shutting the book and returning it to Mr

Kentish with a little bow, 'we have here a bottle. Is Franciacorta, from Piedmont. Italian Champagne. How you say – on the 'ouse.' He undid the wire that held the cork in place, popped the cork and poured four glasses, handing Mrs Kentish hers first, and saying, 'For the hero,' when he handed Sebastian his. When it came to Dominic's he said, '*Permesso?*' to Mrs Kentish and only handed it to him when Mrs Kentish nodded her assent. 'To love!' he said and held an imaginary glass up as if giving a toast.

'Oh, yes' said Mr Kentish, 'I'm afraid we didn't quite catch what Claudia was telling us but we understood that it was something about love.'

'Ah, I will translate. She was saying congratulations to the young lovers, how love saves. Rosetta. She loves your son,' Dario laughed expansively. 'When they carry her to her room, she is unconscious, but she is repeating Sebastian's name.'

The Betters, on the way to their table, stopped. 'That's right,' said Clifford. 'She was quite out of it, the poor girl. All she could say was your name.'

'*È giusto,*' said Mr Cespuglio who was seated with his wife and the Italians in khaki at another table. 'Sebastian, Sebastian, Sebastian!' He placed his hands on his heart and wobbled his head in what Sebastian believed was intended to be either a caricature of a young woman in love or a poor imitation of the semi-conscious Rosetta.

'Who is that vulgar man?' hissed Mrs Kentish under her breath. 'And why is he dressed like his wife?'

'*È vero,*' announced the man in khaki, and imitated his friend.

Clifford laughed. 'That's Giorgio. And that's Emilio. They carried Rosetta to her apartment with me. Don't mind them, they're harmless. And she probably won't remember a thing.'

'Well, naturally she'd mention Sebastian,' said Mr Kentish.

'He was the last person she'd seen before losing consciousness. How is she, by the way?'

'I hear she's quite better. Anyway, enjoy your dinner. And well done again,' he said to Sebastian. '*Bravo.*' He joined Eva at their table.

'This is insufferable,' said Mrs Kentish, sitting straight and so tense that Sebastian feared she might shatter. She put her hand on her fork as though to start eating but just stared at her *antipasto*.

Mr Kentish placed one hand on his wife's and held his glass up with the other. 'Hold on a moment. To Sebastian. For preventing a young woman from falling where she may have injured herself.'

Sebastian said, 'Thanks, Dad.'

Mrs Kentish shook her head and said, 'You two.'

'What do you mean?' said both father and son.

'First, I find *you* asleep where the American left you and then I find *him* in the company of that girl again,' said Mrs Kentish, choosing to reply to her husband.

'I only went to see how she was,' said Sebastian, for whom the evening had already become too much. 'And anyway,' he hissed at his mother, leaning forward in his chair, 'you told me to keep an eye on Francesca. Didn't you?'

Mrs Kentish pursed her lips and narrowed her eyes to stare straight at Sebastian.

Mr Kentish hadn't quite heard. 'What was that?' He smiled sheepishly. 'Anyway, I'm guilty as charged. It was just so hot. And the big lunch. And the beer. I suppose he must have been undecided as to what to do. Which would have been the greater evil: disturb my sleep or leave me to wake on my own? Come to think of it, I'd fallen asleep while he'd been talking! I hope he wasn't offended.'

The family were silent and began eating. Night had fallen and the excited talk from the tables around them had moderated. Candle flames fluttered like butterflies in a light breeze. They ate slowly and deliberately, first stealing looks at each other in wonder and then staring at each other openly, their faces lit from below by flickering tea lights.

'What are we eating?' someone asked.

No-one knew. When Francesca came to take their plates, they repeated the question.

'*Sformata*. Maybe like a flan, maybe like a soufflé. This one is chickpea served in an anchovy sauce. I come back with the *primi*.'

'I never imagined that anything meeting that description could taste as good,' said Mr Kentish. 'You know, one thing the American said that I believe I can share with you was about the Italians and Catholicism. He said something like he didn't approve of the way in which confession allows the Catholics to sin again, to re-set the clock, to pass the water under the bridge – something like that. I see the point but, maybe, in Italy the food serves that function too. After all, when you can eat like this every evening, doesn't everything become more bearable and forgivable?'

Mrs Kentish just snorted.

FIFTEEN

Bravo woke to a sound like artillery fire. It was a thunderclap that, he knew for certain, would have woken every living thing in the valley. He sat upright in bed, his pyjama T-shirt stretched uncomfortably tight around his stomach. He listened to the rain rat-tat-tatting off the patio and the metal garden table. A sergeant-major might have shouted in his ear and he wouldn't have heard him. A lightning flash lit his room monochromatically, despite the closed shutters. He rubbed his chin. He hadn't seen this storm coming. The next peal of thunder rattled the empty bottles of wine and *grappa* that stood together in one corner of his kitchen.

For the brief moment between sleeping and waking he'd thought they'd come for him. Had he really been naïve enough to think they'd let him get away with exposing his country's and Italy's state secrets? He'd run his fingers across his chest and belly feeling, foolishly, for wounds – for bullet holes – and had tried and failed to recall whether bullets travelled slower than the speed of sound.

Bravo stood slowly and, stepping into a pair of slippers and over a bottle, he made his way to the kitchen. Standing by the sink, he couldn't see the mountain opposite for the rain. Rainwater puddled on the kitchen floor by the door. He wasn't concerned. The village had withstood 700 years of sun and rain.

Claudia handed him his second coffee of the day that he drank standing in the doorway to the bar, looking out. It wouldn't do to be staring at her the way he'd like to. The storm had subsided but it was still raining heavily, the raindrops bouncing to knee height off the cobbled *piazza*. The stone was grey, the mountain ahead was the colour of slate and the sky above a uniform sheet of lead. He fingered the guest office key in his pocket. Ah, there was Kentish, skidding on the wet stones as he turned the corner, his cassette recorder carrying case over one shoulder and his satchel carried in both hands above his head in a futile attempt to keep dry. He hadn't travelled a hundred yards from his apartment and yet the sleeves and the back of his light blue linen jacket were wet and no longer so light a blue. 'No umbrella?' Of course, no-one took an umbrella on a summer holiday.

'Well, yes, but it's in the car,' said Kentish, shaking and brushing what water he could off himself and his satchel.

'Just a thought,' said Bravo, after Claudia had passed Kentish his coffee, 'what say you we just sit downstairs today rather than swim to the guest office in this?' He pointed outside. And then he remembered. 'Oh and by the way, I'm so sorry, I just left you asleep yesterday. You seemed to be in too deep a sleep for me to wake you.' He had no excuse. He was embarrassed to think that he'd thought that what he'd done had been amusing.

Kentish appeared embarrassed too. 'Oh, not at all. I quite

understand. And I am so sorry to have fallen asleep while you were talking.'

Touché, thought Bravo.

'Which reminds me,' said Kentish and handed Claudia the napkin Bravo had left him clutching. 'Thank you,' he said to her with a smile. 'Downstairs is fine by me,' he said to Bravo. 'Dario has been allowing me to type there and no-one else has ever come down.'

They tripped down a winding staircase decorated with wine bottles and sepia photographs of peasants at work and made themselves comfortable at one of the tables at the end of the long, vaulted room. Kentish hung his jacket over the back of a chair and Bravo propped his umbrella up in a corner. The room gave the impression of being underground because it was, partially, extending from below the bar to a Dutch door, the top half of which was open onto the path that ran around and down from the square, rainwater gushing and gurgling along its gutters. The room served as a restaurant in the winter and on rainy days but Bravo doubted they'd be inconvenienced – the locals would almost certainly go to the coast where they knew it would be brighter, while the holidaymakers would probably stay in and play Ludo. What plans did Kentish's family have?

'Jackie's never at a loss,' said Kentish. 'She saves postcard- and letter-writing for rainy days. And the boys, well, they, at a guess, will read, get bored, play chess and then come and look for me.' He had his cassette recorder and his notes ready. 'Shall we get started?'

Bravo nodded his assent. He considered the pictures on the wall, framed maps and architectural drawings of the village that showed the interconnectedness of the individual dwelling spaces and the conformity of the whole to the Fibonacci sequence. The

legend below a sepia map explained that the surrounding mountains were of limestone, a sedimentary stone made from detritus
that had sunk to the bottom of seas and rivers and was full of
fossilised shells, and that these layers of sediment had been
compressed to form the rock that Colletta sat on. A drawing of a
Nautilus shell had been imposed on a black and white aerial photo-
graph of the medieval village, making explicit the connection
between the natural marine forms found fossilised in the local rock
and in the village, an explicit link between the past and the present.

'The Piazza Fontana bomb in '69. And you went on to
study for a doctorate in Bologna, where you could better
monitor left-wing student activism.' Kentish gave the faintest of
smiles, as though to say, *See! I remember that much.* 'What can
you tell me about the Peteano bomb in '72?'

'It was felt that we had to act quickly. After the election.
You recall, the Pike Committee was particularly interested in
our financing of the Christian Democrats that year. On the
direct orders of Nixon, our U.S. ambassador in Italy oversaw our
spending of ten million dollars before that election alone.'

'On what?'

'The usual. Covert operations, bribes and general support
for the Christian Democrats. Again, it was felt we didn't really
get value for money. Support for the Left and Right remained
broadly unchanged. So –'

'So two weeks later, an anonymous telephone call summons
policemen to an abandoned Fiat 500 in a forest near Peteano.'
Kentish read from his notes. 'The car is booby-trapped. They
trigger a bomb that explodes, killing three of them and injuring
one of them. Two days later another anonymous phone call
implicates the Red Brigades, a relatively new, supposedly militant branch of the extreme Left, which gives the police a pretext

to round up 200 or so communists.' Kentish looked up. 'The Red Brigades or Gladio?'

'Gladio. Of course.'

'How would someone who wasn't in on this, on this whole Gladio business, have been able to tell? Would there have been any clues?'

'Not really. Maybe the explosives. Earlier, in February, the *carabinieri* had stumbled upon two of our underground arms dumps near Trieste containing weapons and Composition C-4. That's the most powerful plastic explosive and it's used almost exclusively by us, I mean by U.S. forces and NATO. We call it *plastique*. The Brigades, however, they rely on explosives made of gelignite. The *carabinieri* thought they'd discovered a cache of arms that belonged to a criminal network. Actually, the finds were an inconvenience and the C-4 ended up coming from a NATO-supplied Gladio munitions dump hidden in the main city cemetery at Verona. So, maybe a forensic analysis of the explosive would have provided a clue but not a conclusive one.'

'What about the people who planted the bomb?'

'Just members of the state's security apparatus doing their job.'

'And what about the Red Brigades? Did you manage to infiltrate them?'

'Not me in Bologna. Although we did infiltrate them in Trieste and Milan. In '73. We learnt that Bologna's Marxists were happy to talk but not to translate their talk into action. There was a split within the communists. Many splits, actually. Bologna had the idealogues but the universities in the north had the activists.'

Kentish turned a page. 'Brescia. May '74.'

Bravo drummed his fingers on the table.

'A bomb explodes in a garbage bin in Piazza della Logia

during a public demonstration against a group of neo-fascists. Eight people are killed and over a hundred wounded,' Kentish continued. 'Anonymous callers to the police and the press attempt to implicate *Lotta Continua* – another militant communist organisation. They are rounded up but released due to a lack of evidence – the square had been hosed down by the police within two hours of the bombing and all evidence destroyed.' Kentish looked up, the question written on his face.

'Gladio. Led by a Gladio member who'd been receiving regular paycheques from the U.S. embassy.' Bravo shrugged and laid his hands palms up on the table, as though to disclaim personal responsibility.

Kentish turned over another sheet of paper. 'August '74. The bomb on the Italicus Express, the Rome to Munich train, that killed twelve people and injured many more. Aldo Moro, who would become Prime Minister in just three months' time, had only just left the train.' Again he looked up.

Bravo was beginning to find the room claustrophobic. He stood by the half-open door and looked out on to the rough walls of the buildings opposite. It was still raining but not as hard.

'Ours was a monster of many heads. Or maybe it was just one head – a Gorgon – of many snakes.' He sighed. 'What I'm trying to say is that while we were all united by the desire to see communism fail, we weren't all always in agreement about the means. Gladio had splinter groups who were as extreme, on the Right, as the most extreme groups on the Left. The train bombing – that was *Ordine Nero*, neo-fascists, racists and anti-communists who wished to destroy liberalism and create a non-democratic fascist state out of Italy. They maintained that the first phase of political activity ought to be the creation of conditions favouring the installation of chaos that would destroy the structure of the democratic state under the cover of communist activities. They were our bed-fellows for no other reason than that our enemy was their enemy too.'

'What I have heard from you,' said Kentish, 'is that while you may have been in agreement about the *ends* you seem to have not been in agreement about the *means*. By which I refer to the indiscriminate murder of civilians.'

Bravo rested his forearms on the lower half of the door and looked out over it, down into the gutter along which rainwater raced. He leant further, and looked up into a sky the colour of granite and felt the rain on his face. 'You're absolutely right,' he said, turning around. 'Which is why, I suppose, I'm talking to you.' He ran his forearm across his face.

Francesca came down the stairs carrying a tray with two coffees, *cantuccini* and water. 'From Claudia,' she said 'She thought these might be welcome.'

Bravo suppressed a smile as he noted Kentish's stammered thanks and his clumsy making of space on the table for the tray. He watched Kentish stare at Francesca as she climbed the stairs back to the bar. Then Kentish turned the cassette over.

A newspaper cutting had fallen to the floor and he picked it up. '*Juin* 1973,' he read.

'That's from *Le Monde*,' said Kentish. 'It alleges that a collaboration between the Mafia and the Federal Bureau of Narcotics led to raids by Interpol on Corsican drugs laboratories on the French Riviera. These brought to an end the Corsican influence in worldwide narcotics trafficking. It effectively handed the Mafia and the C.I.A. a monopoly.'

Bravo placed the cutting in Kentish's outstretched hand. 'The manner in which the prosaic can impact on the national or international has frequently intrigued me,' he said. 'Let me explain. Sicily was crucial to the heroin production and smuggling businesses that we ran that, for us, was a means of financing our fight against communism in Europe and a conduit for intelligence gathering in the Far East, as the drug trade permitted us to buy arms that we would sell to insurrectionary movements there. Anyway, by then, the Mafia had established hundreds of laboratories in Sicily, which meant the island was now pivotal to the narcotics industry as well as already of strategic importance for us as the location of U.S. military bases. As you know, we never really succeeded in dissuading Italy from its flirtation with communism; its support for the Communist Party in general elections has remained quite steady. What greater punishment – what greater catastrophe – could we – the Mafia, Gladio and the Vatican – inflict on the country than the separation of Sicily, than the breakaway of one of its most important provinces? A plan was hatched for the invasion of Sicily by Gladio and the installation of a right-wing government.'

Kentish blanched.

'It was approved by The White House. Aldo Moro got wind of this and didn't like it. He had become Prime Minister by then. He was summoned to meet Kissinger.'

'Hold on a second. Are you really telling me that just three or four years ago plans for a civil war and secession in Italy had been drawn up with the connivance of the Nixon administration?'

'Don't think we were alone in this.' Bravo found himself to be speaking more defensively than he'd intended to. 'I suppose I should have told you that M.I.6 was in on Gladio from the very beginning. In fact, M.I.6 – and the S.A.S. – provided invaluable help. But to get back to Sicily, a combined briefing from your Foreign Office and your Ministry of Defence that was shared with us showed your Cabinet to be in favour of deposing the

Italian government if the Communists came to power in the '76 election.'

Kentish made as though to protest.

'I'm telling you. Your government was ready to support a coup d'état and any other subversive action – even the restoration of a monarchy in Sicily.'

'But we've had a Labour government all this time,' Kentish said weakly.

Bravo made a gesture intended to convey that that was irrelevant. 'Anyway, the election was a disaster. Not enough to give the Communist Party a majority but, still, it gained almost fifty seats. We paid six million dollars to political leaders and it just ended up in villas, in vacation homes and in Swiss bank accounts. And then there was the "democratic alliance" between the Christian Democrats and the Communist Party that Aldo Moro had embraced in '73.'

'That had been inspired by Allende's government in Chile.'

'Exactly.'

'And look what happened to him.'

'Exactly.' And the same had happened to Moro, the American could see the Englishman thinking. 'Faced with the rise of the Communists, Moro thought like other centrist politicians about how to avoid the possibility of Italy becoming a Soviet-aligned state. He was a conciliator who thought to involve the Communists in government so as to be able to moderate their aims. Kissinger did not like that. He summoned Moro to Washington and made it clear that under no circumstances were the Left to be included in government. In fact, he threatened Moro, telling him that if he brought the Right and the Left into direct collaboration he would pay the price. Kissinger made Moro ill with worry.'

'So here we are,' said Kentish. 'We've arrived at Moro.'

Voices could be heard upstairs, in the bar. Sebastian and Dominic traipsed down, the younger boy carrying the chess set in a plastic carrier bag. They stood in their dripping anoraks by their father. Bravo, on every occasion he saw them, was taken by how much the dark-haired, short younger boy looked like his father and by how much the blond, tall elder looked nothing like him at all. Their mother, the younger was saying, had thought that they could come and play chess here, as it was, anyway, almost lunch time.

'We could sit over there, right at the far end,' said Dominic.

'If that's alright,' added Sebastian, standing behind his brother.

The men watched them setting up the chess board.

'You play, I presume,' said Bravo.

'Yes,' Kentish replied. 'And you?'

'I have played. In my early days in naval intelligence, chess was encouraged. The game was used to illustrate the distinction between strategy and tactics.'

'And now?'

'I have no idea what or how they teach now. But I came to think that chess was not a good guide to, well, intelligence gathering and warfare. Chess is rules-based. Its world is a closed world of sixty-four squares. There's no cheating.'

'No cheating? Didn't Bobby Fischer allege that the Soviets had colluded to prevent him from winning?'

Bravo waved that away. 'Yes, and it's probably true, but that's politics. In the game itself, there's no cheating. I think it was Wittgenstein who said that if you move your knight three squares forward, instead of two, and one to the side, you're not cheating, you're simply no longer playing chess, you're playing a different game. But in the real world of Right versus Left, of the free world versus communism, there's only one game in which only the cheat wins.' He leant over the table and spoke quietly. 'This is what the Right has learned, what it was doing. When you're on the Right you don't attack the state or its representatives. You attack civilians – women, children, people from outside the political arena – for one simple reason: to force the public to turn to the state to ask for greater security. This is the role of the Right in Italy, to create a strategy of tension so that ordinary people will accept that at any moment a state of emergency can be declared, so that people will willingly trade their freedom for the security of being able to walk the street or take a train or enter a bank. This is the political logic behind all the bombings.'

Kentish said nothing.

Bravo looked from him to his children concentrated on their chess board. He consulted his watch. 'Moro tomorrow,' he said, and Kentish simply nodded. Bravo retrieved his umbrella from its corner and didn't go out via the bar but opened the Dutch door fully and stepped out into the rain. Despite the atrocious weather, he thought he might be becoming lighter of step, as though he were divesting himself of a burden that Kentish was now having to carry. He couldn't wait until the day after the rain, when every tree, bush and plant would appear resplendent.

SIXTEEN

Sebastian stood by the open door at the top of the steps, looking out from the apartment over the valley. The body of rain resembled a slowly moving steel box, its edge a perforated metal wall being dragged slowly across the valley by an invisible hand. Sebastian had never seen that phenomenon before: the very edge of rain. He'd of course been outdoors when it had started to rain and when it had stopped raining, always gradually. But never had he seen such a clearly defined boundary between rain and no rain. A man walking briskly and carrying one end of a ladder could remain completely dry while his partner, carrying the other end, would be wet right through.

Their spirits lifted with the clouds, the Kentishes walked to the bar in the early evening sunshine, delighted by the reflections of blue sky and pink clouds in the puddles that forced them to cross the square in skips and jumps if they wished to keep their feet dry. Beads of water on the tables and chairs on the terrace sparkled like fairy lights. The branches of trees and bushes glistened and bowed under the weight of fresh water.

The door to the bar was open, releasing light and noise into the crisp, clean air.

They plunged into the crowded bar, fighting their way amicably through the Italians whose eyes were expectantly on the television set. They went down a winding staircase and shouldered their way to the last unoccupied table in the restaurant where another, smaller television set balanced on a chair placed on a table now showed the Italian and Dutch teams running out onto the pitch in the Estadio Monumental in Buenos Aires.

With little space separating the dining tables, Francesca and Rosetta were having to squeeze and sashay between the chairs and tables as they carried plates and dishes above the heads and gesticulating arms of the diners. They placed carafes of water, white wine and red wine on each table and dishes of grilled vegetables, cold meats and chutneys.

'It's like this,' said Dominic. 'In Group A, Austria has lost two games and West Germany has drawn two games, so neither can go through.'

'And Italy and Holland have three points each, each having won one game and drawn another so they're playing for a place in the final,' said Clifford, standing by the Kentish's table. He called over to the Langemensen's table, 'Kees, so what's your prediction?'

'Two nil to Holland.' Kees rocked back in his chair. If he'd been wearing braces he'd have tucked his thumbs under them.

Dario handed plates of food to Rosetta above their heads. 'Italy will win, easy,' he said deadpan, pretending to ignore Kees while saying it loudly enough for him to hear. Sebastian had cooled towards Dario; he thought the ribbing he'd received about Rosetta the previous night fair enough, he could take a joke, but he'd objected to Dario's having carried it on into lunch.

The clasping of the heart and the fluttering of eyelashes while calling and moaning Sebastian's name had palled. He had dared look neither at his mother nor at Rosetta when she'd been instructed to clean the Kentish's apartment while they'd been at lunch.

'And in Group B,' said Dominic, speaking deliberately, 'Peru has lost two games so can't go through. Poland has won one and lost one, but they can go through if they beat Brazil and Argentina loses to Peru –'

'Which is very unlikely,' said Mr Kentish.

Sebastian always cringed when his father tried to participate in football-related discussions. His mother and Mrs Better, he could see, were doing their best to look interested.

'Both Argentina and Brazil have won one and drawn one,' continued Dominic.

'But Brazil has the better goal difference,' added Clifford.

'So Brazil will likely go through to the final – if they beat Poland – unless Argentina beats Peru by at least a three goal margin, depending on how much Brazil beats Poland by,' concluded Dominic.

'Which must also be very unlikely,' said Mr Kentish, looking around for corroboration but not getting any.

'So, Italy and Brazil in the final,' said Dario, again loudly, receiving plates from Francesca above their heads.

'You're wrong about the final,' said Kees.

'What are you meaning?' said Dario, loaded with plates.

'I know what you mean,' said Clifford. 'It's a fix. That's what he's implying,' he said to Dario. 'Argentina should be playing its game against Peru at the same time as Brazil plays its game against Poland. But now that Argentina is playing later, should Brazil win, Argentina will have the advantage of knowing how many goals they need to win by.'

'Exactly,' said Kees. He tugged at his cap with both hands. 'And Quiroga, the Peru keeper, he's Argentinian.'

'No he's not!' exclaimed Clifford. 'Really?'

'Well, he was born in Argentina,' said Kees.

'Who cares, so long as Italy is in the final! *Vengo! Vengo!*' shouted Dario to Claudia in the kitchen in reply to her calling for him. 'Women! They always want me!'

Two Italian couples dressed similarly, like two pairs of twins – one in Italy's team colours and the other in khaki – and whom Sebastian had come to recognise, squeezed in behind the Kentishes and stood against the wall, dispensing *Mi dispiace*s and *Mi scusi*s as they knocked chairs and elbows despite trying to disturb no-one.

'Sebastian, Dominic...' Mrs Kentish didn't have to finish her sentence for the boys to understand that they were to give their seats up to the ladies, which they did to effusive *Grazie*s. Dominic, with his brother's help, climbed and sat on some wooden cases of wine, dinner plate in hand. Sebastian shook the proffered hand of the Italian in *azzuri* blue who, clearly, was thanking him and introducing himself as Giorgio, as he helped his wife take Sebastian's seat.

Sebastian stood, his back to the wall, drinking from a bottle of beer. Giorgio's cigarette smoke targeted one nostril and his wife's excessively applied perfume sought the other, making him feel light headed. The television set on a chair on a table resembled the peak of a modern art installation, an antennaed robot, its arms those of the wooden chair its head rested on. It squatted just below the dense ceiling of cigarette smoke that obscured the room's arches and gave the impression of a football stadium in the clouds on the point of hosting a football game on Mount Olympus for the benefit of the gods. Darkness had fallen and the Dutch door giving onto the alleyway, now open top and bottom, gave the illusion of a black curtain having been hung over the doorway. When the match kicked off, even the neutrals felt the tension and excitement and even Mrs Kentish angled her chair to better see the game.

Plates of *primi* were passed out of the kitchen and, when Sebastian's reached him, he looked down on a serving of pasta parcels in a creamy walnut sauce and lost himself in the depth and richness of this simplest of dishes.

Sebastian was pleased to be standing where he was, with no-one behind him and not in his mother's line of vision. He watched Rosetta at work and tried to catch her eye but she was too busy. She collected the dirty plates from their table and stood by his mother momentarily, arrested by the drama of yet another Italian attack on the Dutch goal, unwittingly highlighting the contrast between blond and dark, manicured and wild, old and young. She was called away by Dario, returned to wait on another table, took orders from yet another and was stopped to share a joke at a third. Sebastian was jealous to find her attention distracted and the resentment he felt at having to "share" a person was a novel sensation. Kees familiarly put his arm around her waist, slightly rucking her thigh-length dress up so that, had she leant over any more to take his order above the din, she'd have appeared indecent to everyone behind her. Sebastian wanted to thump him. She returned with beers for the Dutch. Gradually, everyone else in the room faded away and Sebastian watched Rosetta execute a secretly choreographed ballet in outer space just for him.

Sebastian was brought down to earth by shouts and exclamations – Italy had scored. Giorgio made as though to hug him then, thinking better of it, hugged his wife instead. Dario danced a jig in the little space available to him. The Italians punched the air in joy. The Langemensens groaned and threw their hands in the air in desperation and cried, '*Buitenspel!* Off-side!' without conviction. Sebastian paid attention to the replay, aware of all heads in the room craning forward.

'It was coming,' said Dominic sagely.

Half-time brought sea bass on a bed of fennel and lemon and roast potatoes and rosemary. The food here, for Sebastian, was more of a highlight than any football match and yet he was surprised, during the second half, to find himself increasingly engrossed in the game, in which the Dutch team seemed to grow in stature, asserted themselves physically and equalised within five minutes.

'What a shot!'

It was the turn of the Dutch to stand with arms aloft and of the Italians to hang their heads in their hands. And twenty-six minutes after that goal, and one minute after Dominic had made his mother promise to ask Claudia for the recipe for her choco-late and *amaretti* cake, the Dutch scored again, with a most audacious long-range shot.

Kees blew his cheeks out and shook a hand in admiration. 'Forty metres! At least!'

'Goal of the tournament,' said the men wisely.

'No question of off-side,' said Mr Kentish.

'Look who's turned up,' said Sebastian to Dominic.

Leaning against the door jamb, lit only by the light from the restaurant, was the Argentinian and, behind him, in the partial obscurity, stood the driver, the television's flickering light playing faintly on his brilliantined hair. The driver's eyes were focused on the television. The Argentinian's were narrowed and restless. He was looking for someone.

'What do you think they're doing here?' asked Sebastian.

'He's Argentinian,' replied Dominic.

'I know that. So?'

'It's Argentina playing next.'

'Right. I forgot. Anyway, I hope he's not going to bother Rosetta,' said Sebastian, feeling protective towards her and brave. Having never been in a fight, he wasn't afraid of getting into one.

Dominic nudged Sebastian. The Argentinian was clearly not that interested in the game that was going to conclude soon anyway, with Holland going through to the final and Italy condemned to the third place play-off. He'd partially turned his back to the restaurant in order to facilitate his pulling his Opinel knife from a back pocket. He transferred it to his breast pocket and then pulled a wooden box the size of a match box out of the same back pocket. He seemed to take great care in selecting a toothpick that he sucked before tucking it in the corner of his mouth and replacing the box. Sebastian looked at his brother and rolled his eyes.

There were to be 45 minutes in between matches and so the bar and restaurant emptied into the night square for fresh air and a change of scene. The square and the gardens were lit by a full moon, reflected in puddles and off still wet leaves and stones that sparkled. There were expressions of jubilation and of heartache, handshakes of commiseration and of congratulations. Above them, by the church and on to the car park, swung the headlights of the returning cars of those who'd gone to Albenga to watch the game. The Italians found themselves to be as tired as if they'd played the game themselves and announced they'd turn in early. The Dutch, Kees announced, would be going back to their apartments to get drunk on shop-bought beer. It's the neutrals that are left, observed Sebastian, and the men more than the women. Dario informed everyone

BRUNO NOBLE

that they'd be closing the restaurant and that the match would be shown in the bar. Claudia, drying her hands on her apron, gave Mrs Kentish a hand-written recipe for the dessert. Rosetta and Francesca appeared with cloths and dried some chairs so that people could sit outdoors. Someone announced that Austria had beaten West Germany by three goals to two and only then did Sebastian realise that Godehard had not been present that evening. Dominic made it his business to learn that in the other match Brazil had beaten Poland by three goals to one and then announced that Argentina would need to win by a four-goal margin to go through to the final. Mrs Kentish told Dominic that it was time for bed and he, for once, didn't complain.

Sebastian's father surprised Sebastian by asking him if he'd stay behind for a nightcap and reappeared from the bar with a beer each. This was unlike him. Sebastian had never been to the pub with his father, as some of his friends had started to do with theirs. Some parents were very strict and tolerated no drinking before the age of eighteen, while others spoke of *educating* their children to drink responsibly and did so by introducing them to pubs early. Sebastian quite liked the French way of treating alcohol as nothing out of the ordinary, of not demonising it and drawing attention to it; his maternal grandparents had, for as long as he could remember, offered him and his brother a glass of wine with their meal that, more often than not, they had declined. When very young, they would have had it diluted, of course. Sebastian's father had been content to go along with the continental way of doing things and, consequently, Sebastian had become aware of missing the matey, man-to-man chats that some of his friends had been subjected to and was rather glad of it. His dad, he knew, was an intellectual – he wasn't a 'bloke's bloke' – and he felt a little remorse for having begrudged his father his attempts at participation in the football-related conversations.

'Thanks, Dad.'

Mr Kentish clinked his bottle against his son's. 'Cheers, Seb.'

They took long swigs from their bottles.

'To my surprise,' said Mr Kentish, 'I'm quite enjoying this World Cup – even though I think I shouldn't be. Actually, it's the football I've enjoyed. It has seemed rather good. Isn't it strange how football is adversarial and yet it brings people together?'

'Yes,' said Sebastian, 'I know what you mean. It's like chess, in a way. But why do you think you shouldn't be enjoying it?'

'Because it's being played in Argentina. It leaves a sour taste in my mouth. You know, we touched upon it the other day. Of course, you know all about it, don't you?'

'What? About "the disappeared" and all that?'

'Yes. But how much do you know?'

Sebastian thought for a moment. 'Well, there was a military coup two years ago. And, ever since, Argentina has been governed by General Videla. Who doesn't like communists and throws them out of airplanes. Actually, Dad, is that true?'

'That's absolutely true. The lucky ones are drugged before they are thrown out. At thousands of feet over the Atlantic. Governed by a complete bastard who said, *As many people as necessary must die in Argentina so that the country will again be secure.* That's clever, isn't it? Create insecurity by killing people and kill more people to make the people you haven't killed feel secure.'

Sebastian wondered how much his father had had to drink with his dinner. 'Mum said that this World Cup is being used as a political tool by the Argentinians. As a means for the military of making Argentinians forget for three weeks that they are living in a dictatorship. She said that if Argentina wins the cup it will extend the life of the dictatorship by a number of years.'

'Your mother is wise.' That was Bravo, coming up behind them.

Sebastian and his father jumped.

'I thought I'd watch the game.' Bravo indicated the bar.

'Don't let us stop you,' said Mr Kentish.

Sebastian had the impression that the men were embarrassed to see each other away from their formal meetings. And then he thought that, as he wasn't present at their private meetings, for all he knew they might be embarrassed to see each other on those occasions too. And then it occurred to him that such convoluted thinking was evidence either of his being drunk or of his being sober. And he concluded that if he couldn't tell it must be because he was drunk. But, then, wouldn't such lucid thinking point to his being sober? He wondered if he would be lucky enough to have a few moments alone with Rosetta that evening.

Sebastian and his father watched the American enter the bar. For a moment they saw him in perfect silhouette, a hulking shadow that blocked the light from the bar, leaving the square lit only by the blue light of the moon. They watched him take a seat at the bar behind the Argentinian and the driver who kept their eyes on the television on the shelf above the bar even as they turned their heads slightly to greet him. He ordered a draught beer from Dario who looked tired under the electric lights of the television and the flycatcher. He was quite stationary as he stood, momentarily, his eyes closed and one hand on the tap. Well, Italy had lost, Sebastian reflected, as he looked around the empty square. The defeat to the Dutch seemed to have drained the energy from the Italians; few had remained to watch the Peru Argentina game.

The television camera that had been panning the cheer-leaders and the crowd in the stadium in Rosario entered the tunnel the players would be appearing from. There was a ratch-eting of expectation. In the bar in Colletta those men standing shuffled forward a little and the three men sitting shifted in their seats. The noise, in that relatively confined space, became muffled but, as though in compensation, was magnified. Sebas-tian expected to see the two national teams lined up but the camera was attracted to a group of men in suits and overcoats. In their centre was a tall, slim moustachioed man in his fifties, with oiled, swept back hair and a military bearing.

'Is that, you know, the dictator?' asked Sebastian.

His father nodded. 'General Videla.'

The Argentinian in the bar in Colletta had sat forward, one foot on the ground as he looked intently at the television.

And then a man appeared next to Videla, a man of the same age but a little shorter, a man with swept back hair in a white raincoat and thick-framed glasses, and the Argentinian and the American leapt off their stools. Sebastian could hear their excla-mations from where he sat even though he couldn't make out what they actually said.

'Who's that?' asked Sebastian.

'That's Henry Kissinger,' said Mr Kentish.

The two men in the bowels of the stadium in Rosario seemed to have their own space despite the crush of journalists around them, as though no-one dared get too close to them.

'What's he doing there?' asked Sebastian.

Mr Kentish raised a hand.

Kissinger had stopped. He was speaking into a reporter's

microphone. 'So, I just wish you all good luck in - in - in the football.' He had a deep and thick, heavy voice.

'He doesn't sound American,' said Sebastian.

'He's German.' Mr Kentish was standing too. 'Where's he going now?'

The two men entered a room behind a door and the camera didn't follow them in but turned around and panned the dense crowd in the confined space the two had just left.

The Argentinian and the driver were now arguing with each other. The American had stood too and seemed to be arguing with the television. Sebastian thought the driver was trying to mollify the Argentinian but he wasn't having any of it. The few *Collettiani* in the bar looked on in amusement until the Peruvian and Argentinian football teams ran out onto the pitch.

The Argentinian stormed out of the bar and strode up the path towards the church and the car park and into the night. He was followed by the American who, head down, ignored the Kentishes, and by the driver who easily kept pace with the other two while seemingly moving unhurriedly. Clifford watched them go from the door of the bar.

'What was that about?' asked Mr Kentish.

'I'm not exactly sure!' Clifford laughed. 'Unless I've got the wrong end of the stick, they think it's a fix. Well, one of them certainly does. Videla and Kissinger entered the Peruvian team's changing room for some reason and the one in the middle – you know, the quarry worker who's here from time to time – he's Argentinian – well, he thinks Argentina and the U.S. have bought the game. I tried to tell him it was already fixed but he wouldn't listen to me! And Bobby, well, he just seemed pissed off to see Kissinger there! Pardon my Italian!' He ducked back into the bar.

The doleful Peruvian national anthem finished and the

military Argentinian one began. The British and the French national anthems were the best, Sebastian had long ago decided. 'Do you want to watch the game, Dad?'

'No, not really.' His father yawned. 'Do you?'

They took a last swig of their beers. The game kicked off.

Francesca came up the stairs from the restaurant into the bar and wished everyone goodnight. She stood by the Kentishes and looked up at a moon so bright it rendered the stars invisible. She wore the jeans and the shirt she'd worn to wait in and carried a cardigan in her hand. Her face was flushed. She and Rosetta had been working hard, cleaning up after them all, Sebastian presumed. 'Colletta. Is nice in the light of the moon, no?'

'Oh, yes,' said Sebastian. In places in this village, one could look up walls of sheer rock and feel one was falling up.

'It feels, well, gothic – not in terms of architecture, of course,' said Mr Kentish. 'In terms of mood, you know, eerie, mysterious.'

'Yes,' said Francesca, smiling disarmingly. 'Sometimes I feel is like a monastery.'

'Erm,' uttered Mr Kentish pointing vaguely at her chest.

Francesca looked down and shuddered. Something indistinct had alighted there, a black blot on a bare breast, a moth perhaps. Francesca made a little face of disgust. She flapped a hand at her chest.

'I think it's gone,' Mr Kentish said. 'You've been working hard,' he added.

'Yes,' Francesca conceded. 'Is not my job, really, but when I am needed, I help.' She looked in at the bar. 'Poor Dario! He wants to sleep but he doesn't want to ask people to leave the bar before the football is finished. He can sleep tomorrow.' She yawned. 'And now, *I* go to sleep. *Buona notte!*'

'Good night,' said Mr Kentish, 'I think we're turning in too. Come on, Seb.'

Sebastian followed his father, looking over his shoulder in the hope of a glimpse of Rosetta.

Sebastian and Francesca were lost in a long slow kiss but his father and the American were waiting to throw them out of the plane that juddered as it climbed the skies over Colletta.

'Seb! Seb!'

Sebastian was reluctant to stop and to have to explain himself to Rosetta. And then there he was, falling, alone and hurtling towards the stream that contoured Colletta, desperate to wake because he knew that if you hit the ground in a dream you die.

'Seb!' Dominic succeeded in shaking his brother awake. 'Listen!'

Sebastian propped himself up on his elbows and listened but could hear nothing. 'What?'

'Listen.' Dominic knelt on his bed and leant out of the window, grabbing the edge of the wide slate sill with both hands. 'There! Did you hear that?' He looked back at his brother.

Sebastian shook his head.

'Come here and listen.' Dominic's voice was pleading and urgent. He made room for his brother at the window.

The village was washed in a pale blue moonlight, the walls and roofs forming geometric patterns in various shades of blue and grey and black where the shadows were deepest. The beauty of it took Sebastian's breath away. He thought he'd ask his mother to paint night scenes for a change. Insects of the night engaged in a macabre dance around the one street lamp attached to the angle of an adjacent building, insect corpses lying thick at its base. He quite forgot he was supposed to be listening out for something.

'There!'

Sebastian had heard it and there it was again, a soft and low moaning.

Sebastian pulled his head in and sat on his brother's bed. He recognised the sound for what it was, but how to tell Dominic? On last year's family holiday in the U.S., they had checked into a motel for a night, the four of them sharing a room next to one occupied by an energetic couple very much in love. Sebastian's father, to save them all considerable embarrassment and himself from having to explain the mechanics of sexual intercourse to Dominic, Sebastian presumed, had turned the television up loud enough to drown the moans of pleasure out, which had been loud enough to bewilder and frighten Dominic.

'Dad!' Dominic had clapped his hands over his ears. 'Why have you made it so loud!'

'Because this is America! Everything is better, bigger and louder here!' Mr Kentish had shouted throwing his arms wide and had then shooed them out of the room for an early and long dinner.

'You heard that then,' said Dominic. 'Someone's hurt.'

'Oh, they'll be alright,' said Sebastian. He didn't feel like explaining the whole sex thing to Dominic either.

'Seb! You can't do nothing!' said Dominic and, when Sebastian didn't move, 'Right, I'll go and tell Dad.'

Sebastian put an arm out. 'Hold on a sec. Don't do that.' He looked at his watch and was surprised to find that he hadn't been asleep for very long. He was quite awake now and if he went for a walk, there'd be a small chance that he'd bump into Rosetta. 'I'll go. You get back to bed.' He pulled a pair of jeans on and slipped a sweatshirt over his pyjama T-shirt and flip-flops on his bare feet. 'Right, then.' He stepped out of the apartment.

Sebastian thought he'd just go for a walk, past the bar to see if anyone happened to be still there and then down by the water troughs and just once around the village by which time, with any luck, the couple would have exhausted themselves and Dominic would be fast asleep. With a little more luck, he'd find Rosetta up. He stuck his hands in his jeans pockets as he wandered along and past the tunnel that ran through the heart of the village, the one he'd taken with Dominic a couple of times. He thought he wouldn't take it, he'd take the longer way, and he felt silly for his reluctance to do so, based as it was on Dominic's encounter with the witch there on one occasion. It was just that, well, at night, Colletta was rather spooky – not that he believed in ghosts, but still.

The slap of his flip-flops was loud on the wet and slippery stones. He stepped in the puddles. He didn't mind his feet getting wet. Sebastian inhaled deeply. The night air was refreshing.

The contrast in the village between day and night was stark. Sebastian stood in a lifeless square, bleached of colour and devoid of noise. This is exactly what the village would have looked like a hundred years ago, he thought, even 700 years ago. The sign on the bar door read *Chiuso*; it was pitch black inside. Sebastian walked around the bar, not down the alley that would take him to the pool, but down the other side, to the water fountain and trough, where he stopped to drink. He turned left along a less frequented path that ran parallel to the road just visible down in the valley, down some more steps, past shuttered stone cottages and up to the swimming pool. He paused and listened to the hum of the pool's water filter motor and to the trickle of water it pumped incessantly out of and into the pool. Water boatmen and water striders skated on the water's surface leaving wakes of elegant ripples. If Sebastian tilted his head to one side, he could just about manage to align the moon with the two globe-like lamps mounted on steel posts at the two ends of the pool. The thought of an earth with three moons tickled him. Up close to one of the globes he could hear the wings of flying insects beating against the glass.

Sebastian stood among the olive trees, deciding whether to take the nearest path, the one that led back via the square, or the one that led back past Rosetta's apartment, but he was honest enough with himself to know that it wasn't a sincere deliberation. He climbed the steps heavily, enjoying the slip-slap of the heels of his flip-flops in the otherwise absolute silence.

At the top of the steps the path was solid rock face, unpaved and uneven where it neared the corner to the stairs to Rosetta's and Francesca's apartment. Sebastian was proceeding carefully along it when he heard a burst of running footsteps, a slip, an imprecation, and the resumption of a thudding, limping running, away down an alleyway and into the tunnel and then silence. The approach to the corner was in darkness so Sebastian kept an arm extended and one hand on a wall, fingers dragging along stone, moss and cement. Past a black, closed and curtained window, around the corner and through the archway shaped by the staircase that led to the apartment. There, at its foot and in the space between buildings, lay Francesca.

Francesca's body was lit by the grey light of the moon and her face by the yellow light of a lamp under the arch, which gave the grotesque impression that her body and her face didn't belong together. She was barefoot, with one foot on the lowest step and another tucked under a leg. Her jeans were unzipped, revealing her pubic hair above her underwear. Her shirt buttons were undone and her chest discoloured. There was blood on her face and on the stone ground. She seemed to be having difficulty breathing. And then she moaned, through swollen lips. It was the moan Dominic and he had heard.

She tried to say something. '*Aiuto!*'

Sebastian knelt and repeated her name. He stood and said he'd get help, he thought he'd run and fetch Dario and the doctor, he'd run to the middle of the square and scream for help if he had to.

And then he heard the running steps again, the same ones but others too this time, getting louder as they came closer. There was Dario, ahead of the limping American.

Dario knelt by Francesca and patted her hand. He spoke to her urgently, almost endearingly, it sounded to Sebastian, as though he were begging her to wake up. He massaged her hands, he pulled her eyelids apart, he brushed her hair from her forehead. The American panted, his hands on his knees. He smelled of alcohol.

'What happened?' asked Sebastian but neither man replied. 'Shouldn't we get the doctor?' He made as if to go.

The American took a deep breath and stood. 'He's away. He doesn't always live here. Claudia is calling an ambulance.' The American winced and rubbed his knee. He said something to Dario in Italian and turned to hobble away. As an afterthought, it seemed, he said over his shoulder to Sebastian. 'I'm going to meet the ambulance at the top of the village. They'll need someone to guide them here.'

Dario had yet to let go of Francesca's hand. Whatever soothing things he was saying to her was having some effect. Sebastian was surprised to find himself thinking that Dario was flirting with her. Her eyes fluttered open and closed and she seemed to be trying to smile.

Dario looked up at Sebastian. 'Okay. The ambulance will be here soon. Go to her room, her apartment – you know where it is? – and pack some things for her, what she will need in the hospital, you know, clothes, toothbrush, find her passport, anything, some ID, some underwear.'

'Er, alright,' said Sebastian hesitantly, not moving.

'*Va bene.* I go. Sebastian, hold her hand. Keep talking to her. Tell her she's beautiful. Say to her how lucky you are to be holding her hand. Yes, you see, she understands! Good! Good, Francesca! Okay, come on.'

And so Sebastian found himself for the second time in a week holding the hand of a young woman on the cobbles of Colletta.

Dario bounded up the twisting staircase, up, up and up once again to the top. Would he find Rosetta there? Sebastian wondered where she was. 'What happened?' he asked Francesca. He was holding her hand, as Dario had commanded him to, and stroking it, as he'd seen him do. 'What happened to you? Who did this to you?'

She could hear him, he knew, and even understand him; she seemed to want to shake her head and mouth something. Her breathing was still laboured. Her free hand flapped against her chest and he looked closely at where he thought she might have pointed, to just above a frayed bra top. He saw that the skin there was red and swollen.

He heard Dario descending the stairs now but with a pillow and a blanket. Sebastian lifted Francesca's head as gently as he could, while Dario slid the pillow under it. He covered her with the blanket while Dario returned for her hospital things. He continued to hold and stroke her hand and suddenly wanted to weep for tiredness and for anxiety on her behalf, for the drama of it all. The faint wail of an ambulance in the distance reached his ears. 'Don't go,' he said, 'don't fall asleep.' He wanted to ask after Rosetta but couldn't bring himself to.

He heard the American returning and was surprised at the lack of urgency in the footsteps.

'Sebastian!' It wasn't the American but his father. 'Good grief!' Mr Kentish looked down at Francesca and his son and then around and around, as though afraid that they'd be found, that his son would be apprehended in the process of committing some horrendous act. He appeared completely out of his depth, as though nothing in his life had prepared him to find his son tending an unconscious and injured woman in a remote Italian village in the middle of the night.

Well, he should have learnt from the first occasion, thought Sebastian wearily.

He was surprised to find himself completely indifferent as to what his father might think. He didn't even want to begin to explain. He looked up at his father and saw that in the light of the moon he looked like stone. His mouth was open but he was saying nothing. 'Go back to bed, Dad. You know you're dreaming.'

Mr Kentish nodded, as though that made absolute sense.

Sebastian wondered where he'd found the courage for that bit of cheek and regretted it. He hoped his father wouldn't remember it. His father was as pale as the stone wall he leant against. He wore a top and trousers over his pyjamas too, Sebastian could see, and slippers that were too warm for this weather. Dominic, worrying that his brother hadn't returned, had probably gone to summon his parents and then his mother had worried and sent his father out to look for him.

Sebastian had not let go of Francesca's hand and hadn't stopped patting, stroking and squeezing it – he hadn't really known what he'd been doing – and now he felt a definite squeeze of his hand. 'Francesca,' he said, 'stay with us. Dad, look,' he added and pulled the blanket down a little, enough to expose her chest.

Mr Kentish recoiled in horror, as though his son were about to do something indecent, and convulsed as he heard footsteps from above suddenly tumbling towards them. Dario stood before them, a small suitcase in one hand.

'Dario,' said Mr Kentish, waving his hands around in a panic, as though it were incumbent upon him to explain this situation. 'We just got here!'

'Dad, be quiet!' Sebastian felt almost ashamed of his father. 'Dario, this is what I think happened. Do you see here?' He pointed to Francesca's chest. 'Dad, please move out of the light. You see, it's red and swollen and irritated and I think she was pointing to it earlier. Well, when Dad and I were talking to her this evening, before we all went to bed, I think something stung her there, she brushed it off, it was black, not a wasp but something like that.'

'*Ahia!* Black hornets. We have them here.'

'Hold on. She's squeezing my hand.'

Francesca was trying to open her eyes and to mouth something through her still swollen lips.

'I think I'm right; she's trying to tell me I'm right. And then she went into shock. Maybe perhaps because she's allergic to stings or something.' Sebastian looked around for affirmation.

Dario got down on his knees and put his ear to Francesca's mouth. 'Yes, yes, *bravo*,' he said to Sebastian. 'She started to undress for bed when she realised.' He shushed Sebastian and his father even though they hadn't said anything. 'And she didn't want to lose consciousness where no-one would find her. *Brava!*' he said to her, 'you did the right but – *ahia!* – you fell on the rocks and you hurt your face. Not too much, eh? I hope, I hope.'

'But what about Rosetta? They share the room, don't they? So where's Rosetta?'

They turned in the direction of the sound of running footsteps. At the end of the alley, the American, his chest heaving, was pointing two stretcher-bearing ambulance attendants their way.

SEVENTEEN

'Good morning, Clifford.'

'Ah! Good morning, Robert.'

'The water a little bit chillier this morning?'

'Just a little. It always is after a storm.'

'No Renzo today? No Kees?'

Clifford laughed while he did a casual backstroke. 'No! Kees is probably hungover and Renzo's probably sulking!'

Bravo considered the unoccupied sunbeds, already steaming in the early morning sun. 'No towels on the sunbeds still, I see.'

'No! That worked a treat, didn't it? Credit to the Germans for taking it well.' Clifford resumed the breaststroke.

Bravo waved and walked on, past where Francesca had fallen, where, pausing briefly, he could make out her blood on the stone. She'd hurt herself quite badly, the poor girl, but he didn't believe she'd fallen face first or her injuries would have been far greater; her legs must have just given way, he thought. The paramedics, after some minutes of seeing to her, had said that she'd had an anaphylactic shock, corroborating what the Kentish boy had apparently guessed to be the case, and had administered an adrenaline injection before lifting her onto a stretcher and carrying her up to the ambulance parked by the church. The church cross that hovered silver in the moonlight by the little campanile had resembled a visual echo of the bright red cross on the ambulance. Theirs had been an almost funereal procession along Colletta's dark alleyways and moonlit paths, but the ambulance men had assured Dario that Francesca was out of danger, that she'd be retained in hospital for one day only, maybe two at the most.

The four of them had walked down from the church in near silence, Dario's hand on Sebastian's shoulder, whispering thanks to him for having saved yet another member of his staff and deaf to the boy's protestations that it hadn't been him who'd found Francesca and raised the alarm. Bravo didn't mind. The boy's embarrassment amused him and, anyway, he'd played his part in ensuring the girl's comfort and safety. Mr Kentish, on the other hand, had been less than impressive, clearly flustered by an event out of the ordinary and visibly more relieved that it held no nefarious consequences for his son than he had been once Francesca's well-being had been assured. Bravo sighed. The image he'd begun to form of Mr Kentish was disquieting. It was at odds with the picture he'd formed of him as a reporter and researcher, where he thought he'd shown courage and original-ity, and of the husband he'd want Mrs Kentish to have – which was a ridiculous thought to have so he cut it dead.

Bravo waved at Claudia and pointed at the terrace. She had understood, he knew, and would appear within minutes with his coffee and a cloth with which to dry a chair and a table for him. She wouldn't dry the others, counting on the sun to do her work for her. Indeed, the black metal chairs and tables were steaming in the sun and the puddles amongst the cobbles were already shrinking. She would ask him if he wanted a breakfast pastry, as she always did, and he would surprise her by saying, yes, as he never did. Last night's excitement had left him hungry. If she remarked that the square was unusually quiet, he would suggest that that was because the Italians were sulking because of their defeat at the feet of the Dutch. He wouldn't worry her with the story of what had happened to Francesca; he'd leave that to Dario.

The wasps, that made their nests in the arched, hollow leg supports, the bowed stretchers that connected and held the table legs in place, began to crawl out and fly lazily away. Bravo contemplated one closely and shuddered. He didn't fancy being stung by one of them let alone by a black hornet.

Ah, there was Kentish, earlier than Bravo had expected him, pointing up at him and, presumably, asking Claudia to bring him a coffee too, managing to make himself understood without his phrase book.

'Did you manage to get some sleep?' he asked.

'Not much, no,' said Kentish, fishing a handkerchief out of his satchel and drying a chair with it. 'Did you?'

'Enough.' He watched as Claudia reappeared with a coffee for Kentish and a breakfast pastry for each of them.

'Ah, I thought I'd said, no, but never mind,' said Kentish and bit into his breakfast. 'So who won? Argentina?'

Bravo nodded. 'Six to zero.'

Kentish whistled, or tried to, losing a morsel of pastry as he did so. 'So it's an Argentina Holland final.'

They walked up, past Francesca's closed office.

'The key,' said Kentish.

'I still have it,' said Bravo, fingering it in his pocket.

'I hope she's alright. It was all a bit much to take in at the time. It was only once I was in bed and explaining what had happened to Jackie that it hit me how fortunate she was that you found her.'

Bravo dismissed this. 'If I hadn't found her, your son would have.'

'You're limping,' said Kentish.

'It's just a knock on the knee.'

They climbed the steps to the guest office and Bravo stopped at the sight of the one cushion that was sodden with rainwater. Of course: Kentish had been sitting on it when he'd left him asleep there and there it had remained in the storm and the rain of the following day. He was sorry that they should have this reminder of his indelicacy but said nothing and simply brought another chair and two cushions out from the office. He left the wet cushion on the grass to dry.

'22 June 1978. Colletta di Castelbianco,' said Kentish into his microphone. He leafed through his notebooks and some loose papers and then placed them on the table. 'We've reached, I think, the end point. Aldo Moro was found dead...' – he made some quick calculations – 'forty-five days ago. His murder, unless I'm mistaken, prompted you to change your mind: you agreed to speak to me.' Kentish had his head to one side, like a bird. 'What can you tell me about the assassination of Aldo Moro?'

Bravo didn't know where to start. In the '40s, when Moro had developed his opposition to fascism? In the '50s when his teacher parents had even talked of returning to Italy so pleased were they with Moro's reforms as Minister of Education? Or in the '60s, when, in his first term as Prime Minister, Moro had sought to integrate the Socialists into the government system and introduced a wide range of social reforms that were considered *socialist* by the Right? No, he thought, in 1973.

'Five years ago,' he said, 'we had the year of the *Compromesso storico*, the Historic Compromise. It allowed for a democratic alliance between the Christian Democrats and the Communist Party and was embraced by Moro. I told you, I recall, that nothing terrifies us – the U.S. – more than communism but that's not quite right, one thing does, and that's the prospect of a *democratically elected, non-violent* communism, one independent of Moscow and resistant to our demonisation of it, one with broad popular appeal. So Moro's proposition, earlier this year, of the formation of a cabinet composed principally of Christian Democrats but also of ministers from the Socialist Party and the Communist Party was strongly opposed – Kissinger had made that very clear to Moro.'

'The cold war of ideology continues,' said Kentish.

'Yes, the participation in government by communists in a Western country would represent a cultural and ideological failure for the U.S. And, in practical terms, the governmental collaboration of the Christian Democrats with the Communist Party would inevitably allow the Communists to gain information on strategic NATO military plans and installations and to pass that information on to the Soviets.'

'So, what can you tell me about the assassination of Aldo Moro?' Kentish repeated his question.

'On the sixteenth of March this year, Moro left home carrying details of the Historic Compromise in his briefcase. He was being driven to the palace of the Italian parliament in Rome where he intended to put his plan – to include communists in the executive – to a confidence vote that he would win. It was to be the day of the opening in parliament of a newly formed government of national unity, this coalition of Christian Democrats, Socialists and Communists, to be led by Andreotti. Moro was being driven in a black Fiat limousine and not, according to one report, in a bullet-proof car, which he had requested on his return from Washington. At some point in his journey, a white Fiat with diplomatic number plates pulled out in front of his car. Two men in the white Fiat and four others in the street with submachine guns opened fire and killed Moro's bodyguards, the two in his car and three who were following in a white Alfa Romeo.'

'I drive an Alfa Romeo,' said Kentish, and blushed.

'Moro was held incommunicado by his captors but permitted to write letters to his family and to politicians – he sent almost a hundred – which magnified the massive sense of national crisis that Italy is experiencing. The Red Brigades assumed responsibility and issued a total of nine *communications* requesting an exchange of prisoners and, amongst other things, bemoaning "the imperialist state of the multinationals" that they see Italy turning into. Andreotti cracked down on the Left – over 70,000 road blocks have been erected, 37,000 houses have been searched and over six million people questioned in just two months. A government announcement that the Red Brigades had killed Moro was later shown to have been false. The images of the Red Brigades have dominated the television and the newspapers' front pages. The message in the press has been clear: *this is what you can expect from doing business with double-crossing communists*. On the ninth of May, Moro's body was discovered in the boot of a red Renault 4, halfway between the offices of the Christian Democrats and those of the Communist Party. He'd been shot.'

'I'm left wondering,' began Kentish seriously, frowning as though wishing to atone for his earlier irrelevant interjection, 'why would the Red Brigades – Italy's militant extreme Left – want to assassinate Moro?' Kentish held a finger up. 'If I can just finish my line of thought. One, before the kidnapping, the

Communist Party was about to assume a direct role in the Italian government's post-war history for the very first time. Two, whatever it was, it has to be assumed that the plan backfired: the assassination resulted in yet another centre-right cabinet under the control of Christian Democrats. Three, do the Red Brigades really have the skills and the capacity to pull off such a coup on their own? And four, if they do and if they really have been infiltrated by the C.I.A. or by Italian intelligence, as you said the other day, can they really have remained undetected for so long and, if they didn't, doesn't this point to collusion with the Right? Might not Moro's assassination fit in with this dictum or principle or whatever that you mentioned previously of selective assassination?' Kentish considered his hand, his four extended fingers and his thumb, as though unsure whether he'd made four or five points and hoping he'd find the answer written on his palm.

Bravo moved his chair so that his head would be in the shade while his knee, on which a scab was beginning to form, would remain in the sun. 'You're assuming, I think, that the Soviets would welcome the participation of the Italian Communist Party in the Italian government.'

'I hadn't really thought about it but, come to think of it, of course.'

'They don't. They fear that the Italian Communist Party in an Italian cabinet would risk emancipation from Moscow and a *rapprochement* to the Americans and are therefore opposed to it.'

Kentish scribbled away. 'So not only would the Red Brigades *not* have been acting on direct orders from Moscow but, if what you say is true, they wouldn't even have had Moscow's tacit approval, they'd have been acting unilaterally.' He closed his eyes and brought a hand to his head. 'Still. This has no bearing on the extent of the involvement of, well, let's say, the Right.'

'That's correct.'

'After all, the government that, one might argue, had been leaning to the Left, has swung back to the Right. One can even see this as the beginning of the end of the Left in Italian politics.' Kentish shuffled through some papers. '"Moro sacrificed for the sake of the stability of the state," was one headline, I think. "The end of Eurocommunism" was another.' He put the papers down and sighed. 'You see, no matter what you say about the Soviets, which I'm sure is all true, I can't help but believe that the Right had so much more to gain from the elimination of Aldo Moro than the Left.'

Bravo pursed his lips.

Kentish turned the cassette over. 'Now tell me, tell me what you know. Are there any connections between Gladio and Moro? Why did you change your mind and call me?'

Bravo shifted in his seat. Why had he called Kentish? Why had this one death, after so many, been the straw that broke the camel's back? He cleared his throat. 'You know, of course, that I'm retired from active service. After I finished my doctorate, I retired formally, officially. That said, one can never leave, in a sense, not after thirty-one years with the Agency. I stay in touch with colleagues, contacts, that kind of thing. They stay in touch with me. And I recognise our fingerprints whenever I see them, in a news article, on the radio, on the television, in the press, wherever. So, what do I know? The connection with Gladio? Practically, I know that the ninety-one bullets recovered at the scene of the attack have been found to have been treated with a special preserving paint characterised by the ammunition kept in the many Gladio munitions stores. And I know that Moro was detained, for at least some of the time, in an apartment owned by SISMI.'

'SISMI?'

'That's the Italian Military Intelligence and Security Service.'

'What else?'

'That's it.'

'Are you saying, then, that Moro died because it suited both the Right and the Left?'

'I think I must be.'

'It's ironic to think that neither the Soviets nor the Americans wanted to see the Communists accede to government positions in Italy.'

'Yes, that was one thing that united them.'

'But while for the Americans it would have been considered a disaster, for the Soviets it would have represented an inconvenience, an aggravation.'

'Something like that.'

Bravo's mind drifted. Kentish was going through his notes, summarising what he had learnt during the seven interviews he'd conducted – Gladio, the Catholic church, the Mafia, the bought elections, the bombings, the murders culminating in Moro's. Who was next? What was next? Bravo shrugged. As he'd said, he was out of the loop. So why had he changed his mind and called Kentish? Twice he'd been asked that question and not replied. He had questions of his own – what was Kentish intending to do with all of the information? Would he take it to a newspaper or to a broadcaster? And in which country? Would it be safe for him to do so? Had Bravo said enough for Kentish to be able to deliver a story but not so much as to lead him into danger? Bravo was sweating.

'It *is* getting hot,' he heard Kentish say. 'Shall we call it a day?'

Bravo thought it a little early to do so; the surprise must have shown on his face.

'We leave on Sunday. Today is Thursday. I need time to go through my notes, to give them, well, some kind of structure. I have some questions and I'm sure that, once I've finished, I'll have some more. On Saturday, should you be around, perhaps we could get together one more time and fill in the gaps – would that be possible?'

Bravo nodded and rose. He collected all three cushions, placed them in the guest office and locked the door after him while Kentish put his cassette recorder and his notes away.

'And perhaps,' added Kentish, 'you could join us for dinner one of these evenings, before we leave.'

EIGHTEEN

Rosetta stood in the square in a kaftan dress of browns, orange and turquoise. A woven cloth shoulder bag hung all the way down to her thigh and drew Sebastian's eyes further down still to the toes of brown, dusty cowboy boots peeking out from beneath the hem of her dress. She raised her arms to tighten the knot of a bow that bunched her hair, a piece of cloth of many colours that reached the small of her back. He glimpsed her armpit hairs and her bra through her wide, baggy sleeves and was instantly jealous of the little crowd about her – Claudia and Dario and some other Italians – seemingly petitioning her for something. It was the first time he'd seen her dressed not for work, he realised, and it gave him a jolt. She wouldn't have looked out of place at Woodstock and yet, despite the hippy vibe, there was something *chic* about her, as though this costume, and not the one that accessorised a bucket and a mop, provided the truest reflection of her. For once, he found himself wishing his mother would show up.

He stood at the periphery of the group trying to catch Rosetta's eye and understand what she was saying. She saw him but carried on talking to the others and answering their questions. He thought she might have smiled at him with her eyes, if one could do such a thing. Approaching further, he heard the repetition of Francesca's name and gathered that Rosetta had news of her.

'*Eccolo!*' Dario had seen him. He put his arm around Sebastian's neck and drew Sebastian to him. He smelled of fresh aftershave and stale cigarette smoke and the cigarette packet rolled into the cuff of his short sleeve dug into Sebastian's cheek.

Rosetta had just returned from visiting Francesca in the hospital in Albenga. Francesca was quite out of danger. The hornet that had alighted on her had not flown away, as she had initially thought, but burrowed its way beneath her shirt only to sting her when she'd disturbed it, once she'd begun to undress. The adrenaline had done the trick but she had bruised and cut herself when she'd fallen and had needed stitches to her chin and her forehead. The hospital had kept her in for the day and the night and would release her in the early afternoon, when Dario would fetch her. In the meantime, she sent her apologies to everyone for having been the cause of so much trouble – and everyone pooh-poohed the notion that she had been – and, Rosetta finished mischievously, Francesca sent a special thank-you to Sebastian. The small crowd turned to Sebastian and applauded him.

'It wasn't me who found her!' protested Sebastian weakly as, once again, he found himself fêted for something that had happened to him rather than for something that he'd done.

'*Bravo!*' said someone.

'*Santo Sebastiano!*' said another.

Saint! Thought Sebastian. *Well, rather pats on the back than arrows.* 'You can let go now, Dario,' he said.

'Okay, is enough.' Dario clapped his hands. 'Claudia,' he

said, pointing to Mr and Mrs Langemensen standing by the bar door, 'I think these people want coffee. We are coming, we are coming,' he assured them. 'Rosetta,' he said and placed his hand on her shoulder before carrying on in Italian. 'And don't forget to dilute!' he finished in English, clearly for Sebastian's benefit.

'Come,' said Rosetta laughing, 'he wants me to finish with the windows I never cleaned before I help with the lunch.' She threaded her arm through his. 'I go to get changed. Come with me.' The sensation of her bare arm against his was electric.

Rosetta pulled Sebastian after her, away from the square, down the path that ran past the open door of the restaurant in which Mr Kentish was busy typing, the sound of the keys hitting the roller as loud, in the confined space, as the clack of her cowboy boots' heels on the cobbles. They took a sharp left into an alleyway, past the apartment of the doctor who, Sebastian could see through the open window, was now back home and reading.

'Where were you?' Sebastian asked, elated and emboldened by Rosetta's new familiarity.

'When?'

'When Francesca fell. And yesterday. I looked for you everywhere.'

'Thursday is my free day.'

'Your free day?'

'My day off.'

'Well, you could have said. And where were you on Wednesday, after dinner?'

'Wednesday, after we finish serving the dinner, after the football, I help Claudia in the kitchen and I clean the restaurant. Like normal. Why do you ask?'

'Fine, but where did you go afterwards? Why weren't you there when Francesca fell?'

'Is my fault?' She let go of his arm.

'No!'

'I have to tell you everything? Alright, I tell you everything.' She placed her hands on her hips. 'On Wednesday, my father picks me up, like on every Wednesday night, when I finish with the serving. He drives me home and I spend Thursday with my family, I see my father and mother and my brothers. On Friday morning, he drives me back here, to Colletta. Exception: this morning I went to see Francesca in the hospital first. Is that enough information for you? Do you want more?' She untied the knot in the cloth that held her hair back and shook her hair free and ran her hands through it.

Sebastian wished he hadn't sounded so plaintive. He'd meant to say something endearing, to show her that he'd missed her, but instead, he'd managed to convey the idea that he thought he could make demands of her. Even to his own ears, he'd come across, at best, like a sulky schoolboy.

They had arrived at the stairs that led up to Rosetta's apartment.

'Goodbye,' she said, effectively dismissing him. She went up the stairs without a backward glance, the Segs on the heels of her cowboy boots sparking on the stone.

Sebastian leant against the warm wall, tilted his head up and closed his eyes. Not even the sun on his face was as warming and as pleasing to him as the sensation of Rosetta's arm in his had been. He was an idiot.

Something light and gritty landed on his hair and on his face and he stepped forward and shuddered and brushed whatever it was off and looked up. Three floors up, there was Rosetta, looking down at him over her terrace wall, one arm around a plant pot and sprinkling earth from it onto him with her free hand. She laughed and then disappeared from view. They had remained friends.

He was still standing there when Dominic found him and, to Sebastian's amusement, he too stood with his back to the sunlit stone and his face to the sun.

Sebastian regarded him affectionately. Younger brothers were so much easier to understand than girls were. The steps to Rosetta's apartment – to Rosetta herself, as she was there – crisscrossed and careened above them in a zigzag of crazy stone work that interrupted the direct sunlight and cut and refracted it in lozenges, triangles and rectangles of greys and browns. The picture of Colletta immediately in front of Sebastian was incongruous, seemingly cubist, if not contemporary, and yet with no visual clues that they weren't in the Middle Ages. If a flock of sheep driven by a shepherd in a jerkin with a crook in one hand and a leather water bottle in the other had passed them, it wouldn't have felt out of keeping.

'Is this where you found Francesca?' asked Dominic, looking down at the uneven stone.

'Yes. Her face was exactly where your feet are.'

Dominic stepped hastily to one side.

'Only kidding.'

'How come,' began Dominic sheepishly, 'you haven't told anyone it was me who heard Francesca moaning and sent you out?'

Sebastian laughed and grabbed his brother in a friendly headlock. 'So you want your fair share of the glory! Come to think of it, I did tell Mum and Dad.'

They walked back the way Sebastian had come, past the doctor at whom Sebastian lifted a hand in greeting and, past their father who sat typing, his back to the open door, his fingers proceeding so violently on his typewriter that the boys felt they oughtn't interrupt him.

Sebastian experienced a sense of mild confusion, a feeling of déjà vu or of being stuck in a time warp. With the exception of the day of the storm, every day had been like the other, a succession of hot and cloudless indistinguishable days. There'd been the two dramas of Rosetta and of Francesca, with the second a near identical repetition of the first; the evening football matches at regular three- or four-day intervals; and, now, there he was, leading a procession – composed of him, his brother, his mother and the American – away from the village in a mirror image of the one on Thursday, when the American and his mother had walked up ahead, his brother had followed and he, carrying the easel, had brought up the rear. On this occasion, he led, still with the easel, his brother following with the basket in which Claudia had packed their lunches, his mother carrying her paints and a blank canvas, and the American at the back, tagging along again, explaining to Mrs Kentish that he just happened to have been setting off on his walk to Veravo and assuring her that he would not be imposing on them for long.

They followed the path down, flanked by the old stone wall on one side and open to the amphitheatre's long grasses on the other, down into the wood, past the man encased in glass, onto the stone bridge and over the stream and then uphill again, out of the wood and into the open.

'Dom,' said Sebastian, slowing so that Dominic might catch up. 'What do you think of Mum's paintings?'

'I think they're good,' said Dominic.

'Is that all you've got to say about them?'

'I think they're better than she thinks they are.'

'What do you think is good about them?'

'I think,' said Dominic slowly, 'that they're good because they're as much paintings about her, about her state of mind, as they are of the things she's painting.'

'Blimey! That's profound! Did you come up with that all on your own?'

'No. I heard Dad say that to Mum once.'

Sebastian made to cuff his brother's ear but had to bring his free hand back to steady the easel.

'Boys!' Mrs Kentish called up. 'That's the spot.'

Mrs Kentish and a perspiring American joined the boys by a wooden bench in the shade of a cypress tree. They looked at Colletta across the valley they had traversed and over a bush blazing with yellow flowers just on the other side of the path from the bench. They hadn't seen Colletta from this angle before, in its long, low profile. With the sun above and behind it, the medieval village appeared to them drained of colour, a random ensemble of barely distinguishable blocks of faint greys, browns and mauves, like so many dice having come to rest after having been rolled by a god.

'I've always thought,' said the American drawing the back of his hand across his brow, 'that Colletta seen from this angle resembles a dragon at rest.'

'Hmm,' said Mrs Kentish noncommittally, the brilliant yellow-flowering bush in front of them having drawn her eye, its stems and leaves writhing with nature's exuberance, its blossom catching and releasing the bright sunlight. She stepped forward and fingered a petal. 'Broom,' she said. 'But Scotch or Lydian?'

'It's just a bush with yellow flowers, to me,' said the American. 'Well, I shall leave you.' He lifted two fingers to his forehead in a parting salute.

'Don't forget to sing. To keep the wild boar at bay,' Mrs Kentish called after him.

'Oh, they won't be out at this time of day,' the American called over his shoulder.

'Here,' said Mrs Kentish and she had Sebastian erect the easel by the bench in the shade. 'This will do nicely.'

Sebastian couldn't keep his mind on his book. He'd been such an idiot. He watched as his mother drew lightly in charcoal, sketching the broad outline of her intended picture. He felt waves of affection for Rosetta, for her having been forgiving. Dominic, besides him on the bench, had let his book fall from his hands. Spittle hung from his open mouth and a gentle rise and fall of his chest betrayed his breathing. His head had slumped forward, revealing a strip of white neck between his mop of brown hair and his T-shirt. It contrasted with his brown arms and legs and made Sebastian realise just how tanned they'd become without realising it. He stretched his arms out and looked at them and then stuck his legs out, straight, like a baby in a buggy. He, like his mother, never caught the sun in the way Dominic and his father did, they never turned brown, but a blotchy shade somewhere between pink and red and orange. He considered his mother's legs. They were indeed the same colour as his.

There was nothing of the stereotypical painter about Mrs Kentish. She wore a crisp blue, buttoned dress that stopped at the knees and at the elbows with lapels as wide as her white belt buckle. Her beige and orange shoes were sturdy without being inelegant and matched a scarf, tied like a neckerchief at her throat. Her hair beneath her straw sun hat drew a perfectly straight line from shoulder blade to shoulder blade, its ends bleached by the sun. The only concessions to her art were her fingernails, cut short but still lacquered. Her hands were surprisingly strong; they adjusted the easel with ease and brought unbidden to Sebastian's mind the memory of Rosetta's grip on his wrists. They'd be leaving in two days. Sebastian stood.

'Mum, I'm bored. I think I'll go back to Colletta.'

'What about your lunch?' asked Mrs Kentish.

'I'll go with you,' said Dominic. He wiped his mouth with the back of his hand.

Sebastian sat down again. 'Never mind,' he said. There'd be no point in going back now. Rosetta would be cleaning windows and then helping with the lunch. He'd try to catch her in the late afternoon. 'I think I'd just be bored there too.' He looked out over the yellow Broom bush, over the valley and at the village where, somewhere, Rosetta would be on a ladder cleaning windows with no-one to catch her if she fell.

Sebastian looked up expecting to see the American returning but it wasn't him. Sebastian thought it was the driver from the first day, stamping heavily with each step as he arrested his speed down the steep incline, releasing clouds of dust around his shoes, but it wasn't him either. It was Mr Pompeo, dressed much as the driver had been – *did they wear a uniform?* Sebastian wondered. The clothes of some Italians constituted a code of sorts: the freshly ironed blue shirt, its collar up and the sleeves rolled to just below the elbow; the V-neck jumper, if not worn then draped casually over the shoulders or, as in the case of Mr Pompeo, held in one hand; the crisp jeans; the black leather shoes that, despite the dust that had accumulated on them, Sebastian could see, had been polished that morning.

Mr Pompeo halted and declared his delight at meeting them, clicking his heels and nodding to the boys before giving Mrs Kentish more of a bow than a nod. His shirt was a darker blue at his chest and underneath his arms where his perspiration showed, and a fresh haircut betrayed the sweat or hair oil that trickled from his temples above each ear. He made as though to wipe his forehead with his jumper and then seemingly thought better of it. And then he inspected the unfinished painting.

Sebastian considered his mother's painting critically. She had intended to paint Colletta from this newly discovered vantage point but what had started as a painting of the village in the distance had become a painting of the yellow-flowered bush in the foreground. It was a painting of two halves. The top half: the village and surrounding mountains were represented by a pastel assemblage of squares and triangles in distant greys and greens. The bottom half: thrashing, intertwining stems and branches in dark greens and browns and exploding yellow flowers seemingly seeking a resolution in an unspecified conflict.

Mr Pompeo stepped back and looked from the painting to the view, back to the painting and then at Mrs Kentish.

'Is perfect.'

'It's unfinished.'

'Is beautiful.'

'The view is beautiful.'

Mr Pompeo pointed at the bottom half of the painting, at the tortured representation of the Broom bush.

'Is... *violento*.'

'Violent? I suppose it is. I was thinking of Argentina.'

'Argentina?'

'Yes, of the violence committed on the Argentine people by the junta.'

Mr Pompeo nodded. 'I buy. For Anna, my wife. How much?' He fetched a wodge of bank notes from his back pocket, licked a thumb and index finger and started counting through them, all in one easy action, while never taking his eyes off Sebastian's mother.

Sebastian looked at her too. He knew what she made of the ostentation, of the not keeping one's money in a wallet, and he knew that she hated talking money and business. She was silent, as though petrified, discomfited, Sebastian knew, by the prospects of a negotiation she didn't know how to undertake. It was incongruous, improper somehow, vulgar, she would say.

'It's unfinished,' she said.

'*Va bene*,' said Mr Pompeo as if understanding that the price of the painting couldn't be settled until it was finished and folding and returning his money to his back pocket. 'When is finished, I buy. I make a good buy. And now, good-bye!' He strode off laughing, pleased to have punned in English.

'Let's have lunch,' said Mrs Kentish.

The three of them sat on the bench and drank bottled water and ate goats' cheese and tomato *panini* while the sun beat down oppressively on everything around them and the cicadas drilled and screamed in protest.

'What did you and the American talk about?' Sebastian asked his mother.

'When?'

'On the way here.'

'Oh yes. I forgot. I bet you can't guess.'

Dominic and Sebastian had just taken big bites from their sandwiches and couldn't.

'*Grand-maman* and *Grand-papa*. I thought that would surprise you. It surprised me. It's funny, I'd had the impression that there was something he'd been keen to tell me ever since we got here. He said he knew them – *had* known them. From before I was born, from the time when *Grand-maman* and *Grand-papa* had just got married and *Grand-papa* had been posted to *Indochine*. It was his first overseas posting. He was a captain then. Anyway, the American said he'd been stationed there too and he'd worked with *Grand-papa*.'

Sebastian had finished his sandwich and looked longingly at his brother's and mother's. It was a shame, really, that Dominic was now of an age to eat his lunch in its entirety.

'The funny thing is he seemed more interested in *Grand-maman* than in *Grand-papa* – well, he asked for news of her mainly, what was she doing, was she happy, did she ever speak of *Indochine*, that kind of thing.' She broke the end of her sandwich off and gave it to Sebastian.

'Thanks, Mum.'

'But when I said, I'd remember him to them, he told me not to bother and please not to and, well, he seemed embarrassed.'

'They had their war there after us,' said Sebastian, 'after the French, I mean. The Americans. Vietnam.'

'Yes.'

'Do you think he saw any fighting?'

'Maybe.'

'Do you think he's ever killed anyone?' asked Dominic.

'You can ask him yourself, over dinner tomorrow,' said Mrs Kentish.

'Can I really?' asked Dominic. He seemed excited at the prospect.

'He's having dinner with us?' asked Sebastian.

'It would seem so.'

'On our last night?'

'It's the final. Argentina against Holland,' said Dominic.

'Yes. He said that there should be quite a good atmosphere. Anyway, Dad invited him to join us and he accepted.'

When Sebastian had reached the age at which he'd started noticing – *really* noticing – girls, he'd also begun to notice men noticing his mother. He could recognise the looks other men gave women because they were his too. He preferred the openly admiring stares to the ashamed, furtive glances when they were directed at his mother. In contrast to his mother's guarded jealousy of Francesca and the obvious appeal Francesca had for his father, his father never seemed bothered by the attention his mother received. If anything, he seemed pleased, proud, even, at times. It was as though having found Jacqueline Panetta (as she had been before they'd married) attractive, he quite understood that other men would too.

Mrs Kentish, in a one-piece red swimsuit and a hair cap of the same colour that resembled an inverted flower, completed lengths of the pool. She swam purposefully and yet gracefully, easily beating Dominic over a length despite, seemingly, making no effort.

She'd declared, after the picnic lunch, that it was simply too hot to paint on, that she'd finish the painting later, that she'd welcome a cold drink and a swim, and so they'd packed up and walked back – down the hill, over the stream, through the wood, past the glass man and up, in the shade now – and into the village and into the bar, where it had taken them a moment for their eyes to adjust to the light. They had carried their cold drinks into the restaurant where they had persuaded Mr Kentish to leave his typewriter for the rest of the afternoon and

223

join them for a swim – once Mrs Kentish had deemed they had digested their lunch, of course.

Sebastian liked that, the family doing something together, all of them in the pool at the same time, his mother completing her lengths while his father, his brother and he just messed about, keeping cool in the pool's lightly chlorinated water. They paddled, floated, trod water, swam above and under water and threw insects and dead leaves from the pool onto the grass. They chatted to the other holidaymakers they had come to know, who would slink off their sunbeds and into the pool, like alligators in search of respite from the heat or, in the case of Renzo, of prey.

Renzo stood in the shallow end of the pool in the tightest, smallest swimming costume Sebastian had ever seen. It was grey and had a snake-skin pattern. Sebastian observed him watching his mother with a ruttish look on his face as she reached the deep end and kicked off, trailing her legs after her as she switched from the breaststroke to the crawl.

'She is your wife?' Renzo asked Mr Kentish. He was tanned like a walnut – wrinkly and brown – and skinny but wiry, with a hollow in his chest.

'She is,' said Mr Kentish. He leant against the side of the pool, his arms along it, the water up to his neck as he kept his legs bent and bounced gently off the bottom of the pool.

'She swims very beautiful,' said Renzo and sighed and slithered back to his sunbed.

Sebastian wished his father would show *some* ownership of his wife and was pleased when she swam back and into his arms and they embraced, momentarily. Dominic and he joined them.

'He's a creep,' said Sebastian. 'Did you see the way he was looking at Mum?'

'Lots of people look at Mum and who can blame them?' said Mr Kentish and his wife splashed him.

'The American does, doesn't he?' said Dominic.

'Yes,' said Mr Kentish, 'he does, but he looks at her a little differently.'

Jacqueline Kentish resumed her lengths.

NINETEEN

Bravo felt buoyant. He rarely swam and, on those occasions on which he did, it was out of a sense of obligation to take exercise or out of a need for a literal cleansing to help address the excesses of the night before. He had a mental picture of himself in water as a bobbing bottle of wine and as aquadynamic. Today was different, though. He swam as though swimming away from a past he was pleased to have left behind for a present he was happy to inhabit. Or away from a present that discomfited him into a future that would embrace him – he wasn't quite sure which, but it didn't matter. He felt better as he powered through the water, despite the drag of his belly, than he had in a long time, some time before he'd lost the naivety and innocence of his youth, his spiritual decline matching his physical deterioration. He'd been surprised recently, when he'd come across a book on Naples published shortly after the war, to recognise himself in one of the black and white photographs it contained in which he was slim, muscular and handsome, and dismayed to have been confronted with the evidence of the change in him. He knew that, once summer over, the first thing he would do on his return home would be to look through old photographs of him in the hope of seeing both Sebastian, who had his looks, and Dominic, who had his colouring, staring back at him.

Three more lengths of the cool water and one last session with Kentish. Kentish had made for an unexpected psychotherapist – no, Bravo had been his own psychotherapist, he realised. Kentish had been more of a priest, listening without passing judgement. Kentish and the swimming pool: confession and benediction.

Two more lengths. He'd been pleased to see Francesca serving at dinner. She'd had band-aids on her chin and forehead and a bruise around one eye but had insisted to Dario that she work. She hadn't discouraged people from praising Sebastian for having come to her succour (again much to the boy's embarrassment) and she had quietly, when fetching dishes in between courses, let him know that she knew she had him to thank and, so, thanked him for it. She had been so gracious and profuse in her expression of gratitude that he'd been moved and hadn't trusted himself to speak but then he'd been distracted by looking over to the Kentish's table and amused to find them all virtually asleep with their heads in their plates, or nearly. The heat and the exercise had taken their toll. Really, when would North Europeans learn that an after-lunch nap was *de rigueur* in an Italian summer?

One more length. As he swam it, he thought of an earlier evening's close, of the guitar-playing hippy providing the underscore to the flute playing of the young girl in the one spot of light in the darkness, her ethereal flute in the ancient village entrancing everyone but none as much as Dominic. The young boy, he thought, was in love without even realising it.

He leapt out of the pool nimbly, in his estimation, at least for someone of his age and bulk, and padded over to where his towel lay. He dried his hair and then, extending one leg at a time, placed his heels on a sunbed to save himself from having to bend over as he dried his blotchy, hairless legs. The Pompeos arrived, waved, showered and took to the water. They swam side by side at the same steady speed, with an economy of movement and without, somehow, leaving a wake behind them. Renzo, after the pretence of a shower, joined them. He was like an eel in the water and as brown as one.

Behind him Kees said, 'Wow, Bobby! You're so white. From a distance I thought you were wearing a T-shirt.'

Bravo considered the contrast of his outstretched hairless leg, a blotchy pink, and, protruding above it, his white belly. He was so infrequently out of a short-sleeved shirt that his torso never saw the sun and he, not owning a full-length mirror, never saw his full reflection in one. He tucked his chin into his neck and to better consider his shoulders and upper arms: white. He extended his forearms: a mottled light brown. His belly: a blinding white.

'And a good morning to you, Kees,' he said.

'An *excellent* morning!' Kees was even louder than usual. He disrobed violently and kicked his sandals off.

Bravo raised his eyebrows.

'Holland wins its first World Cup this evening,' said Kees, 'so a *beautiful* morning! A beautiful *day*!'

'Do you really think you'll win? The Argentinians have home advantage. That must count for something.'

'We beat Argentina four nil last time. In Gelsenkirchen. So,' Kees stroked his chin, 'maybe this time we'll win by just two goals. But we will win.'

. . .

Bravo suggested they walk unencumbered and Kentish acquiesced, saying that he'd return his cassette recorder and satchel to the apartment and would be back in a jiffy.

'A jiffy?' he asked, imagining Kentish in something resembling a colonial hat.

Kentish looked bemused. 'A moment.'

'Of course. Hold on.' Claudia was saying something. Bravo smiled. 'She's asking if, just one last time, you'd ask her a question from your phrase book.'

'Ha ha. Very funny,' said Kentish, smiling to show he'd taken the request in good humour but leaving, nonetheless, without doing so.

Bravo looked at Claudia and shrugged. He was pleased to discover an element of mischief in her. He was impressed with the way in which she scratched her cheek *through* her large gold earring that hung all the way down to her jaw. With her head at an angle, he reckoned she could bite the earring. He wondered if it would complicate things if he invited her out one evening. Had he, too, fallen in love without realising it? No, his asking the question precluded that.

He shoved his hands into the pockets of his shorts, felt something and withdrew the guest office key. 'I'll see you outside the *ufficio*,' he called after Kentish and walked slowly up the wide, sloping steps in the direction of the church. He could hear the voices of families at breakfast as he passed open windows. He stopped outside Francesca's office and listened as *Wasted Time* finished and *Victim of Love* began. He looked up for eagles above the church but couldn't see any.

Francesca stepped out of her little office.

'The guest office key,' he said, holding it out. 'Thank you. We won't be needing it anymore.'

Together, they looked down onto the square, already a little busy.

'Another fine day in paradise,' said Bravo.

'Oh, yes,' said Francesca.

'And how are you?' he asked, looking at her closely. The bruising on her cheek was now more yellow than blue.

'Oh, better, Bobby, thank you.' She smiled with difficulty and ran her fingers through her hair. Small cuts on her knees, he saw, had been treated with a blue-staining antiseptic.

They watched the Kentish family, Mrs Kentish addressing Claudia, Sebastian standing by the easel, Dominic shouldering a bag and Mr Kentish taking his leave of them.

'A very nice family,' said Francesca.

'Oh, yes,' said Bravo.

'Maybe Mr Kentish will read to us from his Italian book. *Ahia!*' she said, bringing her hand to her cheek. 'I mustn't laugh.'

'It's very nice to see you again,' said Mr Kentish, approaching. 'I'm very sorry we didn't have a chance to speak to you yesterday evening.'

'It was my fault. Please don't apologise. It was so busy and when I came to look for you, you had gone.'

'Yes. We were inexplicably tired. We turned in early. Anyway, we are very pleased that you weren't even more seriously hurt.'

'Well, now is my chance to thank you very much for helping me,' said Francesca and she stepped forward and, placing a hand on each shoulder, kissed him on both cheeks.

'Oh, it was nothing, nothing at all,' stammered Kentish, abashed and having to steady himself on the sloping cobbles by placing his hands on her waist.

'You saved my life! Both of you! *Ahia!*' Again, she brought her hand to her cheek.

Both men dismissed the expression of gratitude with a gesture of a hand.

'And Sebastian!' She waved to him down in the square, standing by the easel, his brother and his mother.

Sebastian and Dominic waved back. Mrs Kentish was expressionless behind her dark glasses.

'Come on,' said Bravo to Kentish. 'Let's walk.'

The two men followed a path that led down by the side of the church and cut back around the south of the village, Bravo leading. Glimpsed through olive trees and deciduous bushes and a long way below them to their right, the road wound its way like a grey ratsnake in the morning sun. Above them to their left, Colletta's tall stone walls appeared solid and impregnable. Like the glass sculpture of a man overlooking the pond in the wood, Bravo found the walls comforting, seeing in both the modern art and the ancient architecture fixed in the North Italian landscape something that spoke to the higher qualities of man.

Kentish had asked him how much of the year he spent in Colletta and he'd replied that he'd lived in Bologna for ten years now, not moving on once he'd finished his thesis and formally retired from the Agency but choosing to make Bologna his home. Colletta was where he chose to flee Bologna's soaring temperatures; he found the city uninhabitable in July and August. 'I hole up here in the winter too sometimes,' he'd added.

'How did you find this place?' asked Kentish. 'It's a little out of the way.'

'Through Joaquín.'

'Joaquín?'

'Joaquín. You may recall, I introduced you. A former

colleague. Well, kind of. We occasionally worked together. He works in the quarry you'll have passed on your way here.'

'So what are you going to do now?' asked Kentish, at the point at which the path bifurcated, down roughly hewn steps to Colletta Sottana to their right and up a grassy knoll ahead in the direction of the swimming pool.

'I should be asking you that question.' Bravo headed up and stopped by a gnarled, ivy-covered olive tree. 'How are you going to use what I told you? *Can* you use what I told you?'

'*Can* I?' exclaimed Kentish. 'God, yes! It's dynamite!'

Bravo grunted. Good. Kentish recognised he had a scoop on his hands. 'But you have just my word. No hard evidence. Isn't it all just circumstantial?'

'Leave the rest to me,' said Kentish, determinedly. 'I may need some corroboration on some points, but I know where to take this.'

Bravo extracted a switchblade knife from a pocket, set the lock and stepped up to the tree. 'Ivy,' he said. 'One day, ivy will take over the world. We shouldn't care but I do.' He began by cutting the ivy from around the tree and pulling its roots up. He hated the stuff. 'Ivy competes with the tree for nutrients, for light and water. It strangles the life out of it.'

'Oh, I don't know. It has its own root system,' said Kentish.

'You English like it, you cover your houses with it where it invades the mortar in between the bricks and sucks the moisture out of it and makes your homes unsafe. Where you see ivy and poetry, Italians see weeds and disease.' He was creating a pile of ivy roots, leaves and tendrils that he would have Giulio, the gardener, burn.

'Bacchus crowned himself in ivy.'

'Yes, the old soak.' Bravo was sweating now.

'In early Christian medievalism it was a symbol of the eternal life of the soul.'

'To my mind it's a symbol of corruption. It kills everything it touches in time.'

'I'm not sure that it does. It's also a symbol of love and friendship. Because it endures.'

'Because it remains green while the tree it clings to is dead, you mean. You think it pretty, beautiful even, but it administers a slow death, and it shelters, beneath these broad green leaves, rats and snakes.' Bravo held up a fist full of leaves and shook it. He threw the leaves on the pile and ran his arm across his brow. 'So what are you going to do with what I've told you?'

'I'll let you know. Very soon.' Kentish looked out over the road below. The *tuk tuk* of a farmer's three-wheeler Piaggio Ape on the road below grew louder and quieter.

'So you're not sorry that you came?'

'God, no!' Kentish laughed. He wore socks with his sandals. Without his satchel he no longer resembled a schoolboy so much as a professor – or an archaeologist; Bravo had once accompanied a party of archaeologists around Southern Italy.

'You might have to do more research. Stitch together what is publicly available. You'd be less at risk that way. The Pike Committee report would be a good starting point.'

'Indeed,' said Kentish. 'It's where I started. At risk?'

'You have your family to think about.' Bravo began to cut the ivy at about three feet up the tree's trunk and to strip the vines down carefully off the tree all the way back to its roots. 'The ivy I leave on the tree will die off in a month or two. If I were to pull it all off now, I'd risk damaging the bark.' He worked his way around the tree. When he finished it looked as though the exposed tree were wearing a pale sock. 'I don't mean to worry you unduly. But it should be quite clear to you that there are some parties that would rather remain in the shadows.'

'Thank you for your concern but I'm not worried,' said Kentish. 'At least, I don't think I am. I hope I'd never write anything to put my wife and children at risk. And you can be sure,' he added, 'that nothing I write will point the finger at you.'

'Oh, I'm past worrying about that.' Bravo closed his knife and indicated they resume their walk. From some distance above, came the sounds of children in the pool, splashing and joyous cries.

'I thought you'd have more questions for me,' said Bravo, his back to Kentish and his eyes on the grass verge as it narrowed. To their right was a long fall into bushes and brambles.

'I thought so too. I do, actually. But then, again, what would I do with your answers? Every day, as I typed our conversations up, I thought of one, principally: what has been your motivation?'

Bravo arched his eyebrows. 'I never realised you'd started typing them up. So you have everything in triplicate, in effect – the recordings, the notes and a transcript?'

Kentish nodded.

Bravo pointed to some more ivy-covered trees. 'More work for me,' he said. 'When I moved to Bologna, I rented a small flat in the town centre, but it was too noisy. And smelly. After a year, I bought a house in the *sobborghi* – the outskirts. An old villa with an ivy-covered garden. I think that's why I bought it, to rid the garden of ivy. You know, to tidy my own garden. To make my contribution to the world.' He laughed. It sounded ridiculous, even to him.

They reached the very far end of the village, past the pool and below it. Kentish followed Bravo up some steps onto the patio of a two-story cottage. The two wrought iron garden chairs and table beneath a thatched portico were identical to those outside the guest office.

'Welcome to my summer residence,' said Bravo, throwing his arms wide and bringing them down hurriedly, suddenly aware of just how much he'd been perspiring. 'Please sit down. I'll make us a coffee.'

He put the moka pot on to boil and changed his polo shirt. He placed two cups and saucers on a tray. From where he stood, he could see the back of Kentish's head and the split in the mountains where the valley led to the sea. By the wall of the house, behind Kentish, were three crates of empty wine and other bottles. Oh well, so what. Kentish probably hadn't noticed them. And so what if he had? Bravo looked around him. There were empty bottles indoors too and too few full ones. He hadn't meant to invite him to his home. It had just happened that way. Anyway, he wouldn't invite him *in*.

'It's quite a view you have here,' said Kentish, having thanked Bravo for the coffee.

'My motivation,' said Bravo. 'We've touched upon it. True, I attended the university in Bologna as a sleeper, an infiltrator, an informer – whatever – yes, but I was also pleased to be returning to university, to be studying again. There is indeed a sense in which education is wasted on the young. When young, so much of the philosophy we read had appeared dry and purely academic, and it was only later that I realised that it had a real and practical application.

'I had my thesis to pursue, yes, but I also had to attend the lectures that the young communists would attend and, incidentally, the opportunity of rediscovering some of the thinkers I had barely understood when an undergraduate.

'Take utilitarianism. As a young man, innocent of "life"' – he held his fingers up to symbolise the inverted commas – 'and death too, I suppose, I found this idea of the maximisation of utility or happiness seductive. But then I went back to Immanuel Kant.' He looked at his coffee cup and was surprised to find it already empty. 'I had found him difficult. Too distant, too far removed from my own experience. And then I went to war. Around me, people were making life and death decisions all the time. Literally so. A platoon is pinned down by enemy fire. Everyone in it is certain to die. Do you send a squad in from the flank to save the platoon if it means certain death for everyone in the squad? Of course you do. Ten lives versus fifty. Ten deaths, rather. As I said, it's a no-brainer. Lives are digits, interchangeable units. Company commanders play God. They don't play, they *are* gods. They decide who lives and who dies by means of the simple arithmetic of *for the greater good*. War reduces us all, simply, to a means to an end.

'We had a class on Kant in which the professor would like to pose the trolley problem. A trolley – or a train – is trundling along a track on which four men are working. The train is out of control and they haven't heard it coming. The only way to save the four men is to pull the switch lever to divert the train onto another track on which only one man is working. So you face a choice: do you take one life to save four or do you do nothing and watch four men die? What would you do, Peter?'

Kentish frowned and looked at the coffee grains in his cup for the answer. 'I don't know.'

'Don't think of there being a right or a wrong answer. Just think, what would you do?'

'I think I'd choose to save four lives.'

'You'd choose to take a life.' Bravo nodded. 'That is the reflex answer most people give on first being asked the question. I never *once* heard anyone argue for doing nothing. We were *all* communists in that class – well, utilitarians – with or without realising it. Happy to play God. Incidentally, there were few mature students; virtually all the students had been born after the war. And yet, these young people who had never actually experienced a war had no difficulty in reducing the individual to just another quantifiable unit, a means to an end.

'The thing is, once a war is over, we don't stop thinking that way, that way of thinking somehow imbues society. We claim to have fought for freedom, for the liberty of the individual against the tyrannical utilitarianism of communism – or socialism or fascism; the differences are minor – and what do we do? We come to justify to ourselves the murder of a small number of individuals for *our* greater good, *our* greater good being a democratic society in which the individual reigns supreme, one in which individual freedoms are held up as the ultimate prize. And we are blind to the irony of this, this violent, bloody elimination of some lives so that others might prosper. We fail to see that no-one's rights can be secured by the violation of the rights of others.

'I didn't see this at first. I was taken up in it all. The secrecy. The patriotism. The foreign countries. The intrigue.

'The Portella della Ginestra massacre? Ten people dead. So what? The assassination of 200 union leaders? The future of two million Sicilians was at stake. The smashing of the communists' march through Rome in '63? 200 injured? A small price to pay to secure the prosperous future of fifty million Italians. Twenty deaths from the bomb in the bank in Milan? The car bomb in Petano? The bombing in Brescia? The bomb in the Italicus Express? What's that – a hundred deaths? What's that compared to 170 million Western Europeans living in liberty, free to think what they want to think, to say what they want to say, to vote for whom they want to vote for?'

'Except,' said Kentish speaking slowly, 'they can't be said to be thinking what they want to think if you're influencing their newspapers, they can't say what they want to say if you're killing them for it, they can't vote for whom they want to vote for if you're rigging the voting system.'

'Of course. Believe me, it's been difficult to come to terms with the fact that I'd been living a lie and contributing to this logical contradiction.'

'Why did you? I mean, how come you did?'

'Like I said. Kant.' Bravo sighed. 'Kant argued at length that a man is an end in himself and cannot be reduced to a means to an end. I found the argument complex, but its conclusion touched a chord in me, more than it had when I'd read him as an undergraduate. I could only think, *but that's all I – that's all we – have ever done*. Our foreign policy has only ever seen individuals as dispensable means, to cajole, coerce or eliminate.'

'I understand,' said Kentish.

'What's the point of philosophy if it's not going to inform a life? If you don't take it out of the classroom?'

'And Moro?'

'*Pfff*. If it hadn't been him, it would have been someone else. You can call him the straw that broke this camel's back.'

'And was this gradual epiphany – if there is such a thing – painful for you?'

Bravo wasn't sure how to answer. He was afraid of examining the question too closely, of having to answer honestly. Was his intellectual position sincerely held and, if so, why had he only allowed himself to hold it so late in his career? Was he truly wedded to this principle of Kant's second categorical imperative or was it simply a marriage of convenience? Was he, simply, granting himself absolution and allowing himself the psychological comfort of the repentant sinner? He looked at Kentish looking out over the valley, his sandaled feet crossed at the ankles, his woolly socks pulled up his calves and a white short-sleeved shirt tucked into his cream-coloured shorts and wondered how it was that his country had been on the winning side of two world wars.

'Are you fully retired?' Kentish asked.

'Oh, they keep tabs on me. "Friends" drop by. Sometimes it's social. At other times, they might want to pick my brains about something.'

'I can see why you chose this spot,' said Kentish. It's almost as though, from here, you would see them coming.'

'Yes, probably, if we were living in a Western.' Bravo looked down the V of the valley, between the forested mountain sides in the direction of the Ligurian Sea.

'Are you married?' asked Kentish.

He wasn't surprised by the question. An American would have asked it on day one. 'No. I never married.' *But I may have a daughter*, he thought. *And grandsons.*

Kentish drank from his empty coffee cup and stood. 'Thank you for the coffee,' he said but made no move to go. He too looked out over the mountains.

'You are thinking.'

'Yes,' said Kentish, 'I am thinking how ironic it is that that which is most horrible in man should have been made known to me in a place that I find amongst the most beautiful known to man. It's been almost unbearably incongruous. I've never considered myself a political naïf and I don't think I am, but still. This is – you are – the closest I've come to the horror of the politics you've described to me.' He turned to look at Bravo directly. 'No offence.'

'None taken. You've lost your innocence.'

'Yes, even though I never thought I had it to lose.' Kentish sighed. 'We'll see you at dinner.'

'Yes, thank you. It's the final tonight. In a country in which thousands of people have been murdered by an unelected government sponsored and supported by my colleagues and my country, but never mind. We'll pretend it's just about the football.' Bravo would miss Kentish. Kentish had been the instrument of his catharsis. It had felt good to be able to unburden one's self, to take the lid off one's deep wells of disillusionment.

TWENTY

'I'm sorry, Peter,' said Jacqueline Kentish, putting her hand on his, 'but I do find it remarkable that we can get excited about the football this evening and ignore the desperation of so many thousands of Argentines.'

'Oh, I know,' said her husband. 'I'm with you there. And others are too.'

'Maybe tonight could provide us with a template for the future,' said Mrs Kentish, 'in which we could have disagreements between nations decided by football games rather than by wars.'

'Now that your father has retired from the army.' He gave her hand a squeeze.

'Or by chess,' said Sebastian.

'Or by swim-chess,' said Dominic.

Mrs Kentish raised her hand to her husband's cheek. 'You caught the sun this morning.'

'Probably caught when just standing there watching our friend cutting ivy,' mused Mr Kentish. 'He's joining us for dinner this evening, boys.'

'Mum said,' said Sebastian.

Mr Kentish considered his empty coffee cup. 'He made me a very good cup of coffee this morning.'

'You can finish mine,' said his wife, sliding her cup over to him. 'It's far too strong.'

'We've just finished our last lunch here,' said Dominic.

'It's going to be a long evening,' said his mother. 'We should take a leaf out of the Italians' book and go for an after-lunch nap. You don't want to sleep through the final, do you Dominic?'

Sebastian didn't think he'd fall asleep but he did, creasing the last few pages of his book as he turned in his sleep.

His morning had been a near repetition of the previous day's. He'd watched his mother add the last touches to her painting and, as he so often did, tried to understand the process whereby she'd decide a painting was finished. He couldn't. He'd once asked her why she never painted portraits and she'd replied, 'Because you can never really know someone,' and then he'd heard someone else ask her the same question and she'd said, 'Because I hate being stared at.' He thought both were true. He'd imagined himself painting Rosetta's portrait with a paint-brush and then just with his fingers and he'd fallen asleep.

He opened one eye and saw Dominic, on his side too, breathing deeply through his open mouth while the bell of the church in Vesallo, visible on the hillside behind him, struck the last of four dongs. The open window was a perfect square, inter-rupted by the diagonal of the hill – blue on green – and the church steeple a pale yellow rectangle bisecting the two. Sebas-tian liked the Russian abstract artists his mother had introduced him to.

Sebastian closed the apartment door behind him quietly. He

took the long way to the square, around the houses and down to the pool, even though he knew Rosetta wouldn't be there. It was to him as if the longer he took to find her the more delicious their reunion would be. Three young children were asleep on one sunbed in the shade while their sunburnt mother slept on another right next to theirs with an open magazine on her chest. Sebastian was reminded of a sow and her litter. The rhythmic *put put* of the pool's water filter motor made him realise that he no longer even heard the chatter of the cicadas. The glare from the stone walls, almost white in the bleaching sun, as he walked up from the pool was blinding. He passed the doctor's open window but couldn't see in and, closing his eyes for a dare, felt his way past the doors of the restaurant in the alleyway and the bar in the square, the stone rough against his fingertips. The silence – the absence of people – was almost audible. The sun on his uplifted face was like a warm, stifling cloth. It beat a red tattoo on his eyelids. He imagined the village inhaling and exhaling as it slept, the whole one living, breathing organism comprised of the many individuals asleep between its walls. He felt connected to them and to the thousands of people who'd lived here previously – shepherds, goatherds, farmers, cultivators – people with lives different to his but people who'd loved and desired too. He opened his eyes gradually against the glare and pressed his nose to the windowpanes of the door to the bar, his hands either side of his face. No-one. If Rosetta wasn't there, before her official time off of five to seven in the late afternoon, where could she be? He stood in the centre of the square and spun, nearly losing a flip-flop and getting dizzy as he did so. He stopped to listen to distant voices, a high, weak and whistled series of notes that sounded like *wip* and *wonk* and *wow* with a rising intonation. He shielded his eyes from the sun with one hand and looked up. Far, far above the church flew three eagles in a slow, lazy rotation, pinned like a mobile to the azure blue roof of the world.

Sebastian found himself at the foot of the stairs that led to Rosetta's and Francesca's apartment. He slipped his flip-flops off and, holding them in one hand, tiptoed silently up the stone stairs. He peered cautiously above the top step at a terrace empty of people. He took two more steps and looked in through the open, sliding glass doors at Francesca's sleeping form. No Rosetta. He resisted the crazy impulse to water the plants and made his way down again.

Voices from open windows indicated that people were waking from their siestas. Sebastian wandered slowly back in the direction of the bar but, on a whim, turned down an alleyway and headed in the direction of the public water troughs. An image came to him of Rosetta washing clothes there and beating them dry against the broad stone, much as he'd seen washerwomen in photographs in old history books, their bare arms wet below their rolled-up sleeves, their hair unpinned, their white teeth exposed as they gossiped and laughed, and their cleavages discovered as they bent to their task above the soap suds.

He stopped at the spot at which he'd had his first conversation with Rosetta, when he'd waited for his mother with her easel and Rosetta had appeared from behind the green door ahead of him. He didn't knock but tried the handle, opened the door and closed it behind him, leaning with his back to it while his eyes adjusted to the lack of light. Washing machines and tumble-dryers lined one wall and sinks were on the other. The air was warm and humid. Under the one dim lightbulb above an ironing board covered with bed linen stood Rosetta, the iron in her hand held in mid-air.

'Ha!' Sebastian was pleased to have found her, delighted to

have surprised her and happy to have noticed, before she'd had the chance of hiding it, that she was pleased to have been found. Rather unsuccessfully, he thought, she tried to scowl. 'We never finished that fight,' he said.

Rosetta pointed the flat of the iron in his direction and it released a hiss of steam.

Sebastian could tell from the way in which she cast her eyes about her that she felt trapped and he knew what maybe she didn't, that he was too much of a gentleman to press his advantage. Or not even that, perhaps – even a game of chess palls as soon as it is won. The door closed with his back to it was threatening, he knew. He opened it and let the sunlight in. 'I just thought I'd say hello,' he said.

She resumed her ironing. 'When I'm finished with this, perhaps you can help me,' and she pointed her chin at two plastic laundry tubs full of sheets, towels and table napkins that needed drying.

Together, they carried them up the staircase his mother had ascended nearly two weeks ago now, shaded winding stairs that twisted and turned and bifurcated up outdoor stairwells, each step getting narrower and taller the higher they went into the light.

'Hurry, you don't want your mother to see you with washing,' said Rosetta breathlessly, teasing him.

Sebastian wouldn't have cared.

They stepped into the sun and over a chain with a sign marked *Privato*, onto a terrace not overlooked by any window. Plastic-coated wires fixed in stone walls either side had brightly coloured clothes pegs on them that moved gently in the breeze, like polychrome sparrows on telephone wires. Sebastian sat on the parapet and looked out over the valley and road far below. To his left, he could just about make the swimming pool out through treetops and hear the cries of children playing.

'Careful,' said Rosetta as she began to hang the washing.

'How come your English is so good?' asked Sebastian.

'You only now think to ask? It's not that good, actually. I often have to think before I speak.'

'Most people do.'

She stuck her tongue out at him.

'But seriously.'

'My father's work. Latin America, in American and international schools. And then America. And now here.'

Sebastian wasn't really listening. He felt drunk at the sight of the moist tip of her tongue. Hers had been a thrilling gesture that spoke of a familiarity that had yet to be explored. She disappeared behind a sheet the colour of the now pale blue sky and he couldn't suppress a laugh. It was as if she'd simply vanished.

'What's so funny?'

He told her.

She re-appeared or, at least, her head and shoulders did. She had only a few more things left to hang. When she finished, he would stand, he would take her wet hands in his and bend his arms, bringing her close to him. He would dare her to stick her tongue out at him again. She had just two sheets left to hang.

Rosetta looked at him with her head to one side.

Sebastian thought he heard her name being called.

She walked to the top of the stairs. '*Qui su*,' she called down. 'Dario,' she explained to him. '*Vengo*,' she called back. 'Here.' She handed him the sheet. 'Can you please finish hanging these for me? He's panicking because it will be busy tonight. For the *finale*. Then maybe I see you after the dinner?' And she ran her finger along his cheek and disappeared down and out of sight.

. . .

The hubbub from the square reached the Kentishes through the open window. Sebastian stood with his hands in his pockets looking out. There was a tension in the air, a raised level of excitement and anticipation, that wasn't his alone, he knew, although, of course, not everyone had been promised an assignation with the most intoxicatingly beautiful girl in the world. Sebastian ran his finger along his cheek.

'Come on, Mum!' said Dominic. 'We don't want to miss kick-off!'

'We won't,' said his father, checking his watch.

'We won't,' said his mother, ready. She had taken longer than usual to dress for dinner but now stood before them in a white, beaded evening dress.

'Splendid,' said her husband, admiringly.

'Overdressed?'

'Oh no.' Mr Kentish was dressed in a white shirt and a blue linen suit, the jacket held over one shoulder.

She apprehended, Sebastian knew, the American joining them for dinner. He seemed excessively interested in her and yet bashful in her presence, which made her nervous. She had apprehended even more the negotiation of a price for her painting with Mr Pompeo and so had gifted the painting to the bar – or to the restaurant; Dario could decide where to hang it – as a way out of that difficulty. Sebastian found it endearing that that which made his mother appear aloof – her smart clothes, her formal dress – was, actually, a sign of her vulnerability, a self-defence mechanism.

'Let's go, then!' he said.

The little square was busier than they'd seen it yet, packed with locals and holidaymakers, most of whom they knew by sight now, though there had been some departures and some new arrivals. The Germans had gone but there were the

Langemensens engaged in a conversation with the Betters, shouting because they were standing in front of the television that already had the sound on high. Dario, Francesca and Rosetta ran in and out of the bar, their arms laden with food and drink.

The Kentishes made their way past television images of the Estadio Monumental in Buenos Aires to their table where a place had been added and the American was waiting for them. He stood, looking smarter than Sebastian had seen him previously, in tan chinos, a long-sleeved blue shirt and a dark blue pullover draped over his shoulders. His white hair, oiled and combed back, showed streaks of silver. He held a chair out for Mrs Kentish while saying, 'Peter, I thought I'd leave you to take the head of the table.'

'Can *I* sit there please, Dad?' asked Dominic excitedly and his father allowed him to, good humouredly, understanding he'd have the best view of the television. Dominic, visibly chuffed, took his seat and then asked, 'Is everyone drunk? Already?'

Mr Kentish and the American laughed.

'They're just excited,' said Mrs Kentish, 'about the football. Like you.'

Francesca, bearing faded bruises and still wearing plasters, brought them water and wine and beers for Sebastian and the American.

'What a beautiful dress!' said Francesca to Mrs Kentish who smiled, as though to say she knew it was.

Sebastian and the American clinked bottles in an action Sebastian knew his mother would consider familiar. He didn't like that feeling of seeing things – of judging himself – through his mother's eyes.

Dominic threw his chair back and looked down at his feet. 'It's the wasps,' he said.

'That's okay,' said the American. 'It's nearing sunset. They're just making their way home.'

They watched the wasps buzzing around the hollow cross-pieces that held the table legs in place. The wasps flew in a diminishing concentric formation and entered their nest one by one.

Dominic resumed his seat warily.

'*Allora.*' Dario arrived with an enormous platter of Parma ham and figs, some whole, some quartered. Sebastian couldn't tell if it was an odd quality of the evening light, but his shoes appeared newly polished and his hair only recently oiled; Dario was shiny at two ends connected by a sparkling silver belt buckle half-way between them. He poured Dominic a glass of water and Mr and Mrs Kentish a glass of red wine each.

'We were thinking,' said Mr Kentish looking from his wife to Dario, 'that we'd start with some white.'

'No,' said Dario sternly.

They had come to know Dario and laughed politely, as if in on a joke.

Dario dropped his head into his shoulders and raised his hands. 'Is *prosciutto di Parma*. With figs. You can't drink white.' He pointed at the bottle of red. 'Is a Sangiovese, young, from Tuscany. Trust me, Peter.' He placed a hand on Mr Kentish's shoulder and lifted Sebastian's empty wine glass in the other.

'He's right, you know,' said the American.

'Thank you,' said Dario, holding the glass as if in a toast and looking around the table, 'for holidays with us here and for saving the lives of our staffs.' He winked at Sebastian. 'Signora,' he bowed to Mrs Kentish, 'last but not by importance, thank you for the painting of our lovely village. We put it in the restaurant in the prime position in memory of you. And you will see it when you return next year for holiday.'

The Kentishes reciprocated with thanks of their own, having to raise their voices above the chatter in the square.

Dario removed his lighter from his shirt sleeve and lit the candles on the table. He held the flame in front of Dominic for him to blow out.

The platter passed from Mrs Kentish to the American to Mr Kentish to Sebastian who placed it between him and Dominic and the two of them looked down on the reddish purple of the meat and of the fig flesh, and on the glistening white of the meat fat and of the fruits' seeds.

Dominic shooed an interested wasp away from the figs and shuddered.

The American leant forward and held a fig up. 'Did you know that figs are in fact flowers? Inverted flowers, flowers turned in on themselves? Look.' And he tore open the fig and held its centre up so that, indeed, it resembled a flower with four petals. 'And did you know that without wasps, you wouldn't have figs?'

'No!'

The American talked while the family ate.

'This is a cycle, you know. Figs, if not pollinated, will not develop but will shrivel and drop off a tree, still immature. When a fig is ready to be pollinated, it emits volatile compounds that are attractive to female wasps who home in on the chemical signal and enter the fig here.' He picked another fig up from his plate and pointed at its base. 'Here, is a very small hole, a tiny opening, the only way in. She'll force her way in, losing her wings and antennae as she does so, but she won't need them again. Once in, she'll do two things. First, inadvertently, she'll pollinate the flowers in the fig with the pollen that she's brought in from the outside from another fig. And then, obeying her biological imperative, she'll lay her eggs in the fig and die. The wasp larvae will feed on the fig to grow and, once fully grown, they'll mate.' He paused and took a mouthful of Parma ham. His mother disapproved, Sebastian knew, of a person speaking with his mouth full. 'The male will chew a way through the fig wall and die but not before having created that escape route for the female. She, carrying pollen from the fig she was born in, will fly off to find another fig tree and so the cycle continues.'

But that's incest, thought Sebastian, *in a fig.*

'So a fig,' said the American, now chewing on one, 'is a microcosm of our society – sex and sacrifice, love and death in a universe that fits in the palm of your hand.' He swallowed and then placed another fig in his mouth whole.

Sebastian was never comfortable when sex was mentioned in front of his parents.

'That's disgusting,' said Dominic examining the fig quarters on his plate and moving them about with his fork. 'So, really, we're eating dead wasps.'

'Well, yes and no,' said the American, swallowing again. 'An enzyme in the fig breaks the wasps' bodies down and the fig absorbs them by the time it is sufficiently ripe to eat.'

'How is it that you know so much about figs?' asked Mrs Kentish.

'I have fig trees in my garden in Bologna,' said the American. 'I spent two years liberating them from ivy. Besides, I like figs and I find that when I recount these fig facts to people they tend to leave their figs for me to eat. I'm joking,' he added.

Joke or not, Sebastian thought he wouldn't have any more figs and decided that he was saving himself for the courses to follow.

'They're coming out!' said Dominic and all eyes turned to the television, to Buenos Aires where the Dutch team slouched onto the pitch of the Estadio Monumental, casually and in ragged formation.

The Dutch cheered and everyone in Colletta's square stood taller, and the diners on the terrace angled their chairs to better see the television in anticipation of the imminent kick-off.

Sebastian caught Dominic's eye. There, at the back of the square, was the Argentinian in jeans, jean jacket and cowboy boots again, and either side of him stood two younger men, equally swarthy, with long unkempt hair and dressed in checked shirts and jeans.

'You're not finishing the figs? You didn't like them?' Francesca raised her eyebrows in surprise as she cleared the table of the *antipasto*.

Sebastian turned his head to the sound of booing. Kees and Anouk Langemensen were following the lead of the Dutch supporters in the stadium, their hands megaphones at their mouths. Anouk, Sebastian now noticed, was even more tanned than her husband, and blonder, which made it seem as though she were wearing a wig.

'Boo!' The other Dutch joined in.

'What's going on?' asked Mrs Kentish.

'The Argentinian team isn't coming out.'

'Pure gamesmanship.'

'They should have walked out together.'

'Look at the pitch! It's covered!'

'Toilet paper!'

'Ticker tape. Confetti.'

The Argentinian fans in the stadium were now making more noise than the Dutch. 'Argentina! Argentina!' The delay of their team's appearance was whipping them into a frenzy.

'The Dutch are going back in!'

'No! Argentina is coming out now!'

The Argentinian moved his knife from a trouser pocket to a breast pocket and ran his hands through his thick hair.

Rosetta brought bowls and a large serving dish of pasta in a basil and tomato sauce to their table and returned with a cheese grater and a chunk of parmesan the size of the grater. She had her hair tied in a denim strip of cloth and wore cowboy boots and a mid-thigh denim dress buttoned up the front, a combination Sebastian found exhilarating. The American requested some wine from Rosetta and offered to serve the pasta.

The noise level increased.

Sebastian was surprised to see Anouk shouting at the television. She was even more taken up by it all than Kees.

'What's happening now?'

'The Dutch are furious because the Argentinians are complaining that one of the Dutch players is wearing a plaster cast.'

'But that's ridiculous.'

'He has a broken bone in his wrist.'

'He's been wearing one since the Iran game and no-one has objected.'

'This has been planned. Orchestrated. Rehearsed.'

'Cynical gamesmanship.'

'Surely any legitimate concerns would have been voiced to FIFA before the game?'

'The Dutch are going to walk off!'

'Where's the referee from?'

'He's Italian!'

'Italian! Hey, Dario, what do you make of that?'

'I don't believe it. The ref's insisting he put a bandage over the cast.'

'Huh. What difference will that make?'

'It's already made a difference. Look at the Dutch. They're

freaking out. They've lost their cool, their concentration. Mission accomplished.'

Dominic left his seat to stand by Anouk.

Kees clenched his fists and went to speak to the Argentinian. The Dutchman kept his face in front of the Argentinian while gesticulating in the direction of the television. The Argentinian said nothing but looked at him contemptuously before fixing his eyes on the screen.

When the game finally started, it was brutal. The Dutch players were angry and didn't trouble to disguise it, but the Argentinian players, with the backing of a hysterical home crowd, were more than ready for any physical confrontation. The Dutch had the better of the dour early stages, but then the Argentinians steadied themselves and gradually came back into the game.

Clifford sat down in Dominic's vacant chair without waiting for an invitation and puffed his cheeks out. 'What a match! It's vicious!'

'What we're seeing,' said the American, helping himself to more wine, 'is a contest between soccer as it's played in Europe and soccer the Latin-American way. The Dutch, in common with most Northern Europeans, regard a two-footed challenge and the tackle from behind as fair so long as the ball is somewhere in view.'

'Absolutely right,' said Clifford. 'But the Argentinians, like all South Americans, see it as a crime!' He took a swig from a bottle of beer.

The American nodded. 'Yet the cynical, off-the-ball tripping and elbowing so popular among the Latin nations are anathema to the Dutch.'

'Not to mention the diving!' said Clifford. 'It's been effective, though. I can't believe how the refs buy it! They're so easily conned.'

'They're so impressionable,' said Peter Kentish, making his contribution. 'This one's not so bad, though.'

'What?' Clifford choked on his beer. 'Hey! Kees! What do you think of the ref? Kees,' said Clifford addressing the table again, 'has had something to say about the Italian referee to Dario every time Dario has walked past him. He's been awful. I mean look at that!'

To the despair of the Dutch, the Italian referee awarded the Argentinians a disputed throw-in from which they scored. The neutrals applauded. The Argentinians in Buenos Aires went berserk. The Argentinian in Colletta allowed himself a brief smile but the two younger men either side of him cheered and hugged each other and Sebastian noticed that Dominic, standing by Anouk who had her head in her hands, had also been looking at them. So they were Argentinian too.

At half time Francesca and Rosetta brought them Florentine steak and Clifford stood to cede his place to Dominic, called back to the table by his mother. Sebastian reached for his beer just as Rosetta was placing a dish on the table, so his arm brushed against hers.

'Peter, I'm sorry but the referee is absolute rubbish,' said Clifford before joining Eva in the square, dashing Sebastian's hope that his father's remark had been forgotten. 'And the linesmen. I bet they've been thrown a bung.'

'They've been terrible,' said Dominic scornfully, as if doubting that anyone could have said otherwise.

'Just look at that,' said Sebastian, keen to move the conversation on. In the middle of the table were a salad bowl of tomatoes and rocket and a platter on which sliced, marbled rib-eye steaks had been seasoned with pepper, rock salt and lemon. The heady, fatty smell of the meat invaded Sebastian's senses, the way in which the smell of Obélix's roast wild boar in the Astérix books meandered through the air and split in two just below Obélix's nose before entering each nostril. He was amazed to find he was starving.

'Did your mother cook in Indochina?' the American asked Mrs Kentish. He had some meat fat on his chin.

'I don't know. I doubt it.'

'I meant, did she cook Asian food at home ever? When you were growing up. Presumably not. This steak has made me think of the meat in the street markets there.'

'It makes me think of the grilled meats in the markets in *Alger* and in the Pieds-Noirs cafés in France because of the salt and the lemon. But it's not fine steak like this they serve there but everything that the rich don't eat – what's it called?'

'Offal,' said Mr Kentish.

'Yes. Hearts, liver, *reins*.'

'Kidneys.'

'Yes, kidneys, that kind of thing. On a stick. Barbecued.'

Dario placed more wine and beer on the table. '*Tutto a posto?*' He was querying Mrs Kentish's empty plate.

Mrs Kentish placed her hand on her stomach. 'But it was lovely,' she said.

Sebastian held his plate out for more.

'And what about you, young man?' The American held his wine glass out to Dario while looking at Sebastian.

Sebastian was surprised to be asked. 'What kind of meat does this remind me of?'

'No.' The American wiped his chin with his napkin. 'What happens next? In your life.'

Sebastian looked at his parents, as though they might have

the answer. 'Well, two more years of school. And then university I suppose.'

'To study – what?'

'Politics.' *History of art*, he'd wanted to say but was afraid that the American might be one of those people who looked upon that course of study contemptuously. Anyway, he did want to know more about what was happening in Argentina and why the world tolerated it. He filled his mouth with meat. At least that would give him time to think if he were asked another question. The sensations of the salt and fat on his tongue, the tender, almost butter-like texture of browned beef between his teeth and the sweet and bitter tastes of the meat and lemon juice made him think he might be having a religious experience. He thought of Rosetta and of their meeting later with impatience.

Half-time had brought a brief respite from the tension of the match. Night had completely fallen and in the candles' and television's patchy light, people appeared to be life-sized cardboard figurines. In the square, diners were eating with plates on their laps while others stood with drinks in their hands. In one corner, the Dutch stood despondent, holding bottles of beer and smoking. In another, the three Argentinians sat, bringing pieces of bread and steak to their mouths with their hands, glasses of wine at their feet. The Romanos and the Cespuglios sat or stood around the up-turned barrel halves, precarious rustic tables on the cobbles. Clifford had joined Eva, the Pompeos and some friends at a table at the other end of the terrace.

'They're coming out again,' said Dominic, as Francesca cleared their plates and brought cherry *semifreddo* for dessert.

'Only the Dutch are,' said Sebastian, as the Dutch players assumed their positions. The Argentinian half of the pitch remained empty of players, resembling a chess board when only one set of pieces had been put out. Sebastian sat forward in his seat. 'Look!' he said to Dominic. 'Kees is going bonkers! Ah, here are the Argentinians. This is nice. What is it?'

'Think of it as an ice cream,' said the American helpfully.

'You can have mine,' said Dominic to no-one in particular, pushing his chair back and nudging his mother's elbow so that some cherry *semifreddo* from her spoon fell on her white dress.

'Dominic!'

'Sorry, Mum!' He left the table to go and stand by the Dutch again.

Mrs Kentish soaked a napkin in water and dabbed her dress with it, succeeding only in smearing the red stain like a wound about her waist.

The second half was more open than the first, the Dutch attacking in waves and the Argentinians counter-attacking with long balls. The crowds in Buenos Aires and in Colletta grew quieter as the tension grew. Passes went astray and substitutions were made by both teams. A Dutch player was shoulder-charged to the ground in the Argentinian penalty area.

Kees threw his hands up in the air. 'Penalty! A blatant foul! The referee ignored it completely!' He and Anouk shook their fists at Dario who brought his fingers and thumbs together in supplication and looked around them for moral support – the referee may be Italian but he, Dario, was not the referee!

It was strange, thought Sebastian, that the Dutch were so much more demonstrative than the Argentinians in the square who, with the exception of the goal celebration, had remained quiet. His mind drifted from the game as he looked around him. Italians, Dutch, British, other North Europeans – and the American and the Argentinians, of course. Colletta was the world in microcosm, people from various countries united in an isolated village the size of a football pitch by their love of sun, good food and, well, he wasn't sure how to put it, similar cultural norms based on hospitality, good manners and friendships. And French! He'd forgotten his mother, born in Indochina and brought up in Algeria and France. France's role as the colonial power in those countries left him uncomfortable; he'd only recently begun to wonder what part his grand-father – rising from *lieutenant*, through *capitaine*, *commandant* and *colonel* to *général de corps d'armée* – had played in those countries' histories. Wanting to know more about Vietnam – and Algeria, where his maternal family had spent so much of their lives – Sebastian had asked questions of his mother, who'd answered in generalities, and of his father, who'd answered with chilling stories about isolated incidents, such as the massacres of civilians by the French in My Trach in Vietnam and in Sétif in Algeria, none of which delivered a complete picture of the wars and the motives for them and all of which just irritated his mother. Sebastian had stopped asking.

There was an explosion of noise in the square: the Dutch had equalised. Sebastian stood to watch the replay, a perfect cross met by a majestic leap and a forceful header.

And then a gasp: the Argentinian captain punched a Dutch player with a right hook and floored him. And the referee didn't whistle. No-one could believe it. Kees held his arms outstretched and his mouth formed a perfect O. His blond hair stuck out from beneath his cap like straw. In the weak light, he resembled a scarecrow.

Anouk addressed the Argentinians in the square in Dutch and approached them to better listen as one of them spoke to her in measured tones. She threw her hands in the air and rejoined her husband.

The Dutch team doctor saw to the player, prone on the pitch.

'They've used their two substitutes. He'll have to play on,' said Dominic, and then, after play had resumed and the full-time whistle blew, 'Extra time!'

The diners left the terrace and congregated shoulder to shoulder in the square while Francesca and Rosetta blew candles out and cleared the tables. Dario served *digestivi* and beers. Sebastian found himself standing next to Mrs Better who asked him how he was enjoying the game.

'It's certainly exciting,' said Sebastian, aware that his mind had been elsewhere through much of the second half of the game. 'I've no idea who'll win in extra time.'

'Who do you want to win?'

'Oh, Holland, of course. I think,' he added.

'If it's still a draw at the end of extra time,' said Dominic authoritatively, 'there'll be a replay on Tuesday.'

Dominic tugged Sebastian's elbow. The Argentinian was arguing again with Rosetta, her hands full with dirty plates and dishes, while the two young men stood close, either side of her. One of them placed a hand on her arm and spoke quietly to her. The Argentinian fiddled with his Opinel knife, holding it as if weighing it, opening and closing it before slipping it into his shirt pocket and patting it. Rosetta, clearly tiring of holding the stack of crockery, tossed her hair back and strode into the bar.

'I wish they'd just leave her alone,' said Sebastian.

'Did you see he's got his knife with him again!'

'So what? He's got an Opinel knife. So have I – so have you!'

Dominic was visibly hurt.

'Sorry.' Sebastian put his arm around his brother and gave him a squeeze. He recognised that while he'd grown out of a fascination with knives, his younger brother hadn't. He helped him onto the stone ledge so he could stand and have a clear view of the television. The American, who now stood unsteadily with a glass of wine in one hand and a glass of grappa in the other, shuffled aside to make room for them.

Sebastian suddenly lost interest in the final. It was funny, he knew the game was exciting but he knew with a profound certainty that where he wanted to be at that very moment was wherever Rosetta happened to be. 'I'll be back in a moment,' he said. He walked past and around the back of the crowd, behind the Dutch who had decided they'd stand in a line for extra time, their arms across each other's shoulders, and into the bar.

'Hello,' he said to Claudia who was washing glasses behind the counter. 'About that walk,' he said to Rosetta.

'Wait,' she said, disappearing down the steps into the kitchen. Reappearing, she said, 'Give me five minutes.'

'Who are those men? The ones that were bothering you. What do they want?'

'They want me to go with them,' said Rosetta, 'after the match.'

'Go with them? Where?' Sebastian's nostrils flared.

Rosetta looked at him as though he were an idiot. She placed her hand on his arm. 'Five minutes. By the *abbeveratoi* – you know, where the water is. Behind the bar.'

Sebastian found Dominic. 'Listen,' he said. 'I'm going to go for a walk with Rosetta. She's keen to get away from – you know – the Argentinian and his friends.'

'Are they after her?' Dominic looked at him and opened his eyes wide.

'Yes. But don't tell Mum. If she asks, say I've gone to bed.'

Sebastian made his way down the path and alleyway behind the bar that had become so familiar to him. Just fifty yards from the square, it was to him as though he'd travelled back to an earlier age, one that preceded electric lights and television, one in which only the eternal constants of love and desire were present. He kicked a stone, thinking that he should be kicking himself. Two weeks had flashed by and he was only now making a move! He couldn't understand what had come over him. The heat and the magic of the idyll he'd spent those weeks in had lulled him into inertia. He'd started to take her daily presence for granted and now wondered if he could bear a separation from her. He stood by the water troughs and looked out over the service road into the valley. They could always write to each other, he supposed. He heard applause from the square and assumed that Argentina had scored. Had it been Holland, the Dutch would have made a lot more noise. Turning his head at the sound of steps, he saw Rosetta approaching him, clutching a cardigan about her shoulders.

'Was that a goal?' he asked.

'Yes.'

'Argentina?'

'Yes.' She pulled the denim ribbon from her hair and shook her head and took him by the arm.

TWENTY-ONE

Bravo felt a social obligation to watch extra time with Mr and Mrs Kentish because they'd invited him to dinner, and he thought it rude to desert them once the meal was over. But he'd drunk too much and wanted to sit down. He waved a cigarette he'd borrowed from Dario at them, as if to explain that he was doing them the courtesy of distancing himself so he could smoke without disturbing them. Having made room for Dominic to stand on the stone ledge he was sitting on, he considered the boy's sandaled feet as he lit the cigarette. Next to him there, Bravo experienced a joy that was all the sweeter for its being momentary and for his inability to share it.

Bravo inhaled and caught the eye of Joaquín who only narrowed his eyes for a fraction of a second in salutation. His sons looked at him and nodded just perceptibly, politely.

It would be difficult for Joaquín, he knew. Joaquín had told him of the *Escuela de Mecanica de la Armada,* now a detention and torture centre, barely a half-hour walk from the *Estadio Monumental,* where the screams of unionists, left wing activists and students being tortured merged with the roars of the crowd

in the stadium. Joaquín was a patriot – or at least he had been.
He knew that the sole purpose of the World Cup was, as far as
the junta was concerned, to deliver legitimacy to an unconstitu-
tional, brutal military government. He had placed his head in
his hands and said, 'For our junta generals, Western civilization
is in decay, it's on the brink of destruction – and they want to be
its moral saviours. Its moral saviours!' He had spat. For Joaquín,
a passionate supporter of his national football team born after
Argentina's only other appearance in a World Cup final, the
desire to see Argentina lift the trophy was matched only by the
horror of the thought of Videla's handing it to them. 'Either way,
I lose.' Like him, Joaquín had lost his faith.

In the second half of extra time, the match risked
descending into anarchy but there was some excellent football
in between the fouls. Possession of the ball was lost and
regained with increased frequency as the players tired and
passes went awry. And then Argentina scored. The cheer
roused Bravo from his reflection. He'd been falling asleep. The
Italians in Colletta applauded, admiring the goal, but, with little
invested in the outcome, he guessed that their thoughts were by
now also of bed and sleep. The Dutch bubble, already punctured, deflated completely. '*Ja, dat is het*,' said Kees despon-
dently, turning his back on the television. Joaquín's smile
resembled a grimace. His sons embraced.

Bravo pulled on his cigarette to keep it alight.

Kentish sought him out. 'Now, that was an excellent goal,'
he said.

'Indeed,' said the American.

'I'm glad you agree,' said Kentish.

When the final whistle blew Dario appeared with *digestivi*
on a tray and Argentina's victory was toasted. Bravo took a glass,
thinking the act of drinking would help him stay awake. As he

knocked his grappa back, he caught sight of Joaquín and his boys leaving, surreptitiously, around the side of the bar and down the path that would take them to the troughs and, from there, the long way around to the car park. He wasn't surprised: it wasn't like Joaquín to stay behind and gloat.

The Italians praised the Dutch team and everyone said that it had been a very close contest; the Langemensens and the other Dutch were grief-stricken, which evoked a desire in the locals to comfort them.

Dominic jumped off the ledge and stood among them. 'Hard luck,' he said. 'You really should have won.' Bravo thought that the young boy got by by imitating adults. He was clever, Bravo thought proudly.

Mrs Kentish stood by her husband, wearing his jacket over her shoulders.

'At what time will you be leaving?' he asked, not trusting himself to stand.

'Mid-morning, I suppose,' said Kentish. 'Breakfast, load the car and go.'

He looked up at the cloudless night sky. 'You'll have a clear run of it,' he said. 'Lyon?'

'Yes. Seven hours including a lunch stop.'

He threw his cigarette butt to the ground and watched the Kentishes enter into conversation with the Betters and the Pompeos. Snatches of conversation in Dutch, English and Italian about football and art reached him as though from a jumble of radio stations. The effect of the multi-lingual non-sequiturs was not altogether unpleasant; it was rather amusing. He closed his eyes.

'To be fair, if the Dutch had played the ball and not the man...'

'So, who is your favourite artist?'

'To be defeated finalists two World Cups in a row... It must be hard to take.'

'You must admit, Italian artists are the best.'

'Where is Sebastian?'

'He was around somewhere.'

'Dominic, where is Sebastian?'

'I'm not allowed to say,' said Dominic.

'Don't be ridiculous,' said his mother.

'He's gone to bed,' said Dominic.

'Why wouldn't you be allowed to say that he's gone to bed?' asked his father.

Through half-closed eyes, Bravo looked where Dominic was looking, over his shoulder through the thinning throng of holidaymakers and locals who, now that the World Cup final was over, were handing their empty glasses to Dario, stretching and yawning and saying goodbyes, to where the Argentinians had stood.

'He's taken Rosetta somewhere safe,' said Dominic conspiratorially.

'Somewhere safe? Safe from what?'

Again, Dominic looked around him. 'You know the Argentinian, the man with the knife? Well, he's after Rosetta.'

'Where is he?' said Mrs Kentish, looking around her too.

'He's gone after them,' said Dominic.

Mrs Kentish squatted and took her son by the shoulders. 'I hope you're not being silly.'

'I'm not! I promise!'

'Right,' said Mrs Kentish standing up, holding her husband's jacket tight around her. 'Do something,' she said to her husband.

'What?' Mr Kentish looked around helplessly.

Mrs Kentish emitted an exasperated *pfff*. 'Dominic, run to

the apartment and see if he's there. If he's not, look for him in Rosetta's apartment. Hurry.'

Bravo had followed the Kentishes' discussion as though through a fuzzy membrane, the mother's anxious pitch of voice reaching his ears like static from a radio programme broadcast somewhere far away. He heard Clifford offering to help Dario move the television back in, the deeper, measured voice sounding nearer. He wasn't asleep. It may look to others as though he were sleeping but he wasn't, he knew he wasn't, he was just sitting in the cooling midnight air, his eyes closed and his head on his chest, drooling only a little. He could stand up if he wanted to, in fact, that's what he would do, he would leap up and exclaim, laughing, that Sebastian and they had no reason to fear Joaquín at all, not at all, because... He took a deep breath and fought the weight of his eyelids.

Dominic reappeared in the square, panting. 'He's not there.'

'Not where?'

'Not anywhere. Not in the apartments,' said Dominic excitedly.

Bravo, at risk of falling forward and off the stone seat, leant back and hit the back of his head against the stone, hurting himself a little. A stupid thing to have done. He should have known better. He'd been snoring, he knew. He wiped his mouth with the back of his hand.

'Right,' said Mrs Kentish. 'Dario.'

'*Signora.*' Dario watched as Claudia and Francesca took in the last of the empty glasses and coffee cups into the bar. He made as though to light a cigarette and stopped.

'You need to organise a search party.'

Dario lifted his hand as if to place it on Mrs Kentish's shoulder and then lowered it, as if thinking better of it. 'Mrs Kentish, what have you lost?'

'Sebastian. He's not here.'

Dario looked from Mrs Kentish to her husband.

'Back me up, Peter.'

'He's probably in the apartment,' said Dario, waving an unlit cigarette.

'He's not. He's not in her apartment either.'

'Whose apartment?'

'Hers. Rosetta's.' Mrs Kentish spoke through her teeth.

'Why would he be there?'

'You need to organise a search party.'

'I see,' said Dario. 'Francesca, do you know where is Rosetta?'

Francesca shook her head.

'Mrs Kentish, why are you so worried? Just two lovers –'

'Don't make fun of me.' Mrs Kentish raised her voice. 'Don't try to make light of the situation.'

Bravo pitied Dario. The day of the World Cup final had been a long one and tomorrow, that would bring departures and new arrivals, would be the busiest day of the week.

'For God's sake, say something, Peter.'

'Well,' said Kentish.

'Tell him, Dominic, tell Dario what you told me.'

Dominic was very happy to do so. 'You know the man who was here, the man with the knife? Well, he's out to get Sebastian.'

'What does it mean, to "get" Sebastian? Why does he want to "get" Sebastian?'

'Because he wants to get Rosetta.'

'Who wants to get Rosetta?'

'Oh, for God's sake,' said Mrs Kentish.

'The man with the knife,' said Dominic.

'What man with a knife? There was fifty people here

tonight! I can't watch everybody! I saw no-one with a knife! Only the diners...'

Dominic held his hands out exaggeratedly. 'It's this big!'

'*Mon Dieu!*' said Mrs Kentish. 'Dario, we have no time to lose!'

'But *Signora* –'

'If you won't help, I'll call the police.'

It was remarkable, thought Bravo, how perfectly one could see through closed eyelids. Dario, he believed, had accepted the fact that he would get no sleep until Sebastian and Rosetta had been found and so had taken action, mobilising a search party equipped with torches, and pointing the tired and yet willing mix of locals and tourists in different directions: the path to the stream; the path to Colletta Sottana; the area by the swimming pool; the service road; the main road; the fig and cherry orchard; the area behind the church.

There was something Bravo wanted to tell them all but he couldn't remember what it was.

TWENTY-TWO

Sebastian and Rosetta tramped up the service road, past Colletta's shuttered windows and banks of lavender that, in the dark, gave itself away by its sweet smell. Far below, the river ran silver in the moonlight alongside the gleaming, winding main road. Across the valley, dark purple mountains butted their tops against a black sky pierced with white stars. They entered the yellow light cast by the last of the boundary-marking globular lamps and heard the quiet drumming of the beating wings of moths and night beetles against its glass and stopped to watch the desperate insects, Sebastian shuffling the corpses of species of insects that he'd never seen before with the toe of a white plimsoll. They resumed their walk, holding hands now, following their lengthening shadows into the night along the white ribbon of the chalky gravel road, lit, once their shadows had vanished, only by a perfect half-moon. The sounds of rushing water and the rhythmic crunch of Rosetta's cowboy boots on the unmade road were constants, giving Sebastian the illusion that they were making no progress and would never reach anywhere. He imagined that just up ahead an invisible hand was unwinding the road like a cotton thread while an unseen accomplice behind them wound it up again. One of his plimsolls began to squeak with each step, which he found embarrassing until Rosetta giggled.

On reaching the road that had led him to Colletta two weeks ago and that would lead him from it tomorrow, they turned left and down, down past the hollows that the wind had, over millennia, shaped out of the soft rock face. Rosetta slipped her hand from his and he felt its absence, the cool air on his palm, the moisture from hers evaporating from his as she ran and stood where he couldn't see her in the middle of the largest, deepest cave and hollered, 'Oo-ee! Aa-oo!' Her voice was deepened, rounded, scooped up by the cave and hurled at the mountains across the valley that flung it back at them, 'Oor-eer! Aar-oor!'

Sebastian joined her and howled, his hands cupped around his mouth, and Rosetta barked and the mountains howled and barked and laughed with them, making them laugh even harder.

They descended, stamping militarily, Rosetta kicking her heels and sparking the Segs on her boots against the road, until they came to the main road where two houses stood like sentinels at the turning. One was in darkness but the other, an *osteria*, had lights on in a sitting room on the ground floor where a television showed the conclusion of the World Cup. They stopped and looked in. Framed by the house's dark stucco, the picture was like an extended family portrait of a dozen or so people of three if not four generations arrested in the moment of watching the celebrations in Buenos Aires. So Argentina had won. Sebastian wasn't that bothered. He had the sentiment that he alone was in possession of an important underlying truth that others were overlooking, namely, that who won didn't matter, that the emphasis of these sporting contests was misplaced, that what was meaningful was that everyone participated if only as spectators, that it wasn't about the competing but about the coming together of strangers and friends and family, as in the domestic tableau in front of him. An elderly man rose from an armchair assisted by a younger man and kissed the crown of a seated woman before making his way from the room. A man carried a child who rubbed her eyes and lay her head on the man's chest. A woman entered the room with a tray and began to clear cups and glasses from a coffee table. Scenes like these were taking place all over the world and some people imagined it was just about the football.

The smell of fresh mint filled his nostrils – Rosetta was waving mint leaves under his nose. 'Eat,' she whispered. At their feet was not just a single mint bush but a low hedge of them running the length of the building.

'No thank you.' He pulled his head away.

'Go on! You don't have to swallow it. Just chew and spit it out.' She plucked some of the leaves from the bunch and set the example.

'Do I have to?'

'You want to kiss me, don't you?'

He allowed her to feed him leaves of it and chewed, wondering if she could see him blushing in the dark, an explosion of mint – of pepper and citrus – going off in his mouth and up to his brain.

She laughed and a couple indoors turned and looked out of the window, lazily, as if not ready to believe that they really had heard a noise above the cheering on the television.

'Come,' she said and took his hand in hers, spitting the mint out and wiping her mouth with the back of her free hand.

They trekked back the way they had come, having to stand to one side as a car drove by, its engine revving hard as it came uphill at speed. Close to them, the car slowed, the driver braking and changing down a gear, to pass them at a walking pace. It was the Lancia, the driver on this occasion accompanied by two men who, one in the passenger seat and one in the back, sat hunched, their heads in the middle of their chests and yet up against the car roof, so big were they. In the little light there was, the men's faces were grim, grey masks, their eyes fixed on the road ahead.

Rosetta dropped Sebastian's hand and shielded her eyes from the glare of the car's headlights. She stood uphill from him and he saw her silhouetted in the red light of the Lancia's brake lights as the car turned off and down the gravelled service road he and Rosetta had walked up not long ago.

They resumed their walk, turning up by the side of the church and along a path bordered by shrubs and bushes on one side and olive trees on the other. It became steep and rocky and narrow. Rosetta used both hands to steady herself and climbed above him, pausing to tie her cardigan around her waist. Sebastian found himself staring at the exposed flesh between the top of her boots and the hem of her denim skirt, the backs of her knees pale in the little light there was. He fought an urge to kiss them. Looking back, he was surprised to see how far they had climbed since leaving the road. The church was some way below them, its glinting metal cross now superimposed on Colletta's square that was lit faintly by the light from the bar. Seen from above, the village resembled a medieval castle, the square the open courtyard between its walls. Sebastian could see movement but no sound reached him.

The path widened and disappeared so they found themselves walking up a grassy slope, Sebastian's plimsolls slipping on the earth and dry grasses. Rosetta giggled and said, 'Race you!' and ran to the lip of the hill.

'Unfair! You had a head start!'

One moment, Colletta and the church had been in view and, the next, when Rosetta and Sebastian had crested the hill and taken only a few steps down its other side, they had suddenly found themselves on their own, Sebastian feeling as if they'd entered through a door to a private world.

They lay on their backs on the grass, panting. Sebastian felt for Rosetta's hand. As his eyes became accustomed to the night sky, more and more stars appeared, as though shyly, as though deciding only after some persuasion to reveal themselves to him.

'Beautiful,' he said. 'There must be a thousand stars there.'

'A million,' she said.

He thought he'd find Orion and point it out to her. It was the only constellation he knew. 'Do you know the names of the constellations? I know Orion but I can't see it.'

'It's not visible at this time. Orion will rise in the East some-time this morning. With the sun. Look. That one is Ursa Major.'

'Where?'

'The other side from the moon.' Rosetta raised her arm and drew an arch across the sky from East to West. 'There.'

'Oh yes.'

'Americans call it The Big Dipper.'

'I think we call it The Plough.'

'And once you've found that you can find Ursa Minor, just above it – see? And somewhere there's Neptune and Pluto.' Rosetta pointed vaguely South. 'And there – see that W?' She lifted the hand holding his and they pointed vaguely North. 'That's Cassiopeia.'

'Cassiopeia. How do you know these things?'

'One of my brothers. He's crazy for the stars. For example, he knows that Cassiopeia was a queen who boasted about how beautiful she was and was put in the sky by Poseidon as her punishment.'

'Was she as beautiful as you?' Sebastian raised himself on one elbow and looked down on her.

'Ha ha,' said Rosetta but she wasn't laughing. Her lips were parted and she was breathing deeply.

Sebastian could smell the mint on her breath, he could feel the rise and fall of her chest against his arm. 'I can see every star reflected in your eyes,' he said. 'Except the brightest one.'

As they kissed for the first time, Sebastian felt the earth melting from below him. They were no longer nestling on a grassy bank but floating in inky space, suspended in a weightless world empty of everyone but him and her and the stars. There existed only love and sensation, the sensations that lived at the tip of his tongue and at the inside of his lower lip, senses of wet and warm, of two constellations interlacing, of an expanding universe and of the tug in his jeans. Sebastian smelled her neck, he inhaled deeply and he licked her there and behind her ears without really knowing what he was doing or why, he took in her heady animal fragrance through dilated nostrils. He ran his fingers through her hair and one finger along her chest, down her cleavage and followed it with gentle kisses. He placed his hand on her knee and then just above it, on her inside thigh, and she held his hand there and cupped his chin with her free hand and lifted his head and they kissed again. The universe throbbed in time with his heartbeat and bestowed its cosmic benediction on him. The stars were calling his name and hers.

'Sebastian!'

'Rosetta!'

The stars called in a rising soprano and then in a ringing tenor but singing the same tune.

'Sebastian!'

'Rosetta!'

Sebastian lifted his head. 'Do you hear that?'

They stood, Rosetta pulling at her dress and running her fingers through her hair.

'Sebastian!'

'Rosetta!'

They walked hand in hand to the top of the hill and looked down, down to the church and to Colletta and to the beams of electric torches fanning out on all sides like search lights from the heart of the village. Two were making their way in their direction now and Rosetta and he trudged sheepishly down to meet them, her hand having slipped from his.

'*Eccoli!*'

It was the Romanos, in pyjamas, dressing gowns and stout walking shoes with walking sticks in one hand and torches in the other that they waved excitedly as soon as they saw Rosetta and Sebastian.

'*Eccoli!*' Emilio turned and hollered and waved his arms and swung his torch in an arc above the church.

'*Eccovi!*' exclaimed Emilia, blinding them with her torch, so that they had to hold their hands in front of their eyes. 'You are alive, thanks God!'

'Why wouldn't we be alive?' asked Sebastian. 'Could you please stop shining that torch in my eyes.'

'You are not hurting?'

'No,' said Sebastian. 'Please stop touching me. We're quite alright. Well, we were,' he grumbled.

'Here is not the man with the knife?' Emilio swung his torch around and shook his walking stick aggressively.

'What on earth are you taking about?' asked Sebastian, thinking, *They even have matching khaki pyjamas.*

Sebastian followed Rosetta and the Romanos, slipping and

sliding on the grass and once sitting heavily on his backside to add to his embarrassment, while they spoke urgently in Italian. He could tell from the tone of Rosetta's voice that she was asking questions and was unhappy with the Romanos' answers. It sounded to him as though she were arguing with them but then all spoken Italian sounded like an argument to him.

'Rosetta, what are they saying?'

Rosetta ignored him.

They passed the church in single file, Sebastian at the back feeling as though he were heading into trouble and resentful of it. He looked down from the top of the village to the people in the square below and at others arriving from all directions, the beams from their torches preceding them.

Emilio and Emilia waved their torches and then stood at the top of the steps their arms aloft. '*Li abbiamo trovati!*' they cried and the light from their torches lit the lower boughs of the fir tree above them like a triumphal arch. It was gone two in the morning but there could be no-one in Colletta left asleep now. The torch bearers below trained the beams of light from their torches on the four of them; it was, to Sebastian, as he followed the Romanos and Rosetta down the long, sloping steps to the cheering crowd in the square, as though he were entering the coliseum.

Mrs Kentish ran to Sebastian and clasped his face in her hands. 'Sebastian! I am so relieved!' she cried but her look betrayed relief and anger in equal measure.

'Mum!' Sebastian shrugged her off and stepped back from her. 'Don't behave like a crazy woman!'

His father put his arm around her.

'Are you alright?'

'Thank God they're alright!'

'They're alive!'

'So he didn't catch you.'

'Did anyone see him?'

'I thought I saw someone.'

'Please!' Sebastian shouted.

There was a snore and then a snort and people turned to see the American rubbing the back of his head and rise unsteadily to his feet from the stone ledge by the bar. He appeared bemused to see so many people in the square and looked down at his watch and up in surprise. 'I must have fallen asleep,' he said sheepishly.

Sebastian looked at the faces lit from waist level around him. He was surrounded by spooks with raised cheekbones, sunken eyes and shiny foreheads. His mother's open mouth was a wound across a face that, crossed intermittently by the light from the torches brandished by the Collettiani, resembled a grotesque theatre mask. Incongruously, her head of fair hair lit from below formed a blond busby.

'Can someone please tell me,' he said in the momentary silence, 'what on earth is going on?'

Everyone spoke at once, many of them in Italian, which did nothing to assist Sebastian's understanding. Dominic's name was mentioned. And his mother's. Rosetta's eyes widened, as if in disbelief. Dominic stood by his brother and held his hand. Rosetta shouted at Dario who raised his hands, shoulders and eyebrows.

Rosetta looked at the American. 'But you know also,' she said. 'You knew. You were here. You could have told them.'

'I intended to,' said the American. 'But...' he shrugged apologetically.

'Please,' repeated Sebastian, placing his hand on Rosetta's shoulder but she brushed it off and stooped to be eye level with Dominic.

'So you're the little hero,' she said, 'who saw the man with the knife who wanted to kill me. Or Sebastian. Or both of us. And who frightened his mother so our lives could be saved.'

'Yes,' said Dominic proudly.

'The quiet man with the long hair and the jean jacket and the two sons? And the big pocket knife?'

'Yes!' said Dominic, nodding eagerly.

Mrs Kentish stood protectively by Dominic and put her hand on his shoulder. 'You could at least thank him,' she said to Rosetta. 'You don't know what might have happened. We might have saved your life from that man.' A beam of torch light rested on the cherry *semifreddo* stain on Mrs Kentish's dress.

Rosetta stood, her untied black hair an Amazonian's silhouette against the light from the bar, while his mother's fine blond hair, now lit from behind and below by the light from hand-held torches, resembled dandelion florets. His mother adjusted his father's jacket, still on her shoulders, holding it tighter to her, as if suddenly cold or sensing her disadvantage.

'That man,' said Rosetta majestically, 'is my father.'

'Your father?'

'Her father!'

'Him!'

'So we've been afraid of her father?'

'And the two young men are my brothers. He is the manager at the career – *la cava – come si dice?* – the quarry. For his work he has the knife. Sometimes he gets his hands dirty and sometimes he uses the knife to clean the dirt from his nails. So thank you,' said Rosetta, having to raise her voice and looking from Dominic to his mother, 'for thinking my father is a murderer, for wanting to save me from my father!'

'But...' said Dominic, his voice trembling and his lower lip quivering.

'But,' said Sebastian, dizzy with the effort of understanding and obeying the impulse to come to his brother's defence, 'we often saw the two of you arguing, we saw him pulling you by the arm and –'

'Yes! He wants me sometimes to go home for the night! He doesn't always like me working here, especially not when he sees the sons of tourists sniffing around me like dogs and trying for a bit of fun with me, and then they go home and forget all about me completely!' She finished by shouting at Sebastian and looked defiantly from him to his mother, to Dario and to the American.

'I say,' Sebastian heard his father say. He stood by his wife.

Francesca, whom Sebastian hadn't noticed to this point, pushed her way through the crowd to Rosetta and took her by the arm.

Dario clapped his hands. 'Come on, people. Breakfast will be soon! We get some sleep. Anyway, everyone is safe – thanks God!'

The night sky had turned from black to a dark blue, the horizon only just distinguishable by the presence of stars above it. There was Orion now, but Sebastian thought he wouldn't point it out to Rosetta. People started drifting home, yawning. Francesca looked sympathetically at Sebastian and mouthed, 'I take her home.'

'*Buona notte!*' said Emilio Romano waving his walking stick at them. 'All is good that ends good, no?'

'Kentishes,' said Dario solemnly, 'you give us much excitement.' He spoke to the American in Italian.

'I know, I know,' said the American. He addressed the Kentishes. 'I kind of only just understood that you were talking about Joaquín and –'

'You drink too much,' said Mrs Kentish.

The American looked at his feet. He brought the tips of his fingers and his thumbs together like a supplicant. 'On the subject of fathers –'

'Stop it,' cried Mrs Kentish, aghast. 'I don't want to hear another word!' She looked at her husband and clutched his arm, 'Please take me home.'

Sebastian looked back at the square. Rosetta had left with Francesca. It had only the American in it, standing unsteady on his feet alone in the night and looking after him and his mother with longing.

TWENTY-THREE

Bravo pirouetted slowly about the silent square. He looked up. At least he had stars for company. Tomorrow, the Kentishes would be gone – no, not tomorrow but today, he realised. He missed them already. Suddenly desperately thirsty, he thought to return home via the drinking fountain. Feeling his way with outstretched fingers along the exterior stone wall of the bar and stepping deliberately on the uneven cobbles, he rounded a corner and reached the top of the roughly hewn flagstones that heralded the top of the steps leading down to the gravelled service road. He contemplated it, a chalky, silvery dead-end track, bulbously wide where it reached the water troughs so that cars might turn. Looking down into this natural bowl, hemmed in by mountains on one side and circumscribed by Colletta's climbing walls on the other, he saw a subaquatic world of greys, faint mauves and blacks. He stepped heavily down to the olive trees – seaweed fronds swaying in the current around and above him – and to a parked Lancia, immobile and yet rippling muscle and latent menace, a grey shark at the bottom of this ocean bleached of colour. Warily, he turned his back to the car and drank from the fountain. He splashed cold water onto his face and neck and rested his knuckles on the rough edge of the stone trough and watched the ripples subside and the reflected constellations take shape in the black, stilling water. It amused him to be looking down into the sky from the bottom of a sea. His face was a dark featureless blot in the gloom, his head and shoulders just the cut-out of a man. Hastily, he reached out a hand and stirred the water violently. He backed away from the car and hurried as best he could up the grassy knoll that led to the swimming pool and on to his apartment, following the path he'd led Kentish along only hours earlier.

If the Lancia was here then Luigi – its driver and Joaquín's colleague – must be here too and, indeed, there he was, sitting upright on a sun lounger by the pool and seemingly quite relaxed as though it were the most natural thing to be doing, sitting on a sun lounger in the dark just before the dawn.

Bravo stopped by him. 'Luigi,' he said and inclined his head. He looked in the direction of his apartment and could tell, from the flickering light shining on the trees and bushes that surrounded his patio, that his front door was open. And that someone was moving around inside. He sat down suddenly on an adjacent sun lounger.

'*Signor* Bravo,' said Luigi respectfully, but he didn't stand. He ran one hand through his hair, swept back and jet black, and felt for his polo shirt collar with the other, tugging it at the corners as though to ensure it was up. He looked down at his spotless white training shoes and rubbed an invisible mark off them.

Two silhouettes blocked the light from his apartment door momentarily before making their way up the steps to the pool and materialising into two very tangible bodies. Bravo knew himself to be large but these men were something else – taller, broader – and younger. Perversely, he felt flattered. One man wore a blond crew-cut and was clean-shaven – C.I.A., undoubtedly. The other was swarthy with a low brow and a protruding lower lip; Bravo guessed him to be Sicilian. It was typical, he thought: the C.I.A. and the Mafia working hand in hand, the one as responsible for the dirty work as the other, their histories and their futures forever entwined in a sinister compromise.

The Sicilian turned to Luigi and handed him the clear plastic bag in which was the American's FP-45.

Luigi held the *Liberator* in his open palms as though weighing it. The steel pistol caught the light from the pool lamps and glinted dully. All four men looked at it, momentarily immobile in an act of obscure supplication.

Luigi raised his eyebrows. 'Is this it?'

The Sicilian nodded.

'This is the only gun you keep?' There was a note of incredulity in Luigi's voice.

Bravo nodded too.

The giant American with the crew-cut stepped forward. He held a towel – one of his, Bravo noticed – neatly folded in one hand.

'Please,' said Luigi, rising. 'If you don't mind.'

Bravo pushed himself unsteadily to his feet and allowed himself to be frisked. It was a cursory search, for form's sake, as it would have been immediately obvious that he didn't have a weapon concealed about his person. The Sicilian remained expressionless as he ran his fingers nimbly around the waistband of his pants.

'So, how are we going to do this?' asked Bravo wearily.

Luigi appeared pained. 'Well,' he said in the manner of a

man who had long wrestled with an insurmountable problem. 'We thought it would be best...' He looked around at the sleeping apartments beyond the pool and the olive trees, at the shuttered windows and empty terraces. 'We don't want to wake anyone up, you see.'

'Of course not,' concurred Bravo. Of course not. So not a bomb, not a gun, but a knife, presumably. It was that time of morning when the land and everything of it remained obscure but the sky was blue and lightening. He had an urge to switch a light on as a waking dreamer might to banish a nightmare.

'We thought,' said Luigi, 'that if you'd be so good to kneel by the edge of the pool –'

'Hence the towel,' said Bravo.

'Yes – we would then perhaps encourage you to take a long drink.' He spoke Italian, with, the American noticed, a nasal accent that marked him out to be from Piedmont. 'We would then sit you down at your kitchen table with, you know, some empty grappa bottles around you and maybe one in your hand and one or two smashed on the floor.'

'There'll be an autopsy.'

Luigi shrugged. 'You drink too much. You are of the age to have a heart attack. Anyway, the doctors around here are our friends.' Luigi waved his hand as if to indicate a lack of concern.

Bravo could picture it. No-one would miss him for a day or two and then, perhaps on the third or fourth day, Dario or Claudia would come looking for him. Pushing open his front door, they'd find him exactly as Luigi had described him, at a kitchen table a raft in a sea of empty bottles, his shirt and hair dry.

Luigi looked up at the sky and down at his watch. 'Shall we?' he proposed.

Bravo felt himself lifted by two pairs of strong hands at the elbows and arms and, before he knew it, before he could even contemplate protesting, he found himself kneeling on his towel by the side of the pool, his arms locked behind his back. He felt grateful for the towel, for the softness beneath his knees, even though he knew that it had been placed there not for his comfort but to avoid any difficulty ensuing from scuff marks on the knees of his chinos. He knew he was still drunk, sober enough to know he had something to say but too drunk to remember what it was. He wondered whether if he hadn't been drunk he'd have put up a fight.

The Kentishes! He'd remembered. Bravo craned his neck and looked up. 'One last request. Please.'

Luigi looked down at him with raised eyebrows.

'The Kentishes. Please do nothing to harm them. Please.' From where he knelt, looking up at Luigi, the moon appeared a halo around Luigi's head and the image struck Bravo as inappropriate, blasphemous even.

Luigi grimaced, as though to suggest Bravo's request risked inconveniencing him.

'He keeps his recordings and his notes in the carrying case for the cassette recorder. You only need to take that from him.'

Luigi sighed and shifted from one foot to the other. He scratched the back of his neck.

'I gave him no names, I promise you.' Bravo tried to keep the desperation from his voice.

'I know that. I know.' Luigi nodded.

'Really, he has nothing, no hard information, nothing that could incriminate anybody.'

'I know, I know,' said Luigi, adding, 'It's the principle – you know. But what have you started, you don't know.' He grimaced and shrugged as if to say this was out of his hands, which, Bravo knew, it was.

'The Kentishes. Promise me.'

'I can't promise you nothing.' Luigi sucked his teeth.

'You can. You can try.'

'Alright. Maybe. Maybe I will try,' added Luigi solemnly. He looked from him to the Sicilian and to the C.I.A. agent.

For the second time that night, Bobby Bravo found himself looking down at the featureless outline that was his reflection against a starlit sky and rising to meet it. The water stung his eyes and entered his ear canals. It felt cool to the back of his neck. He held his breath without difficulty for a moment or two and entertained the crazy idea that he might be able to hold it for longer than they held him. He'd waded ashore in Licata, arriving in Italy wet to the chest up and here he was 35 years later leaving it wet *from* the chest up. His position was ridiculous. To think, children would be playing and splashing in this very water just a few hours hence! Clifford, Kees and Renzo would complete their lengths oblivious to the murder the water bore witness to. They would assume he was sleeping off a hangover while they chatted about the night's excitement surrounding Rosetta and Sebastian. If only he knew definitively that he had a daughter and grandsons. If only, knowing that he did, he could have felt their love and expressed his for them. If only he could have done some good with his life. If only he could take the deep breath necessary to gather the strength to raise his head from the water. If only he weren't going to die. The full nelson his captors had him in tightened as he struggled. The pain across his shoulders was intense. The more he tried to raise his head, the more they bore down on him. He flexed his knees and straightened them as best he could, in effect diving off the pool's edge and into the water and taking the C.I.A. agent and the mafioso with him but they never for a moment loosened their grip. He lost a shoe as he kicked ineffectively behind him;

his head held at the level of his tormentors' knees, he couldn't get both feet on the pool floor so that he might push off and up. He resented the ignominy of his situation. The cold water cut through his lungs like a knife. He watched as far away below him, a soaring eagle toyed with a snake in its talons dropping it and catching it repeatedly, shredding his lungs.

TWENTY-FOUR

The family stood by the open door, their luggage at their feet, the mid-morning sun streaming in. Sebastian looked out over the woods and at Vesallo's church steeple.

'Another beautiful day –' said Dominic.

'Not another word,' said Mrs Kentish.

'Right,' said Mr Kentish but no-one moved. 'I think they'll still be serving breakfast.'

'I suppose,' said Mrs Kentish, 'that there's no way out of running the gauntlet of the square.' She wore dark glasses and her hair in a scarf that formed a triangle at the nape of her neck.

'We could go around the back, behind the bar, along the service road and up by the church,' said Sebastian.

'I don't fancy lugging our suitcases that distance,' said Mr Kentish. 'Besides, I'm not going to leave here with my tail between my legs. Anyway, all the talk will be about the football. There's just been a World Cup, remember.' He slung his satchel and cassette recorder carrying case over his shoulders and picked two suitcases up. 'Come on. We'll load the car, have a quick breakfast and go.'

They walked in single file, through the stone archway and along the slabs of mountain rock that formed their pavement, until they reached the steps up and around to the square into the chattering hubbub. Mr Kentish dropped the suitcases. 'Hello,' he said. The small crowd of bleary-eyed holidaymakers and Collettiani fell momentarily silent before erupting into ironic cheers.

'Hooray!' Clifford laughed as he slapped Sebastian on the back.

The Langemensens, occupying a breakfast table on the terrace, applauded.

Someone shouted, 'So, you finally got lucky!'

'Why does he think you were lucky?' Dominic asked Sebastian.

'Dad. Let's just go.'

'Did you manage to get any sleep?' Mrs Better asked Mrs Kentish sympathetically.

'The adventurer!' roared Dario, absent-mindedly offering Sebastian a cigarette before lighting it for himself. He considered their luggage. 'Maybe we get some sleep this night!' He laughed at his own joke. *'Va bene.* Coffee?' He raised his eyebrows at Mr and Mrs Kentish as he tucked his packet of cigarettes and lighter back into his sleeves. He ran a hand through his slicked-back hair and stroked his unshaven chin. He had bags under his eyes.

Sebastian looked around him. Everyone looked exhausted.

'No coffee, thank you,' said Mrs Kentish. 'I think we'll just load the car and go.'

Mr Kentish picked the suitcases up then put them down again. 'Damn it,' he said. 'I forgot I have to settle up.' He extracted the travel bag from his satchel and waved it at Dario. 'You'll have to tell me how much I owe you.'

'*Certo.*' To Mrs Kentish: '*Signora*, come and see where I hanged your painting before you go.'

'No thank you.'

Mr Kentish followed Dario into the bar.

'Sebastiano.' The Cespuglios stood in front of him in matching shorts, T-shirts and insect bites. 'We go to find you by the river and we find only the mosquitoes – *guarda*.' They showed him their arms and legs, covered in bright red weals.

'I'm sorry,' Sebastian mumbled.

'But is alright. We did not find the *assassino*! And 'e did not find us!'

'Mum,' said Sebastian under his breath, 'can we just go?'

'As soon as your father is back,' said Mrs Kentish, equally quietly.

'Is alright.' Giorgio Cespuglio patted Sebastian on the back. 'But you had *fortuna*, I 'ope!' He brought his hand to his elbow and raised and bent his arm to laughter all around.

'He can '*ope* all he bloody wants,' said Mrs Kentish through gritted teeth.

'Mum!' said Dominic.

Mr Kentish emerged from the bar and handed his wife the travel bag. 'You'd better hang on to this,' he said, 'We're clean out of travellers' cheques.'

'What?' she said.

'He cleaned us out. Dario. I didn't think we'd spent that much.'

'Did he show you a bill?'

'No. He said it was all in his head. I think he just made it up as he went along. Anyway, we have some *lire*. In cash. The worst thing is that it came to more than I had in travellers' cheques so he said he'd do me a discount, now that we're friends. Mates' rates, or something like that. As payment for all of the entertainment we provided them with.'

Mrs Kentish placed her head in her hands. 'The humiliation! I could scream!' And she did, quietly.

'Steady on, Mum,' said Sebastian.

'He could have said as payment for my painting!' said his mother angrily, raising her head.

'Listen,' said Mr Kentish distractedly, 'I feel I should say a proper good-bye to the American.'

'Dad, let's just go,' pleaded Sebastian.

'I'll be quick. I'll catch you up.'

'Good morning! You are leaving us! It's been our pleasure to have you here.' Francesca was as charming as ever, despite appearing tired. The bruising had nearly gone from her face and she'd replaced the large plasters with smaller ones. 'I'll take that, thank you,' she said, taking the apartment key from Mrs Kentish and, picking up her case, 'and I'll help you with this.' Her hair fell like two curtains when she leant over.

Sebastian followed Francesca's sandalled feet up and out of the square and stopped when he heard Claudia calling after them, '*Arrividerci!*' He turned and waved at her and turned again. Laden as he was, he had to take two steps for each long, sloping cobbled step. Goodbyes and *buon viaggio*s followed him up and once at the top by Francesca's office, Sebastian, Dominic and their mother dropped their luggage and waved good-bye to the Betters, the Cespuglios, the Langemensens and the Pompeos below. Renzo was there and the witch and guitar-playing hippy with his wife and daughter but neither Rosetta nor the American. The child of a family of new arrivals pointed at the sky above the church where, just visible, an eagle hung, barely moving the spread of its wings, kept in place by the rising and warming morning air. 'An eagle has come to see you go,' said

Francesca, also pointing. 'Look!' While they raised their heads and a hand to their foreheads, Sebastian felt her slip a scrap of paper into his hand. She brought her finger to her lips before pointing to the eagle again. 'Look! It means you will have a safe journey.' He put the piece of paper into a back pocket of his jeans.

Francesca hung the apartment key on a hook in her office. 'You like the music?' She turned the volume knob of the cassette player up.

> *They call it paradise*
> *I don't know why*
> *You call someplace paradise*
> *Kiss it good-bye*

'I like it. Ah, here is Mr Kentish.'

Giulio stood behind him, carrying the two suitcases as easily as if they were feather dusters. Mr Kentish looked droll, with his cassette recorder and his satchel slung across both shoulders and crossed at the chest like bandoliers.

'Good-bye, Mrs Kentish.' Francesca shook her by the hand.

'Good-bye, Dominic.' Francesca stooped to kiss him.

'Good-bye, Mr Kentish.' She shook him by the hand.

'And a special good-bye to Sebastian, who I will never forget for saving me,' she said while holding his hand in both of hers before kissing him on both cheeks.

They walked up to the parking lot where Giulio deposited the suitcases by the boot of the car and touched two fingers to his forehead when thanked. He wore a sleeveless T-shirt because, Sebastian surmised, he'd had trouble fitting his muscles into one with sleeves.

Mr Kentish arrived, breathless, with the rest of the luggage.

'Just load the car,' said Mrs Kentish to her husband and then surprised Sebastian by calling after Giulio, 'You're the gardener, aren't you? *Le jardinier?*'

'*Il giardiniere?*' Giulio nodded.

'Thank you. The gardens are beautiful. I can't believe you do all this yourself. Anyway, *bravo.*'

Sebastian watched his father pack the boot. If his father took pride in one thing, it was this, the space-efficient packing of the boot of a car. The large cases first, then the smaller ones, the overnight bags, the cassette recorder carrying case, the satchel and the chess set. The folding easel on top of them all. His father looked at the packed boot with satisfaction before closing it.

The family stood by the loaded car, the rear wheel arches now in line with the tops of the wheels. It was as though, despite everything, they were reluctant to get in and drive away. They looked over the village, the cherry and olive trees, the fig trees and the woods. The felt, brilliant green peaks around Colletta reared like waves around a sandcastle. Sebastian was already missing it, the pool, the food, the easy camaraderie – and Rosetta. He wished they'd parted on a better note. He felt a contraction in his chest.

Mrs Kentish turned from the view to her husband. 'Did you see him? Did you say good-bye to him?'

'Yes. No,' said Mr Kentish. He kept his eyes on the mountain opposite. 'There was no sign of life. So I looked through his kitchen window and saw him asleep at the kitchen table. Sitting up, with his head on his chest. I tapped on the window with a fingernail, quietly just in case he was snoozing. I suppose I didn't really want to wake him.'

'I'll bet he's hung over,' said Mrs Kentish coldly.

Sebastian thought it was unlike his mother to sneer.

'I don't think it's been that easy for him.' Mr Kentish turned to look at his wife. He sighed. 'Anyway, what a mess his kitchen is in! Bottles everywhere. I feel sorry for him in a way.' He looked at his watch and opened his car door. 'Come on. We should get going.'

Mr Kentish started the engine and Sebastian revelled in the Alfa Romeo's growl. 'Started first time!' said Mr Kentish. 'You know, I think I'll miss this place, despite everything.'

'Just drive,' said Mrs Kentish.

The car slalomed down, past the hollowed caves where the engine roared and Sebastian and Rosetta had hollered and howled less than a day ago, and turned left in the direction of Martinetto and Albenga. They drove with the windows down, Sebastian and Dominic with their heads on the rear doors and their faces to the wind. Mountains either side and the valley ahead and Rosetta's face filling the sky. Was this love, this aching constriction of the chest, or was it, simply, missing someone?

Mr Kentish suddenly sat straight up in the driver's seat, checked his rear-view mirrors and glanced over his shoulder.

'What is it?' asked Mrs Kentish.

'I don't believe it! It's that Lancia again. And he's flashing me again!' he added.

Mr Kentish slowed and waved his arm through the open window, indicating that the Lancia should overtake.

'He's still flashing me,' said Mr Kentish and pulled to the side and stopped.

The Lancia stopped behind them. The driver got out. He

was on his own on this occasion. He was unshaven and dressed in tight trousers and a blue polo shirt. '*Buon giorno!*' He appeared tired and yet delighted to see them. He rested his forearm on the roof of the Alfa and withdrew it suddenly. 'Is 'ot!' he exclaimed. He looked in, past Sebastian's mother to his father. 'You have a – *come si dice* – your wheel, she is broken.'

Mr Kentish got out and had a look. 'He's right! We've got a puncture.'

'I thought it sounded funny,' said Dominic.

'I 'elp you,' said the driver.

'Shouldn't we move to where it's a bit safer,' asked Mr Kentish uncertainly.

'No, is alright, here. After, I take you to the garage in Martinetto.'

'I think I can manage,' said Mr Kentish. 'I don't want you to get dirty.'

'No! Is alright! I 'elp!'

The men and the boys unloaded the boot while Mrs Kentish stood in the shade of a tree. Their suitcases and bags lay in a line in the dust by the side of the road. 'This,' said the driver, locating the warning triangle and handing it to Sebastian, 'you put at fifty metres.'

Once the spare wheel fitted, the driver looked at the time and seemed to remember that he had to be somewhere. 'We be quick,' he said, and then, 'No, is alright,' and made them understand that they shouldn't be too difficult as to how they loaded the boot, as they were only going to unload it and load it again once the tyre mended. ''Ere,' he said, indicating the middle seat at the back, 'We can put some things 'ere for the moment. You,' he added pointing at Sebastian and back up the road, 'don't forget the *triangolo*.' Sebastian carried the folded warning triangle back with him and added it to the pile of bags on the back seat between him and Dominic for the short drive to the garage.

The Alfa followed the Lancia into the woods and past the quarry with its silent, brooding bulldozers and a crane arm lifted as though to bid them adieu. It had to be the one Rosetta's father worked at. What had she called it? A *career*. Sebastian couldn't help but smile. The mountain side, where it had been cut into and sheets of slate gouged out of it, turned from green to black almost violently abruptly, exposing, at its very edges, the roots of trees through a thin topsoil. Sebastian shuddered, discomfited to be a witness to this sudden despoliation of nature. Maybe human emotion too was superficial; love too might be only skin-deep. There would be no mountain left after some more years of excavation, but how many? Twenty years? Fifty? A hundred? Anyway, enough so as not to trouble Rosetta's father.

They crossed a bridge and pulled into a dusty petrol station forecourt by a café across the road from a garage. The driver of the Lancia hooted his horn and spoke to a mechanic in a blue overall while pointing to the Kentishes. He then drove off with two toots of his horn and a wave of the hand.

'That's all a bit sudden, isn't it?' said Mr Kentish. 'I mean, I didn't even get a chance to thank him properly.'

'He's not gone far,' said Sebastian. He'd watched as the Lancia had entered the dim interior of the garage and parked alongside a Fiat on a ramp with its bonnet open. The driver spoke a word to two big men standing idly by the car and strode to a wall-mounted telephone, stepping around car parts and old tyres to reach it.

The mechanic rested a hand on Mr Kentish's open car window and indicated the café with the other, where they were to wait for him to repair the punctured tyre and where Mr Kentish could wash his hands.

'I'm starving,' said Dominic.

'I'm famished,' said Sebastian, taking a seat close to the open window. He watched the mechanic park their car next to the Lancia and the men unload the boot and consider the easel as though it were a mechanical object they'd never seen before. The driver was still on the telephone, his back to the street and his shoulders hunched. The coiled telephone cord extension resembled a puddle around his feet.

'I think we're all hungry,' said Mrs Kentish and they sat down to a breakfast of coffee and fruit juices and pastries and *panini* in paper napkins fetched from behind a big glass counter by a young, dark-haired waitress.

'Isn't she the woman at the tollbooth, you know, when we arrived?' asked Sebastian. 'It's either her or her sister.'

'There's no point asking your father,' said his mother. 'He never notices pretty women, do you darling?' She ran her fingers through her husband's hair.

'Don't be embarrassing, Mum,' said Sebastian, while noting the change in her in the short time since they'd left Colletta, thinking that, if she were ready to make jokes about his father, she might be close to forgiving him for, well, he wasn't sure why *exactly* he should have a cloud of guilt hanging low over his head.

'I could ask her,' said his father, producing his Italian phrase book. Loose pages stuck out of it at all angles and some fell to the floor when he opened it.

'Go on, Peter,' said Mrs Kentish, 'what would you ask her?'

'I might say, *"È stato costretto alla corde ed ha getato la spugna."*' Mr Kentish read from a page he'd picked up from the floor.

'Give me that, please,' said Mrs Kentish. She pushed her sunglasses to the top of her head and leafed through the remaining pages of the book. '"He was pushed to the ropes and threw up the sponge." That won't do. Would you like to try again?'

Sebastian considered his family. He watched a slow kaleidoscopic ballet of bare brown arms moving across the sunlit café table in pursuit of sugar and jams and fruit juices. There was the one obvious mark of change – their suntans that, literally, ran only skin deep – but Sebastian felt that something had shifted within them all, that the embarrassment he'd brought upon them was one that they'd had to share in because they were family. He sat back in his chair and watched his brother's swinging, sandaled feet under the table not quite reaching the floor. Dominic's legs were a nut brown, like his father's; his and his mother's, despite two weeks of sun, were still only a blotchy beige. His mother put her sunglasses back on to look out of the window, so he couldn't make her eyes out. She'd had an epiphany of sorts, he felt, but he couldn't put his finger on it – maybe it was to do with her having to recognise that her children were growing up. Anyway, the American had discountenanced her.

'You forgot to ask the American if he'd ever killed anybody,' said Sebastian to Dominic.

'I didn't forget,' said Dominic. 'I just decided that I didn't want to anymore.'

'His name is Bobby,' said Sebastian smugly.

'Did Dad tell you?' asked Dominic, evidently stung that a secret might have been shared with his elder brother and not with him.

'No. I heard Clifford call him that.' Sebastian ruffled Dominic's hair.

'How many Italians does it take to change a tyre?' asked Mr Kentish rhetorically.

His wife and children followed his gaze to the mechanic who was supervising the two big men load the spare wheel and the large suitcases and easel into the boot. The driver was now facing the street, the telephone handpiece cradled between his ear and shoulder, and his hands together, clasping the long telephone extension cord between them like a rosary as if in supplication.

The mechanic sauntered over to the café.

'*È pronto*,' he said and solemnly handed Mr Kentish a gleaming three-inch nail. '*Tutto a posto. Olio e acqua – bene.*' He brought the tips of one thumb and forefinger together.

'He's saying he's checked the oil and water,' said Mrs Kentish.

'*Il pieno?*'

'Yes, please. Fill her up.' said Mr Kentish. He held the nail up. 'So you're the culprit,' he said and passed the nail to Dominic who'd held his hand out for it. 'Right, let's settle up and get the things off the back seat and into the boot.'

The waitress brought the bill, tucking thick brown hair behind both ears and smiling at them over her blue buttoned shirt.

'Go on, ask her,' said Dominic cheekily.

'I would if I knew how to,' said his father. '*Grazie,*' he said to her, adding, 'Gosh, that was cheap.' He looked around him. 'And the place so clean, too.' He kept the *lire* in his hand as he went to pay the mechanic. There followed a moment of negotiation at the end of which the mechanic held both hands up and then gently extracted a small number of notes from Mr Kentish's outstretched hand rather than take them all. 'That was kind. He insisted I pay only for the petrol. I understood the tyre repair was a favour. Or free. Something like that. Right, I'll finish with the car.'

Sebastian and Dominic wandered over to the bridge and leant over its railings. The roiling river was too far and turbulent for them to even think of playing Pooh sticks. Dominic dropped the nail and they watched it hit the water soundlessly.

'If it's like this now, what must it be like in winter?'

'Dad's calling us,' said Dominic.

They took their seats in the car.

Sebastian noticed that the Lancia had gone. 'Did you get to say goodbye to the driver?'

'No. I didn't see him go.' Mr Kentish was gripping the steering wheel with both hands but the engine wasn't even on.

'Then what are you waiting for, Dad?'

'My cassette recorder carrying case is missing.'

'What do you mean, it's missing?'

'I can't find it.'

'And the cassette recorder itself? And the cassettes?'

'All missing.'

'I'll look in the garage,' said Sebastian, reaching for the car door handle.

'I've looked. There's nothing there, nothing that's been left behind near where the car was. Those two chaps in overalls looking at us now seemed a bit put out, frankly. I wouldn't want to get on the wrong side of them.'

Mrs Kentish put a hand on her husband's arm. 'Are you certain we didn't leave it by the side of the road?'

'I'm sure. We left nothing behind. I checked. And double-checked in the rear-view mirror.'

'I didn't see anything,' said Sebastian, 'when I ran back with the warning triangle.'

'Ooh, look at that,' said Dominic. A bright red Alfetta GTV had pulled in for petrol. It was the fastback coupé version of their car. 'Can't you get one of those, Dad?'

'Maybe it's for the best,' said Mr Kentish.

'Look. *He* gets special treatment,' said Dominic. They watched as the mechanic cleaned the windscreen of the GTV.

Mr Kentish spoke quietly. 'Jackie, if someone knows enough to be after the cassettes, they probably know enough to want the notebooks. But their problem is that the notebooks have never left my side.'

'And their problem might become our problem.' Mrs Kentish squeezed her husband's arm.

'Yes.'

'Who's they?' asked Sebastian, sitting forward.

Mr Kentish ignored his son and changed his grip on the steering wheel. He lifted his satchel from the passenger footwell and opened it, revealing notebooks and pages of typed manuscript. 'Oh, sod it.' He removed his notebooks and a sheaf of paper from the satchel and got out of the car. He waved to the garage mechanics. His family watched him run to the bridge, kicking little clouds of dust up behind him, and throw his notebooks off the bridge, his arms describing exaggerated arcs as he hurled the books high in the air, one by one. He turned and looked towards the garage as though to check that he was being watched and then deliberately dropped the pages of manuscript over the side of the bridge.

'Mum!' exclaimed Sebastian sitting forward. 'What's he doing?'

'Has Dad gone mad?' asked Dominic.

Their mother didn't reply.

Mr Kentish leant over the railings and stayed there for a moment in which Sebastian couldn't help noticing that his hair had grown so that it hung forward, obscuring his cheeks, and that the backs of his knees were still pale. He pushed his hair from his face and walked back, looking pleased with himself. He leant into the car and rummaged in his satchel. 'While I'm at it,' he said smiling and extracting his Italian phrase book. He ran back to the bridge and threw that over too but didn't wait to see where it landed. He returned the mechanics' looks of interrogatory surprise with a wave and a show of empty hands. 'Right,' he said, 'they definitely saw that,' and he started the car. He looked pleased with himself.

They drove back the way they had come two weeks ago, south now until they reached the motorway by Albenga where they passed the tollbooth, turned west and drove with the Ligurian Sea to their left and Ligurian villages and mountains on their right. His father and mother had the car's sun visors down. Dominic was already asleep, testimony to the lack of sleep they'd all had. His mouth hung open and the wind ruffled his hair.

Sebastian used the momentum of his body's shifting weight as his father took a turn at speed not to lean into his brother but to extract the scrap of paper Francesca had given him from the back pocket of his jeans. He unfolded it. Written on it, in looping handwriting and in red ink, was the name Rosetta Ciottolo and an address. Sebastian held the piece of paper tightly between his thumb and forefinger out of the open window. He closed his eyes against the wind that buffeted his hair and his face, and he felt the warmth of the sun on the eyelids. He knew that if he released his grip just a little the wind would snatch the slip of paper irretrievably from him.

EPILOGUE

At 10:25 on the morning of Wednesday 2 August 1980, just over two years after the assassination of Aldo Moro, a bomb went off in Bologna train station. The bomb had been hidden in an unattended suitcase in an air-conditioned waiting room in which men, women and children were waiting for trains to take them on to the next stage of their lives. The explosion brought the roof of the waiting room down. It destroyed most of the main building and it destroyed a train on an adjacent platform.

The bomb killed eighty-five people and injured over 200.

The explosion was attributed to an old boiler in the station's basement and then to a bomb planted by the Red Brigades before Italy's leading wire service received a call from someone who claimed responsibility on behalf of *Nuclei Armati Rivoluzionari* (NAR), a group of neo-fascist militants. Subsequently, the call was found to have been made by the Florence office of SISMI, Italy's military intelligence and security service.

Four court cases and subsequent appeals over twenty years convicted members of NAR and of SISMI charged, variously, with murder, forming an armed gang, subversive association, defamation and obstruction.

The Italian courts effectively delivered the verdict that the bombing was executed by Italy's secret intelligence services with the assistance of their associates in the criminal under-world of Italian neo-fascism that Gladio, created over thirty years earlier by American and European intelligence services to repel Soviet invasion, had become. It's hard to avoid the conclusion that the atrocity at Bologna, like so many that preceded it, was conceived in the very heart of the Italian *deep state*, if not by *the* government, then by senior and powerful members within it.

The existence of Gladio would only be revealed in 1984, at the trial of a terrorist, and only officially acknowledged by an Italian prime minister in 1990.

ACKNOWLEDGMENTS

My thanks to my first readers – to Jeremy Bolland, Neil Burgess, Adriana Noble, Amy Noble, Gabriella Noble, Ludovic Noble and Marc Noble for their edits and recommendations; to Francesca Dizer and Federica Nistri for their advice on things Italian; to Elizabeth Haylett Clark at The Society of Authors; and to Virginia Jennings and Jamieson Wheatley for their loans of 1978 World Cup CDs and Leonard Cutts' *Teach Yourself Italian Phrase Book*, respectively.

Particular thanks to Collier Street Fiction Group, namely, to Wave Davis, Josephine Bruni, Jonathan Dancer, Cathy Evans, Alex Norris and Maud Waret for their contributions to everything from the *big picture* to the minutiae of the text; and to Jodie Evans, my editor; to Callum Hood, my cover designer; and to Allison Noble, my proofreader.

Profound gratitude to Damien Mosley who accepted my novel onto Indie Novella.

I am indebted to Neil, from whom I first heard of Operation Gladio, and to those writers whose work formed the backbone of my research, namely, to William Blum (*America's Deadliest Export: Democracy – The Truth about US Foreign Policy and Everything Else* and *Killing Hope – US Military and CIA Interventions since World War II*); Richard Cottrell (*Gladio: NATO's Dagger at the Heart of Europe – The Pentagon-Nazi-Mafia Terror Axis*); Daniele Ganser (*NATO's Secret Armies – Operation Gladio and Terrorism in Western Europe*); Max Hastings (*Vietnam – An Epic Tragedy 1945-1975*); Henrik Krüger (*The Great Heroin Coup – Drugs, Intelligence and International Fascism*); Norman Lewis (*The Honoured Society – The Sicilian Mafia Observed, In Sicily* and *Naples '44*); and to Paul L. Williams (*Operation Gladio – The Unholy Alliance between the Vatican, the CIA, and the Mafia*).

And to Rosetta, wherever you are, thank you.

i

n

Indie Novella

www.indienovella.co.uk